THE CLAUSE IN CHRISTMAS

a *Poppy Creek* novel

RACHAEL BLOOME

Cover design: Ana Grigoriu-Voicu with Books-design

Editing: Beth Attwood

Proofing: Krista Dapkey with KD Proofreading

SERIES READING ORDER

The Clause in Christmas

The Truth in Tiramisu

The Secret in Sandcastles

The Meaning in Mistletoe

The Faith in Flowers

The Whisper in Wind

The Hope in Hot Chocolate

The Promise in Poppies

Husby,

I look forward to creating many more traditions together in the years to come

LETTER FROM THE AUTHOR

❄

Dear Friend,

Thank you for joining me on this journey to Poppy Creek. The town
and its quirky, kind hearted characters are dear to my heart, inspired
by people and places I love. I hope you'll feel at home here and visit
again soon!

The idea for this story first came to me two Christmases ago, when a
friend commented on how many traditions my husband and I
celebrate during the holidays. Many carried over from our families
and some we started ourselves.

I'd love to hear some of your family traditions! You can share them in
our Facebook Group, Rachael Bloome's Secret Garden Book Club.
And maybe discover some new ways to celebrate the *Most Magical
Time of the Year*.

Blessings & Blooms,

Rachael Bloome

CHAPTER 1

C assie Hayward hated Christmas. Candy canes made her cringe. Santa Claus made her shudder.

And tinsel... don't even get her started on the lowliest of holiday decorations.

To Cassie, arriving in the quaint, postcard-perfect town of Poppy Creek days before December was akin to stepping foot on the studio lot of a holiday-themed horror flick.

Murder in Mayberry: Poison in Plum Pudding.

Chuckling at her fictitious movie title, Cassie clutched her insulated thermos filled with life-inducing caffeine. She'd savored every sip of the earthy, exotic Sumatra blend while she drove the three-plus hours northeast from her apartment in San Francisco. Now, huddled against the winter morning chill, Cassie relished the piping-hot liquid as it warmed her from the inside out. Plus, her favorite beverage had a special way of grounding her, providing a sense of calm in less than ideal circumstances.

And being in Poppy Creek definitely qualified as less than ideal.

Even if it *was* technically her hometown.

As her heeled ankle boots tapped against the cobblestone

sidewalk, she tried to ignore the extravagant holiday displays crowding the shop windows of the Western-style shiplap buildings. But the further she walked down Main Street, the more claustrophobic she felt.

The square configuration of the town center meant all four streets, with their garland-entwined lampposts and bedecked storefronts, seemed to close in around her. Cassie picked up her pace, scanning the whimsical names of the various establishments as she breezed past them.

Thistle & Thorn: Curiosities and Collectibles.

Mac's Mercantile.

The Buttercup Bistro.

Hank's Hardware and Video Rental.

Cassie did a double take. Video rental? Hadn't the town heard of Netflix?

Shaking her head in disbelief, she glanced at the crisp white envelope in her hand. The return address read L. Davis Law Office. Squinting across the town square, she studied the surrounding buildings again. Only one storefront on the far corner lacked signage. At least, she couldn't see it behind the absurdly enormous wreath and larger-than-life nutcrackers flanking the front door.

Cassie sighed. Just her luck. She could only hope her late grandmother's attorney, L. Davis, wasn't clothed in a flimsy red suit and Santa hat. And if he even *tried* to hand her a candy cane...

Cassie wrinkled her nose at the thought.

Rather than continue down Main Street toward Dandelion Drive, Cassie decided to cut across the expansive lawn in the center of town. A gentle gust of wind fluttered the fringe of her plaid scarf, carrying the festive aroma of pine garlands and sugary cinnamon rolls.

Good grief, Poppy Creek even *smelled* like Christmas.

Thud!

Startled, Cassie turned to see a baseball roll down the

2

angled roof of a white gazebo and plop into an oversized mitt worn by a small child. After brushing aside his shaggy blond bangs, the boy plucked the baseball from the tattered leather glove and lobbed it back onto the roof.

Thud!

Cassie's features softened as she watched the ball roll past the gingerbread trim and topple, once again, into the boy's outstretched hand. While she'd never played catch a day in her life, the sight stirred memories Cassie wanted to forget. Memories of lonely Sunday mornings when her mother had yet to return from her designated booth at the neighborhood bar.

Cassie tucked a strand of dark hair behind her ear, as though sweeping away the unwelcome thoughts. Glancing over her shoulder one last time, she caught sight of the boy scrambling up the side of the gazebo. Teetering precariously on the railing, he stretched his scrawny arms toward the roof, where his ball lay wedged in a crevice. When he couldn't reach, he jumped, missed the edge, and tumbled to the ground.

Cassie's internal debate lasted only a second.

Crossing the distance, she set her belongings on the gazebo steps and lifted the boy to his feet. "Are you okay?"

He nodded, wiping both hands on his grass-stained jeans.

"I commend your effort," Cassie told him with a smile. "But you have to work smarter, not harder."

"What does that mean?"

Cassie strode toward the giant oak tree a few feet away and returned with a long, mossy branch. "Here, I'll show you." Standing on the top step, she grabbed a post for support and stretched onto her tiptoes, jabbing the stick at the baseball. "Come on," she cajoled the branch. "A little bit further."

Still a few inches shy, Cassie groaned. Why had she worn her most expensive pair of skinny jeans? Not to mention the incredibly impractical high-heeled boots.

Swinging her left leg, she placed one foot on the railing and tried again. In full lunge, she prayed her fitted jeans wouldn't rip at the seams. She really couldn't afford to buy another pair. Three months of unemployment meant her credit cards were maxed out on rent and ramen noodles.

This time the tip of the branch made contact with the scuffed leather, and with one solid nudge, it popped over the edge.

The boy cheered and raced over to collect his recovered treasure. "Wanna play?" He thrust the baseball toward her, his huge chocolate eyes filled with hope.

Cassie tossed the stick into the grass and brushed her palms together, scattering flecks of bark and moss. "Sorry, I can't."

"Okay." The boy hung his head, tugging on Cassie's heart-strings.

"I would," she added. "But I'm meeting someone." She gestured toward the door guarded by nutcracker infantry.

A delighted grin spread across the boy's ruddy face. "Uncle Luke!"

Cassie offered a short, half-shrug in response. She supposed the *L* could stand for Luke. But it didn't really matter. "Be careful where you throw the ball, okay? Try to stay away from the corners."

To her surprise, he sprang forward and threw his arms around her waist. "Thanks!"

She awkwardly patted his back. "No problem."

"Say hi to Uncle Luke for me."

"Sure. See you around."

Cassie cringed as the perfunctory expression escaped her lips. Why had she said that? Once she signed the necessary paperwork to claim her inheritance, she'd put Poppy Creek in her rearview mirror quicker than jolly ole St. Nick could down a glass of ice-cold milk.

Gathering her things, Cassie said another silent prayer the proceedings with the attorney would be brief.

But once inside the law office, her stomach flipped with

uncertainty. Had she mistakenly stepped into someone's living room?

The expansive space boasted a fully decorated Christmas tree, complete with presents underneath, a cozy, crackling fire in a brick hearth, the mantel strung with homemade stockings, and...

Cassie blinked in surprise. An elderly woman swayed in a rocking chair by the fire, her knitting needles click-clacking in rhythm with Dean Martin's "Jingle Bells" emanating from an antique record player. A gargantuan tabby cat purred by her feet on a plush ottoman, its ears twitching ever so slightly at Cassie's entrance.

"Have a seat, dearie," the woman said without glancing up. "Luke's in with Frida Connelly, and you know that woman has the gift of gab."

Confused, Cassie hesitated. Surely, she had to be in the wrong place. "Is this the law office of L. Davis?"

The knitting needles paused as the woman raised her head, studying Cassie through thick-rimmed glasses.

For the first time, Cassie noticed how much the woman resembled Mrs. Claus.

"You're new in town?" Her question sounded rhetorical.

"Yes, I am." Cassie didn't bother to explain she'd been born in Poppy Creek, but her mother had relocated them to San Francisco before her first birthday.

The woman smiled, her plump, rosy cheeks appearing even rounder. "Well, welcome, dear! Always happy to see more young people moving into town. Luke should be out shortly. Help yourself to some coffee and gingersnaps. I made them myself. The cookies, not the coffee." Tipping her head toward an empty chair, she added, "Sit a spell. Do you knit?"

"I'm afraid not."

"Well, that's all right. There's always time to learn. Harriet Parker hosts a knitting circle every Thursday night."

"Thanks. I'll keep that in mind." Eager to avoid more

chitchat, Cassie made a beeline for the refreshments. An exquisite foyer table, with the most intricate engravings Cassie had ever seen, offered a welcoming display of gingersnap cookies, mismatched china teacups, and a silver coffee urn.

Cassie unscrewed the cap of her thermos and filled it halfway with the lukewarm liquid, already passing judgment on its lackluster aroma.

Her mother always said you could tell a lot about a man from his favorite whiskey. But Cassie preferred to judge a man on a different beverage of choice.

And if this coffee tasted half as bad as it smelled, Cassie wasn't impressed with Luke Davis.

Not one bit.

❄

L uke Davis nodded as Frida Connelly described—in excruciating detail—the latest quilt she wanted added to her last will and testament. It didn't matter how many times Luke told the elderly woman she didn't need to update her will each time she finished another quilt. Or bring him photographs. She could email him. Or call. Or, better yet, they could update her will once a year, as he'd suggested a hundred times before.

Still, while it drove him crazy, it also made him feel closer to his dad, who held the position of the town's lawyer before Luke. He warmly recalled countless stories his father shared over family dinners of pot roast and fingerling potatoes. For as long as Luke could remember, Mrs. Connelly insisted her will be as current as possible, even calling his father as often as six times in one day the occasion her yellow Lab, Goldie, had a litter of six pups, each left to a different grandchild.

Luke supposed his father's anecdotes could be considered a breach in client confidentiality, but things like that didn't matter much in a town like Poppy Creek where everyone knew what you had for breakfast before the eggs were fried.

"Can we add… Oh, what do you call those things?" Mrs. Connelly scrunched up her face, doubling the number of creases in her wrinkled brow. "A clause? Yes, that's it. Can we add a clause stipulating Francine only gets the quilt on the condition she hangs it in her dining room as a decoration? It really is too pretty for everyday use."

Luke's lips twitched, and he cleared his throat, suppressing a chuckle. "Of course." He jotted the note down on a yellow legal pad. "Anything else?"

"That'll do." Easing herself from the leather club chair, Frida narrowed her eyes with a sudden thought. "Actually, would you tell Dolores to keep her nosy opinions to herself? I don't need her and that obese tabby cat judging me every time I pop in here. You know, she had the nerve to tell me I was wearing a hole in your welcome mat?"

Luke smothered another laugh. "I'll have a word with her."

Although it would most likely be to thank her. Over the last year, since her husband Arthur's death, Dolores Whittaker had become an unofficial greeter in Luke's office. At first, he thought she simply didn't want to be alone in her large, rambling farmhouse. She kept showing up with one excuse after the next. Sometimes bringing him cookies or knitting him a sweater. Until Luke made her a rocking chair and set it by the fireplace, inviting her to hang out whenever she liked. But unlike Frida, Dolores and her tabby, Banjo, didn't have a penchant for trifling and tiresome addendums.

Luke led Frida back into the reception area and nearly stumbled over the braided area rug after catching sight of a stunning brunette standing near the refreshment table.

Their eyes locked, and a guilty blush swept over her cheeks. It took Luke a moment to realize he'd just caught her spitting coffee into her thermos.

"Hi," he said lamely, immediately wanting to kick himself. *Hi?* Was that the best he could do? *Get it together, Luke.*

He cleared his throat. "Hope you haven't been waiting long." That was better. But had his voice raised an octave? He heard Frida snicker.

"Well, I'll scurry on home and let you get to your other *client*." She wiggled her eyebrows and exchanged a grin with Dolores.

Luke tugged on his collar, suddenly feeling too warm in his thick sweater. *Oh, no... the sweater.* Until that moment, he'd forgotten he'd worn the sweater Dolores made him. The one with Frosty the Snowman appliquéd on the front. He suppressed a groan. "Bye, Frida. See you soon."

Heart hammering in his chest, Luke forced himself to meet the stranger's eyes. Her mesmerizing, almond-shaped green eyes. The exact color of the holly wreath on his front door. "What can I do for you?"

Stepping forward, she held out a white envelope. "I'm Cassie Hayward. You contacted me about my grandmother's will."

Luke's heart stopped. *This* was Edith Hayward's grand-daughter?

Oh, great. What he was about to do would be a whole lot harder than he'd thought.

CHAPTER 2

C assie pressed the back of her hand to her flushed neck, wondering when the reception area had become a sauna. But then, that was a silly question.

She knew exactly when.

Her cheeks had decided to double as a furnace the moment Luke Davis stepped into the room. Well, more like *stumbled* into the room. Why on earth did it have to be the exact millisecond she'd spit the horrid-tasting coffee back into her thermos? She silently cursed her refined taste buds. Not that it mattered. She'd sworn off dating until the end of eternity. Plus another five years.

Fortunately, his office felt a few degrees cooler than the reception area, and Cassie gratefully sank into the smooth leather of the club chair.

"First," Luke said, gazing at her across the expansive oak desk with the most perfect hazel eyes Cassie had ever seen.

Drat.

She'd noticed his eyes. Mistake number one.

"Let me say how sorry I am about your grandmother," Luke continued. "She was loved by everyone in Poppy Creek and has been missed by all of us."

Cassie squirmed, causing the slick upholstery to squeak as she shifted her weight. "Thanks." She couldn't think of anything else to say. Her own feelings on the subject would take a slew of shrinks to untangle.

Luke cleared his throat. "About your grandmother's will..."

Cassie held her breath, waiting eagerly for those magic words: *She's left you her charming, picturesque cottage, which is sure to fetch you a small fortune.* But the only noise filling the silence resembled something sharp tapping against metal. Glancing down, Cassie realized she'd been strumming her fingernails against her thermos. She quickly set it on the desk, not wanting to reveal her scrambled nerves *or* how desperately she needed this inheritance. The truth was, she could only afford to pay rent for one more month. After that...

Clearing his throat again, Luke reached into a file drawer and pulled out a festively printed binder of sorts. "The details of the will are... unusual."

Panic rose in Cassie's throat, but she swallowed it down, scooting toward the edge of the chair. "You mean there's a contingency? Like a waiting period or something?"

"Something like that." He placed the binder on the desk and slid it toward her.

Cassie stared at the garish red-and-green plaid fabric with the words *Christmas Calendar* stretched across it in gold foil lettering. "What's this?"

"This is your grandmother's Christmas Calendar." He said the words as though something called a Christmas Calendar was the most commonplace thing in the world.

"I don't understand."

"Here's the thing." Luke took a deep breath, stretching his sweater across his broad chest in a way that made Frosty's eyes bulge.

What was a grown man doing wearing such a ridiculous sweater, anyway? Cassie steered her attention back to Luke's face, trying to focus while he explained the fine print that could change her entire life.

"There's a small clause in your grandmother's will. To inherit the house, you have to complete her Christmas Calendar. For each day in December, she's listed a different festive task for you to carry out until you reach December 25. As the executor of her will, I'll oversee your progress. If you can check off each day's task, come Christmas day, the house will be yours."

Cassie nearly fell off the chair. He couldn't be serious! "Please, tell me you're joking."

"Afraid not."

"But that's crazy!"

"I'll admit it's unorthodox."

"It's certifiable!" Cassie sprang to her feet and paced the hardwood floor. "I don't know how you do things in this town, but you can't—you can't expect me to…" She halted mid-stride and whirled back around. Flipping open the Christmas Calendar to a random page, she read, "Make a gingerbread house."

"A house for a house." Luke chuckled at his own joke.

"This isn't funny."

His eyes still dancing, Luke muffled his laughter behind a cough. "Of course. And no one is forcing you to do anything. If you don't want the house, then…" He reached for the Calendar.

Cassie squeezed her eyes shut. She *needed* the house. She'd applied for several dozen jobs in the past few months and had been rejected by all of them. Beggars couldn't be choosers. But could she really do this? The so-called most wonderful time of the year had only brought her heartache. And the mere suggestion of the Christmas Calendar made her insides clench. But at this point, did she have a choice?

"Wait." Cassie opened her eyes, and before she could change her mind, blurted, "I'll do it."

"Great." Luke rose and handed her the Calendar. "You have

a few days until December 1. I suspect you'll need some time to settle in."

Cassie squashed a groan. She hadn't thought about that. "I'll need to go back home to pack a few things. Since I'll be staying a while, apparently." She tried not to sound as bitter as she felt. But honestly, what were these people thinking? It wasn't as if her grandmother had known she didn't have a job—or a life—that would preclude her from carrying out the ridiculous clause.

"Of course. As long as you're back by the first." Luke pulled a small envelope from the top drawer of his desk. "You'll find the key to your grandmother's house inside, as well as directions from Main Street. It's the last cottage at the end of Walnut Lane. You can't miss it." He held it out to her, then paused, appearing conflicted. "I realize all of this might be a tad inconvenient. If you'd like a letter explaining things to your place of employment…"

"That won't be necessary." Cassie snatched the envelope, resisting the urge to shout, A *tad* inconvenient? Are you kidding? "Thanks," she mumbled insincerely and spun on her heel.

"Oh, one more thing."

Cassie turned back, hoping the entire exchange had been one ginormous, ill-humored prank.

A slow, sincere smile spread across Luke's face, reaching all the way to those dazzling—and downright disconcerting—hazel eyes.

"Welcome to Poppy Creek."

❄

As Luke closed the front door behind Cassie, he felt a pang of disappointment. He wasn't sure why—he'd known the woman all of two seconds—but he didn't want her to leave. And it wasn't just because he felt guilty for springing

12

the Christmas Calendar on her. Although he *did* feel terrible about it. It was clear she'd been caught off guard. And Luke couldn't blame her. It wasn't easy to uproot your life and move to a strange new town for an entire month. Most people only had two to three weeks of vacation time. Not to mention the toll it would take on a relationship.

For some reason, the thought of Cassie Hayward happily coupled with another guy deepened the crease in Luke's forehead.

"Pretty girl, don't you think?" Dolores interrupted his thoughts.

Although she sent an innocent sideways glance in his direction, Luke wasn't fooled by her casual tone. The wily, though well-meaning, woman had an agenda. But then, the entire town had an agenda when it came to Luke's love life. Which was ironic considering they were the main reason he didn't have one.

"Sure, I suppose." Luke strode to the fireplace and added another log, stoking the fire until it crackled and sparked up the brick chimney.

"You don't see eyes that green very often, do you? And her lovely long hair… The color reminds me of my gingersnaps."

"Or chocolate molasses cookies," Luke added before snapping his mouth shut.

Dolores smirked, and Luke couldn't believe he let her rope him into having this conversation.

"Yes, you're right. Definitely molasses cookies." Dolores pushed her heels against the braided rug, setting the rocking chair in motion.

Luke knelt in front of the hearth, giving Banjo a good scratch behind his ears as he watched the sleek lines of the rocker glide back and forth. He still felt proud of that rocking chair. Besides the farm table in his mother's dining room, it was his favorite piece of handiwork. In fact, looking at it made him itch to get back to his shop and design something new.

"She's Edith's granddaughter?" Dolores asked, interrupting his thoughts again.

"Yeah. Crazy, huh? Until a few months ago, I didn't even know Edith had a granddaughter."

Luke's throat tightened at the memory. Edith Hayward, a feisty five foot two, had given him the news of her stage four cancer diagnosis as nonchalantly as a recipe for fried chicken. She even had her last will and testament typed out on her old Remington typewriter, ready for him to look over. Less than six weeks later she was gone. Which came as a shock to everyone but Luke. Given the clause in her will, he suspected Edith somehow knew she didn't have much time left.

But that's how cancer was... sometimes. Other times, it disappeared for a while, long enough to give a person hope. Until it returned, even more aggressive than before. At least, that's how it had been for Luke's dad.

"Edith didn't like to talk about it much," Dolores told him. "It was a difficult time in her life, you know. When her daughter left, taking her newborn baby with her."

"What happened?" Luke asked, surprised by how badly he wanted to know.

Dolores stopped rocking and adjusted her glasses, both eyebrows raised. "Why, Luke Ryan Davis, you don't take me for a gossip, do you?"

Playing along good-naturedly, Luke feigned surprise. "Of course not! I know better than that."

Dolores sniffed and continued rocking. "That you do. This town has enough busybodies, if you ask me." She paused and glanced down at Banjo, who was in heaven thanks to Luke's ear scratches. "For goodness' sake, he sounds like Arthur's old Cadillac DeVille."

Luke chuckled. "Before he replaced the engine."

Dolores smiled at the fond memory before her brow furrowed. "Now, tell me, why did that poor girl seem so upset when she left?"

Luke's lips curled in bemusement. Apparently, Dolores's aversion to gossip didn't extend to listening.

"There's a clause in Edith's will that prevents her from inheriting the house right away."

"Oh?" Dolores set down her knitting needles and unraveled a few more inches of the burgundy yarn. "I suppose that doesn't surprise me. Edith never did like to do things the normal way. What's the clause?"

Luke's features softened. Dolores was right. Edith Hayward was an unconventional woman, but her nonconformity usually benefited someone she loved. She'd even waived her client confidentiality, knowing once her granddaughter undertook the tasks of the Christmas Calendar, she would need all the help she could get.

After Luke filled her in, Dolores threw her head back in laughter. "Ol' Edie sure did love her Christmas Calendar, didn't she? Not a year went by that she didn't do every single thing on her list. But why would a thing like that make her grand-daughter so upset? It's only a bit of holiday fun."

"Yeah, but it's also pretty inconvenient. The strange thing is, when I pointed that out to Edith, she merely waved her hand as though it wouldn't be a problem." Luke shook his head in incredulity. "I offered to send a letter to Cassie's employer explaining the situation, but she didn't take me up on it."

"Well, I sure hope it works out. You know…" Dolores gazed at him over the rim of her glasses. "You two would make quite the handsome couple."

Luke groaned, pushing himself up from the floor, much to Banjo's annoyance. "Don't start, DeeDee. You know I don't have time to date right now. In fact, I'm heading over to Jack's diner so I can look over a vendor contract for him. Some new, fancy steak house in Primrose Valley wants to serve his special barbecue sauce. Can I grab you anything for lunch while I'm there?"

Dolores pursed her lips. "Don't think I don't know what

you're doing, changing the subject like that." Her features softened. "And no, thank you. Banjo and I still have leftovers of the yummy casserole your mom dropped off last night."

Luke smiled. That was just like Maggie Davis. It wasn't enough she ran her own bakery. She still had to cook for everyone in town. "Okay, then. I should be back in an hour. Bill Tucker is coming by later this afternoon. If I'm not back by then, you know what to do."

"Ask him about Peggy Sue."

Bill Tucker couldn't resist bragging about his prize pig. Grinning, Luke tugged the front door open, letting in a rush of cold air. "See you later."

"Luke," Dolores called out after him. "About you and Edie's granddaughter… think about it, okay?"

Luke sighed. His problem would be trying *not* to think about it.

CHAPTER 3

As the car crunched down the narrow gravel lane and approached the clearing at the end, Cassie gasped in spite of herself. The quaint Victorian-style cottage looked like the prettiest girl at the party with her pristine white siding and inviting front porch complete with twin rocking chairs.

"Don't get any ideas," Cassie told the house as she hip-checked the driver's door shut. "I don't care how cute you are. I'm still going to sell you to the highest bidder."

Cassie popped open the trunk of her blueberry-colored Prius and hauled out her enormous suitcase. As promised, she'd returned to Poppy Creek the morning of December 1, prepared to fulfill her contractual obligations. With any luck, the next twenty-four days would fly by quickly. *If* the Calendar didn't drive her completely crazy first. Already, visions of unsavory sugar plums danced in her head.

Lugging her suitcase up the drive, Cassie tried to ignore the whimsical and endearing details of the house, like the exquisite corbels, intricate gingerbread trim, and stunning bay window with a perfect view of the walnut tree.

"It's not going to work," she insisted. "As soon as I sign the deed, you're going on the market. Maybe some yuppie couple with two point five kids and a Goldendoodle will buy you."

The porch steps creaked in protest as Cassie trudged to the front door where she was greeted by the cheerful, cherry-red paint. And if that wasn't bad enough, a welcome mat announced *There's No Place Like Home*.

"You're really laying it on thick, aren't you?" Cassie dug the key out of the small envelope Luke had given her and jammed it into the brass lock. As the front door swung open, her heart plummeted to her stomach.

The inside of the cottage was even more enticing than the outside. A discovery Cassie found unsettling. Her mother never shared details of her childhood or the home where she grew up. But based on impressions Cassie gleaned—mainly from the haunted expression her mother wore whenever Cassie asked about it—she always pictured the house from Hitchcock's *Psycho*. Nothing like what lay before her.

Stepping into the foyer felt like stepping back in time. Ornate molding, a winding staircase, and a striking open-hearth fireplace taunted Cassie with their perfection. And to make matters worse, everything about the decor invoked a feeling of warmth, coziness, and welcome—from the lush vintage furniture to the homey touches of antique collectibles and bric-a-brac.

At first glance, Cassie marveled at how her mother could have left a place so charming and idyllic. But, if her track record had taught her anything, Cassie knew things that looked too good to be true usually were.

As Cassie's heels clattered across the worn parquet floor, she wondered how many times her mother had traveled the same path, enveloped by similar scents of lemon wood polish and dried lavender.

Directly off the living room, she found a kitchen so lovely, Betty Crocker herself would have been jealous. And although

Cassie barely knew how to boil water, she could almost picture herself baking an apple pie in the 1930s mint-green oven.

Setting her oversize handbag on the butcher block island, Cassie retrieved her most prized possession: a polished silver French press, lovingly wrapped in a swath of crushed velvet for safe traveling. She placed a portable hand grinder next to it, followed by a bag of Colombian Supremo—a splurge courtesy of her favorite artisan roaster.

Considering she still had to settle in and start day one of the Christmas Calendar, which had her decorating the entire cottage, inside and out, Cassie would need all the caffeine she could reasonably consume without triggering a heart attack.

Given her experience with the town lawyer, she could only imagine the eccentricity she'd encounter in the doctor's office.

At least Cassie could think of one perk of being stuck in Poppy Creek.

Derek Price would never find her here.

❄

As Luke's ancient faded-red Ford pickup rolled up the gravel lane toward the cottage, a shallow sigh escaped his lips as memories washed over him.

For as long as he could remember, Edith Hayward had been on her own. Which meant Luke's father came by every Saturday—often dragging Luke along—to trim her rosebushes, restock her supply of firewood, and rake the leaves in the fall. Ever since his dad's passing, Luke maintained the weekly tradition, joining Edith afterward for a slice of mulberry pie and pleasant conversation.

Even after she was gone, Luke came by every Saturday afternoon to pull a few weeds or prune the walnut tree. He couldn't bear to see Edith's home fall into disrepair. For the same reason, his mother, Maggie, popped by every now and then to dust the banister or fluff the pillows. In a way, it meant they didn't have to say goodbye.

Luke pulled up behind Cassie's Prius and shifted into park.

Now, someone new would be taking over the beloved cottage. And more than a tiny part of Luke hoped it would be Edith's granddaughter.

His eyes drifted to the insulated thermos lying on the worn upholstery of his passenger seat, and his lips curled into a smile. Despite his busy schedule, he hadn't been able to stop thinking about Cassie Hayward since the moment he'd caught her spitting coffee into her thermos. Even now, the vision of her flushed cheeks and captivating green eyes made his stomach flip-flop. A fact he found baffling. He'd seen plenty of beautiful women in his thirty-one years. Many, right here in Poppy Creek. Why this one set his pulse on overdrive, he couldn't figure out. But lucky for him, she'd left the accessory to her crime behind, giving him an excuse to stop by.

Luke hopped out of the truck and grabbed the thermos and a welcome basket, courtesy of his mother. She'd stuffed it full of local favorites like a bottle of Jack's BBQ sauce, a plate of her jumbo-sized cinnamon rolls, and a jar of The Buttercup Bistro's Mother Lode Stew, which was a secret family recipe. One Luke still wasn't privy to, even after dating the owner's daughter.

After knocking on the front door, Luke took a step back and drew in a slow, calming breath, savoring the crisp air as it filled his lungs.

When he didn't receive a response, he knocked again.

Still no answer.

Luke set the thermos and welcome basket on the porch, figuring the near-freezing temperature would preserve the food until Cassie came outside and found it, when a loud crash thundered from somewhere upstairs.

Prepared to whip out his backup key if necessary, Luke tried the doorknob. Finding it unlocked, he pushed his way inside and bounded—two steps at a time—up the staircase and into the first bedroom, planning to check each room for the source of the clamor.

A large box lay in the center of the hardwood floor, its contents strewn about in every direction. Cassie's lower body hung from a small cutaway in the ceiling that led to the attic. Her backside faced him as she swung her long legs, attempting to reach the pull-down ladder with her foot.

As the adrenaline rushed from his body, Luke released a deep belly laugh, both from relief that she wasn't in any real danger and amusement.

"Hello? Who's there?" Cassie asked, still squirming.

"It's Luke Davis. It seems like you're in a bit of a predicament."

"I slipped trying to carry that box down. Can you give me a hand?"

"Sure, no problem." Luke stepped beneath her, then hesitated. How would he help her down without... well, *touching* her? Telling himself not to overthink it, he wrapped his arms around her legs. "Okay, you can ease yourself down now."

Slowly, she slid down the length of his body until they were face-to-face as he held her in his arms.

For reasons outside his control, Luke couldn't move. It was as if his muscles had stopped working, and his arms were incapable of releasing her.

An awkward moment passed before she cleared her throat. "Uh, thanks."

Color swept across his face as he plopped her on the ground, and he hoped his five o'clock shadow covered it. "I see you're already undertaking day one of the Christmas Calendar."

"Might as well get it over with." Cassie stooped to gather the scattered decorations, tossing them back inside the box unceremoniously. Plucking a headless Santa statue from the floor, she giggled. "Yikes! It kind of looks like Armageddon at the North Pole, doesn't it?"

Luke chuckled as he sank onto his hands and knees, searching for the rest of Saint Nick. "Morbid, but yes." Reaching under the iron bed frame, he retrieved the missing head, noting Santa's jolly smile took on an eerie tone when it wasn't attached to his rotund frame. "It shouldn't be too hard to glue back together."

Cassie shrugged. "One less decoration to deal with doesn't bother me."

"I take it you're not a fan of decorating?"

"I'm not a fan of Christmas."

Luke cocked his head, eyeing her curiously. "What do you mean? Everyone likes Christmas."

"I don't," Cassie said softly, dropping her gaze. Then, almost instantly, her expression transformed. Her full lips stretched into a broad smile that didn't quite reach her eyes. "I guess I'm in good company with Scrooge and the Grinch."

"You know Scrooge and the Grinch like Christmas at the end of the story, right?"

Cassie flushed and busied herself with refilling the box. "Truthfully, I haven't seen either of those movies. So, I guess it's just me, then. The only person in the world who doesn't like Christmas."

"What's not to like?" Luke settled two reindeer figurines carefully in a bed of faux greenery, casting a sideways glance in Cassie's direction. He couldn't help noticing the way her brow creased ever so slightly, or the nearly inscrutable clench in her jaw.

Cassie waved a hand over the mess scattered before them. "It's so excessive. I hate all the commercialism."

Luke nodded slowly, although he could tell she wasn't telling him the entire story. "Sure, there can be that aspect. But isn't Christmas what you make of it? We have a choice to go overboard or focus on the things that really matter. Like family and friends."

Cassie leaned back on her heels and stared at him like he'd grown reindeer antlers out of his head. Clearly, she had some issues with Christmas. Luke only hoped he could help change her mind.

"I can see Christmas decorating isn't your thing. So, how about I help you out? I'm an expert at hanging Christmas lights. In fact, Clark Griswold *wishes* he could string lights as well as me."

"Who?"

"Clark Griswold. From *National Lampoon's Christmas Vacation*."

Cassie's blank expression indicated she still had no idea what he was talking about.

"Wow. You really *aren't* into Christmas, are you?"

"I told you. And before you ask. No, I haven't seen *White Christmas* or *Miracle on 34th Street*, either."

"Okay, Cassie Hayward. I'm about to give you a Christmas Calendar of my own. The twenty-five films of Christmas. Beginning with my favorite, *Home Alone*." Standing, Luke reached out his hand to help her up.

Cassie grinned as he pulled her to her feet. "*Home Alone* sounds like a horror movie, doesn't it? I can already hear a sinister voice saying, 'The call is coming from inside the house.'"

Luke chuckled at her impression of the raspy-voiced intruder. "Let's start with the basics, then. You decorate the inside of the house, and I'll decorate the outside. Deal?" He held out his hand again, already missing the feel of her soft skin against his own.

"Deal."

As they shook on it, Luke realized he didn't want to let go.

Cassie didn't seem to be in a hurry, either, until her phone buzzed in her back pocket.

Luke couldn't bring himself to look away as her phone screen came into view.

He wasn't sure what he expected to see, but he instantly felt the retribution for his curiosity.

No name appeared on the screen, only a number.

But the message... *that* was the real kicker.

It might as well have been seared into his brain by a pyrography pen.

Three simple words that weren't simple at all.

I miss you.

CHAPTER 4

Cassie had only decorated for Christmas one other time in her life—when she was nine years old.

Armed with a wooden spoon and ceramic mixing bowl, Cassie uprooted a shrub from the alleyway behind their apartment building. After planting the foliage in the makeshift pot, she proudly displayed it in the center of the coffee table before scrounging around their studio apartment for random odds and ends to use for decoration. A few hair clips, a pair of her mother's earrings, and a red satin bow she tore off her favorite dress all did the job nicely. The pièce de résistance was the star on top—a gold star, to be exact. A reward for lasting until the final round of her third-grade spelling bee. First place received a shiny blue ribbon, but she cherished her third-place plastic star as if it had been made of real gold. It was the first and only thing she'd ever won.

After nestling the treasured star near the top in the thin, prickly needles of the shrub, Cassie stepped back to admire her masterpiece.

She couldn't wait for her mother to see it, hoping against all reason it would spark a glimmer of festive cheer in their otherwise dreary lives.

The next morning, Cassie woke to Donna Hayward passed out on the couch, the Christmas shrub in a pile of dirt and broken pottery on the floor. The gold star lay snapped in two pieces, as though someone had trampled on it, along with Cassie's youthful hopes and dreams.

She wanted to cry, but even at nine years old, Cassie knew it wouldn't do any good. Instead, she pushed a rickety chair against the kitchen counter and set to work brewing a pot of fresh coffee—the only cure for what Donna dubbed the Whiskey Blues.

Now, as Cassie surveyed her handiwork twenty years later, she couldn't believe she was responsible for the festive sight before her eyes. Even Martha Stewart would be proud.

The tall pillar candles in red, green, and gold that lined the oak mantel were nestled in a fresh cedar garland—courtesy of Luke's pruning skills—filling the entire living room with a heavenly, woodsy aroma. An antique sled rested on the hearth, stacked high with pine logs and cinnamon-scented fire starters. A quilt, each square depicting one of the twelve days of Christmas, rested across the back of the cozy loveseat. But Cassie's favorite touch was an exquisite, hand-carved nativity set Luke said he'd made for her grandmother a few years ago. For some reason, Cassie liked knowing he had crafted it with his own two hands, and she'd given it the prized position in the center of the coffee table.

"Wow." Luke wiped his boots on the Christmas-themed welcome mat before coming to stand beside her. "I'm impressed."

"I'm rather pleased myself."

"Oh?" His hazel eyes shone with a mischievous glint. "Getting into the Christmas spirit, are you?"

"Don't get too excited. I only meant at least it doesn't look like Rudolph barfed everywhere."

He let out a deep rumble of laughter. "Okay, fair enough. For what it's worth, though, I think it looks great."

At his praise, a warm glow spread over every inch of her. "Thanks."

"The sun is setting." Luke strode toward the bay window to peer outside. "In twenty minutes or so we can step out front, and I'll turn on the lights."

Cassie smiled at the way his face lit up in childlike excitement. She had a feeling she'd rather gaze at *that* illumination over some gaudy Christmas light display.

"It's already sunset?" She reached for her phone to check the time, then remembered she'd banished the traitorous device to the darkness beneath her pillow.

No matter how many times she blocked Derek's number, he got a new one. And the longer she ignored him, the more he persisted. She had hoped he would at least have the decency to leave her alone at Christmas. Was he clueless to the cruel irony? Or did he simply not care? When it came to Derek, both scenarios were equally plausible.

"Yep." Luke rested one knee on the window seat as he leaned forward for a better view. "Judging on how low the sun is in the sky, I'd say it's just past five o'clock."

As if on cue, Cassie's stomach rumbled, and she placed her hand over it as if her palm would somehow muffle the noise.

"If that means you're hungry, you're already on Poppy Creek's dinner schedule." Luke's eyes twinkled with humor.

Cassie blushed. "I don't normally eat this early. But I forgot to have lunch. And breakfast, actually." Her stomach emitted another growl, and Cassie gave it a small, appeasing pat. It could be upset all it wanted, but it wouldn't do any good. She hadn't packed a single thing to eat.

"That reminds me!" Disappearing outside, Luke returned with the thermos she'd left at his office and a large wicker basket bursting with goodies. "I should have brought this in earlier, but it's cold enough outside, the food should be fine."

Cassie followed him into the kitchen, her heart beating in a strange rhythm, as though trying to keep up with her conflicting emotions. On the one hand, she was starving and already eyeing the colossal cinnamon rolls like a ravenous reindeer. On the other hand, it unsettled her that everyone she'd met in town seemed so kind and welcoming. It didn't add up with the picture she'd formed in her mind.

"You really didn't have to do this," she told him, although her mouth watered as he unpacked the contents of the basket on the butcher block island.

"I didn't. You can thank my mom. She's the unofficial welcome committee in Poppy Creek." With all the items lined up on the counter, Luke said, "Take your pick. Personally, I'd start with the stew. No one knows what's in it, but I promise it'll be one of the best things you've ever tasted."

Cassie eyed the quart-sized mason jar warily. "It's not squirrel meat, is it?"

Luke sputtered with laughter. "I didn't mean it was mystery meat! But nice to know what you think of small towns." He set a copper saucepan on the stove and unscrewed the lid of the mason jar. "It's beef. But the recipe is a secret. Believe me, some people in this town have been trying to figure it out for years."

Cassie slid onto the backless stool and rested her elbows on the smooth wooden surface of the butcher block. "You really like living here, don't you?"

Luke glanced over his shoulder as he stirred the stew on the gas range. "Yeah, I do. I like that the beauty of nature is right outside my back door. And the people here can be nosy, but they look out for each other. I can't imagine anyone *not* wanting to live here."

"My mom didn't." The words slipped out before Cassie even realized the thought had crossed her mind.

Luke's hand stilled a moment before he resumed the figure eight pattern in the simmering stew. "Do you know why she left?"

Cassie ran her finger along a nick in the countertop,

wishing she'd never brought up the subject. "No, not really. But she hated it here. That much I know."

Luke stirred in silence, and Cassie stole a glance in his direction, noting the deep lines etched into his forehead.

"I'm sorry to hear that," he said softly.

Uncomfortable with the sympathetic edge to his voice, Cassie sprang from the stool and busied herself with finding two bowls.

Cassie had only ever broached the subject of why they left Poppy Creek once. And the haunting reflection of anguish that sparked in her mother's eyes had been visceral enough to forever silence her on the subject.

Even now, being in the home where her mother grew up felt like a betrayal.

More so because she found herself enjoying it.

Luke clicked off the burner and set a lid on the saucepan. "Let's leave the stew to sit a minute and go check out the lights."

At the look of pure excitement on Luke's face, Cassie tried to muster some enthusiasm as she followed him outside.

Standing in the gravel driveway facing the house, Luke said, "Close your eyes."

Cassie wrinkled her nose. "No way."

"Humor me."

"Okay, fine." Cassie sighed dramatically.

"And no peeking!"

Cassie would have rolled her eyes if they weren't already shut, deciding to respond with a sarcastic quip instead. But as soon as her lips parted, her breath faltered.

Luke's large, rough hands grabbed both of hers, drawing them toward her face. His touch sent her heart racing, although she tried to pass it off as purely surprise.

He placed her palms over her eyes, his hands lingering on hers as he said, "Stay here, and don't open your eyes until I tell you to."

Cassie held her breath. He stood so close his body heat spanned the short distance between them. He couldn't have been more than a few inches away. Why did the realization send tingles down her spine?

"Okay," she murmured, embarrassed by the catch in her throat.

She felt the absence of his presence before she heard the sound of his heavy footsteps against the wood planks of the front porch. Even behind the shield of her hands, Cassie could tell the instant the light changed.

"Ready?" Luke asked, standing beside her again. His husky tone conveyed his eager anticipation.

Cassie slowly lowered her hands and her eyelids fluttered open.

She gasped in astonishment as the brilliance of the golden glow overwhelmed her in the best way possible.

Luke had strung white glittering lights across every eave and roofline, along every window and door frame, and even around the porch columns and railings.

"What do you think?"

"I—" Cassie hesitated, unsure how to describe her rush of emotions. "I think it's magical."

"Good." Luke nudged her playfully with his shoulder. "That's what I was going for."

Cassie glanced up, losing her breath for the second time.

Something in the way he looked at her made her at once thrilled and terrified.

❄

Luke pulled into the weathered barn and shifted his pickup into park as the automatic overhead lights flickered to life. He let the key dangle in the ignition, debating on whether or not to listen to the five voicemails cluttering his mailbox.

His gaze drifted to the other side of the barn, which he'd converted into a makeshift woodworking shop. It wasn't fancy, but it served its purpose. And with the help of a few space heaters, the bone-chilling air would warm up in no time. The unfinished rocking chair he'd started a few weeks ago beckoned to him.

Luke sighed, glancing at the voicemail icon on his cell. He knew the messages could probably wait. And no one would mind if he didn't call them back until tomorrow. But the burden of "what if" weighed heavily on his shoulders.

He lifted the phone to his ear, rolling his eyes toward the roof of the pickup as he listened.

As he suspected, no emergencies. Well, no *actual* emergencies. Frida Connelly seemed to think every tweak to her will was of national importance, but Luke could return her call in the morning.

Climbing out of the truck, his boots sank into the thick layer of sawdust covering the dirt floor. The fresh scent of cedar and sap filled his nostrils as he drew in a deep breath. Few things in the world smelled better than his workshop. Not even his mother's bakery, although he'd never say so.

Kneeling in a patch of sawdust, Luke ran a hand over the rough walnut, deciding he'd spend a few hours sanding, smoothing out the surface.

Maybe he'd even smooth out his thoughts in the process.

Spending the day, and a good chunk of the evening, with Cassie left a disconcerting churn in the pit of his stomach. He enjoyed being around her more than he wanted to admit. And catching a glimpse of her text message elicited a stronger reaction than seemed reasonable. After all, what did he care if she had a boyfriend back home who missed her? Even if she didn't, she'd be leaving town at the end of the month, anyway.

Plus, he barely had time to sand a two-by-four, let alone date anyone.

As if on cue, his phone rang, disrupting the still night air.

Recognizing the number of his mother's bakery, Luke answered. "Hello?"

"Uncle Luke!" The chipper voice of Ben Carter spilled from the speakers.

"Hey, bud. What's up?" Luke picked up a loose square of sandpaper and gently ran it along the arm of the chair.

"Whatcha doing?" Ben asked casually.

"Working on something in my shop. What are you up to?"

The boy released an exaggerated sigh. "Hanging out with Mom and Grandma Maggie. But they're still working, and I'm bored. Can you come pick me up so I can hang out with you?"

Luke's hand stalled over a particularly rough patch. He'd hoped for a night alone, but how could he turn Ben down?

While Ben wasn't blood-related, he might as well be. Luke had stepped in as a father figure the moment his childhood friend, Eliza, gave birth without Ben's biological father in the picture.

"I'll leave in two minutes."

Ben whooped into the phone before shouting, "Mom! Uncle Luke is coming to get me!"

Luke heard muffled sounds on the other end before Eliza picked up.

"Hey, Luke. I'm sorry he called. You don't have to come. Your mom and I are working on a big order for the Wilsons' anniversary party, but we should only have a few more hours left. He can wait."

"I don't mind." Luke gave one more pass with the sandpaper before letting it flutter to the ground. "We're in the middle of a cut throat game of Monopoly, anyway."

Eliza laughed, sounding relieved. "Okay. But only if you're sure. He *is* driving us a little crazy. With my parents watching *The Nutcracker* in the city, he's been cooped up here since school let out."

"I'm on my way."

After ending the call, Luke slipped his phone inside the back pocket of his faded Levi's.

Sure, he wouldn't make any progress on the rocking chair. But babysitting Ben would have its benefits, too. Least of which would be serving as a much-needed distraction.

The last thing he needed was free time to daydream about Cassie Hayward.

Especially if she wasn't even single.

CHAPTER 5

C assie toyed with the silver heart charm draped against her throat as she debated her next move.

She *could* delete the voicemail and block the number. But considering Derek left the *I miss you* text last night, followed by a voicemail the next morning, he would only get a new number and try again. Apparently, Costco sold unlisted numbers in bulk.

Gritting her teeth, Cassie pressed play.

"Hey, stranger!" Derek's slick baritone assaulted her eardrum, and Cassie yanked the phone away, switching to the speaker.

"Listen, we need to talk. It's important. And it'd be nice to hear your voice, too." A heavy sigh filled the pause. "I miss you, Cassie. Call me, okay?"

Click.

Tears burned her eyes as Cassie hurled the phone onto the quilted mattress.

How dare he sound so casual! As if nothing had happened. As if—

Dismissing the painful memories with a sharp shake of her head, Cassie snatched her phone and deleted the message before adding the number to the slew of others she'd already banned.

The tiny upstairs bedroom she'd chosen as her temporary abode suddenly felt cramped and suffocating. Grabbing her purse off the antique Singer sewing machine that doubled as a table, she stuffed her phone inside.

She needed fresh air.

And a double shot espresso.

While she'd decided to limit her time in town, save for a few trips to the small market when necessary, Cassie needed a haven—somewhere she could get a calming cup of coffee and clear her mind.

But as she strolled down the cobblestone sidewalk along Main Street, her optimism evaporated. While the town boasted an entire store dedicated to yarn—seriously, was knitting an epidemic here?—there wasn't a single coffee shop in sight. Her only hope was a run-down bakery called Maggie's Place. Fortunately, the tantalizing aroma of vanilla bean and toasted chestnuts overpowered the pink, sun-bleached awning and peeling paint of the same Pepto Bismol color.

A bell jingled overhead as Cassie pushed through the front door, the frosty air dispersing into the warmth generated by a grand river rock fireplace. While the prosaic decor was underwhelming at best, the glass pastry cases burst with the most delectable confections Cassie had ever seen. Rich, gooey brownies drizzled in gallons of chocolate fudge sauce. Buttery lemon scones with an icing glaze so thick it defied all reason. And the pies—mulberry, apple, elderberry—all so huge they could double as private islands.

"Welcome! And what can I get for you on this lovely morning?" A motherly, rosy-cheeked woman greeted Cassie from behind the counter.

Maybe it was the way her silver-streaked ebony curls framed her round features or the kind sparkle in her hazel eyes, but Cassie instantly liked her.

"Do you serve lattes?"

"Oh, dear. I'm afraid not."

"A regular coffee, then?" Cassie asked, hopefully.

"Self-serve at the end of the counter," the woman said with a smile. "How about a nice pastry to go with it? On the house."

"Oh, you don't have to—" Cassie started.

But the woman merely waved away her protest before selecting an enormous brownie covered in crushed pecans and toffee chips. "I know a gal in need of chocolate when I see one." Her eyes crinkled around the corners as she handed a day's worth of calories to Cassie.

"I, uh, thank you very much." Dumbstruck by the woman's generosity, Cassie slowly made her way toward the dubious-looking air pot.

In Cassie's experience, air pots were rarely a good sign.

Setting the brownie on the counter, she selected one of the white ceramic mugs and tentatively pumped it full of the luke-warm liquid. Cassie cringed, noting the contents of her mug more closely resembled a storm drain than a proper cup of coffee.

"It tastes as bad as it looks."

Startled, Cassie darted her gaze to a blonde woman scooping fresh cranberry scones into one of the pastry cases. She appeared to be in her mid to late twenties, maybe a few years younger than Cassie.

An amused smile tugged at the corners of the woman's mouth, and a guilty blush crept up Cassie's neck.

"Oh, well, it doesn't look so bad," she stammered, certain her cheeks were as red as the plump cranberries.

The blonde snorted. "You're a bad liar. And you're also new in town, aren't you?" She scrunched her pretty features, as though trying to read Cassie's mind, when her dark eyes suddenly widened in realization. "Wait! You must be Cassie! I've heard all about you! And the clause in your grandmother's will."

"Must be impossible to keep a secret in this town," Cassie teased.

The blonde's friendly expression faltered, and she dropped her gaze, leading Cassie to second-guess her choice of humor. But before she could apologize, the woman's dazzling smile returned.

"So, tell me," she said brightly. "What's on the Christmas Calendar for today? I'm Eliza Carter, by the way." She held out her hand, which was covered in flour.

"Nice to meet you." Cassie returned the handshake, wondering whether or not it would be rude to wipe her palm down the front of her sweater. Considering she'd already offended her new acquaintance with the crack about her hometown, she decided it was best to let the dust settle. "Today I have to cut down my own Christmas tree." Cassie couldn't help a grimace.

"How fun! My son, Ben, is obsessed with Sander's Christmas Tree Farm. He'd live there if I'd let him. And considering we live with my parents, there are days I'm tempted." Her infectious laugh was loud and boisterous for someone with such a petite frame, and Cassie found herself joining in.

"I wish you could go in my place. I'm dreading it," Cassie admitted. "I have no idea what I'm doing. Or how I'll get the tree from the farm to the cottage in my tiny Prius."

"Don't you worry about a thing! Ben and I would love to go with you! I get off work around five."

"Oh, you don't have to do that!" Cassie said hastily, not wanting to develop more connections in town than necessary. "I was only kidding."

"Nonsense." Eliza flicked her wrist, flinging flour into the air. "We *want* to. Besides, you can't tie a tree to a Prius. As much as I'd love to see someone try."

"Well…" Cassie chewed her bottom lip, ready to make an exception to her no-fraternizing-with-the-townsfolk rule for the sake of convenience. "Do you have a truck?"

Eliza leaned across the counter, her dark eyes twinkling. "No. But I know someone who does."

✳

Luke's pulse lurched at the look of surprise that flickered across Cassie's face when she opened the front door. Hadn't Eliza told her he'd be coming to pick her up?

"Hi." Her surprise softened into an irresistible smile. "So, *you're* the friend Eliza was talking about?"

"Guilty."

"Speaking of Eliza..." Cassie peered over his shoulder. "She's not with you?"

"They're running late. She said they'd meet us there."

A shadow of hesitation clouded Cassie's green eyes as she looked from Luke to his pickup idling in the driveway. His heart flip-flopped. Did she think this was a date? Not that it wasn't possible—or even probable—for Eliza to attempt a setup, but if Cassie thought *he* had something to do with it...

He tugged on the collar of his jacket, feeling the heat of embarrassment creep up his neck.

"Sounds great." Her hesitation seemed to evaporate as she tossed one end of her plaid scarf over her shoulder before bounding down the front steps, leaving a faint trail of spicy bergamot behind her.

Luke quickly followed, almost breaking into a trot to beat her to the truck.

Cassie raised one eyebrow as he sprang for the passenger door, jiggling the finicky handle a few times before jerking it open.

"Sorry." He flashed a lopsided grin. "Blame my dad. There wasn't a day in his life when he didn't open the car door for my mom." Luke could have kicked himself as he realized how his words might be misconstrued. "Or for any woman," he rushed to add.

The corners of Cassie's lips quirked ever so slightly and Luke suppressed a groan. Was he that obvious? Eager to change the subject, he said, "You're going to love Sander's place."

As Luke's pickup rolled to a stop in the dirt parking lot of Sander's Christmas Tree Farm, they were greeted by endless rows of pine and fir trees jutting into the moonlit sky. Luke stole a glance in Cassie's direction, watching her face brighten with awe at the sight of the roaring bonfire and canopy of twinkle lights stretched overhead, illuminating their path.

"Pretty, huh?" Luke asked, helping her down from the truck.

Cassie nodded as she took in the idyllic scene of families roasting marshmallows around the crackling fire, serenaded by two harmonizing cowboys plucking "Silent Night" on their guitars.

"Uncle Luke!" Ben tore across the parking lot before Eliza even closed the driver's door of her run-down Honda Accord.

Luke chuckled as Ben tackled him with a bear hug. "A little excited, are we?"

Ben grinned and whispered loudly in Luke's ear, "They let you have as much hot chocolate and s'mores as you want."

"You don't say." Luke turned his smile on Cassie. "Did you hear that? All the hot chocolate you can handle."

Releasing his hold on Luke's waist, Ben glanced at Cassie, his expressive brown eyes widening in recognition. "Hi!" He flapped his gloved hand in an enthusiastic wave.

"You two know each other?" Joining them by Luke's truck, Eliza raised her eyebrows in question as she pulled her Santa hat over her ears.

"We met my first day in town," Cassie explained. "I lent a hand when his baseball got stuck in the roof of the bandstand."

"Thanks for that! Otherwise, this little daredevil would have tried to climb on top and wound up with a broken arm." Smiling affectionately, Eliza tossed what looked like a green elf hat at her son. "Cover your ears. It's freezing out here." Her words escaped in a puffy white cloud.

Ben jammed the pointy hat over his shaggy blond hair, squirming in anticipation. "Can we go? Can we go?"

Eliza laughed. "All right. Let's go roast some marshmallows." She reached for her son's hand before turning to Luke and Cassie. "You two ready?"

"Not yet." Luke retrieved a chainsaw from the back of the pickup. "We have some work to do first."

Cassie's face registered her shock. "We're cutting a tree down with *that*?"

"No, *you're* cutting a tree down with this." Luke's lips twitched, betraying a playful smile.

"Great. I knew this Christmas Calendar would kill me," Cassie muttered, hugging herself against the cold.

"You two have fun!" Eliza winked at Luke before tugging Ben toward the firepit.

Luke cringed at Eliza's lack of subtlety. Hoping Cassie hadn't noticed, he hoisted the chainsaw over his shoulder. "Okay, what kind of tree do we need?"

"The Calendar said to get an eight-foot Fraser fir."

"Of course. Only the best!" He led her down a row of towering fir trees, enveloping them in the sharp, poignant scent of evergreens. "Tell me when you spot the one you want."

"Can't we cut down the first one we see?" She let her gloved hand brush against the prickly branches as they walked past.

"Is that how you picked your boyfriend?" he teased, instantly regretting it. The last thing he wanted to think about was her doting boyfriend back home.

Cassie paused, her lips slightly parted as though about to respond. Then her eyes widened, focusing on a point over his right shoulder. "There it is!"

Luke turned, following the direction of her finger until his gaze rested on a bushy, lopsided fir. "That one?" He tried to keep the incredulity out of his voice but didn't succeed.

Her bottom lip protruded in an adorable pout as she crossed her arms. "Remind me *whose* tree we're picking out?"

He chuckled. "Fair enough."

Lifting the superfluous branches near the bottom, Luke bent down to assess the trunk. Then he walked around the perimeter to determine the correct direction to safely fell the tree. Satisfied with his assessment, he slipped a pair of safety goggles from the inside pocket of his ski jacket and handed them to Cassie. "They're not stylish, but they'll protect your eyes."

"From what?" She glanced nervously at the gargantuan safety hazard. "If that thing falls on me, I doubt a pair of goggles will be much help."

"They'll protect you from any wood particles that might blow back while we cut through the trunk."

"And what'll protect me from death by tree-crushing?"

Luke passed her the chainsaw. "I will." Stepping behind her, he slid a second pair of goggles out of his bulky jacket. "First, take off your gloves. You'll get a better grip without them."

He waited for her to stuff her gloves inside the pocket of her black peacoat before moving in closer. With his chest aligned with her back, he moved his arms around either side of her, situating her hands in the proper position around the handle of the chainsaw. "The vibrations will take some getting used to, but whatever you do, don't let go."

She glanced over her shoulder, her eyes filled with uncertainty.

Luke couldn't help noticing how close their lips were. It would be so easy to—He swallowed, pushing the thought as far down as possible. "Don't worry. I'll be here to help until you get the hang of it." His fingertips found the pull cord, and he drew in a deep breath, trying to ignore the sweet scent of her silky hair as it grazed his chin.

"Ready?"

She nodded slowly, giving him the go-ahead.

Their bodies vibrated as the chainsaw rumbled to life, and Luke heard Cassie's sharp intake of breath. He helped her cut a notch at the base of the trunk, then shouted over the noise, "It's all yours! Just keep doing what you're doing."

Stepping back, he watched the chainsaw bore deeper into the trunk, all of his senses on high alert. Cassie's slight frame shook with the force of the power tool, but her features set in determination.

Suddenly, a large crack rang out, and the massive tree toppled over.

Luke rushed to Cassie's side, retrieving the chainsaw and killing the engine.

Breathless, Cassie pushed back the goggles, her green eyes bright and sparkling. "That was incredible!" Shaking out her hands, she hopped in excitement, a huge grin illuminating her face. "I can't believe I actually did it!"

A vision of pure joy, Luke wanted to hug her on the spot. Instead, he slapped her on the back like she was one of his buddies. "Nice job. I think you've found your calling as a lumberjack."

"I think you're right."

"And now," he said, bending down to grab the trunk. "You've earned yourself a hot chocolate."

Cassie seemed to glide on air as they made their way back to the truck with her hard-won prize.

Luke had grown up cutting down their own Christmas tree every year, and while he always enjoyed it, nothing compared to seeing the experience through Cassie's eyes. Her fervor was infectious.

Taking in the velvety black silhouette of the treetops against the star-studded sky, the brisk, wintry air, and the intoxicating scent of pine needles and fresh sap, Luke couldn't imagine a more perfect night.

Until Cassie said eight little words that sent his already soaring heart plummeting over the edge.

"I don't have a boyfriend, by the way."

CHAPTER 6

Cassie groaned, burying her face in her hands while she waited for her morning caffeine fix to steep in the French press. The subtle fruity flavor notes of her favorite Colombian roast only slightly served to calm her erratic heartbeat.

Why had she told Luke she didn't have a boyfriend? Momentary insanity? That was the only logical explanation. Her body had been pumped full of adrenaline while cutting down the Christmas tree, and the minute it drained from her body, it took her common sense with it.

Cassie rinsed her favorite mug in the porcelain sink and set it next to the French press, admiring the gentle curve of the delicate handle. Although she'd only been staying at the cottage for a few days, it hadn't taken long to choose a favorite mug. It had little to do with the color or design. Although the vibrant red poppies made for an eye-catching pattern. The immediate connection stemmed from the way its weight settled in her palm, instantly finding an equilibrium as though it belonged there.

In two days, Cassie had managed to make herself more or less at home. The only room in the house she hadn't explored was her grandmother's. For some reason, Cassie couldn't even bring herself to crack open the door. Although the soft white paint and brass doorknob caught her eye every morning as she passed the narrow corridor off of the kitchen.

She would have avoided her mother's room, too, but Cassie had no way of knowing which one belonged to Donna Hayward. Both upstairs bedrooms were practically identical, and neither showed any sign of a former teenage inhabitant. Almost as if her mother never existed.

Forcing out the unwanted air, Cassie rolled the top of the craft coffee bag down as far as it would go before securing it with a rubber band. Her heart sank, realizing she'd gone through her supply much quicker than she anticipated, prompting another trip to town in search of more.

Mac's Mercantile sat on the corner of Main Street and Dandelion Drive, its expansive green awnings shading both streets. Stands of seasonal fruits and vegetables like hearty kale, nutty parsnips, and plump persimmons spilled onto the cobblestone sidewalk, intermixed with freshly bound bouquets of carnations, chrysanthemums, and holly berry. Wrought iron bistro sets studded the colorful display. Although the winter chill precluded most people from sitting outside, each table still offered a free copy of the *Poppy Creek Press* and a vase displaying a single Christmas rose.

Cassie brushed past the oak barrels of individually wrapped taffy candies and licorice shaped like lumps of coal to the back of the store, which catered to locals more than tourists. In between a row of baked beans and canned corn, Cassie stumbled upon a single can of ground coffee. Not one row. One *can*. Considering the odd assortment surrounding it, Cassie wondered if it had been misplaced.

"Hi!"

Still clutching the container of nondescript coffee, Cassie swiveled to see Eliza cradling a sack of flour nearly half her size, her dark eyes bright and cheerful.

"Hi." Cassie returned Eliza's smile, surprised to find herself happy to see her new acquaintance.

"Snatching the last can of coffee, I see," Eliza teased.

"Actually, I was wondering if someone accidentally placed it on the wrong shelf. It doesn't seem to belong here." Cassie set the can back inline.

Eliza eyed the row of seemingly random items. "Nope. That's right. Coffee. In between baked beans and canned corn."

Cassie couldn't hide her confusion, and Eliza shook so hard with laughter, Cassie feared she might drop the sack of flour, turning the entire aisle into the scene of an avalanche.

"Mac likes to organize things alphabetically, not by like items," Eliza explained when she finally caught her breath.

At Cassie's horrified expression, Eliza grinned. "Don't worry. You'll get used to it."

Cassie doubted it but kept the thought to herself. "What I *can't* get used to is being without good coffee."

Eliza's features softened in sympathy. "Wish I could help you, but Poppy Creek is a little behind the times when it comes to coffee."

"Only coffee?" Cassie raised her eyebrows, her green eyes twinkling playfully.

"Okay, we're behind in a lot of things," Eliza admitted with a giggle, adding, "There's only one place in town to get coffee that isn't"—she wrinkled her nose as she pointed toward the can—"that stuff."

Cassie's pulse quickened with an inkling of hope. "And where's that?"

"Oh, trust me. You don't want to go there."

Clearly, Eliza didn't understand how seriously Cassie took her coffee. "Please. I'm desperate. I only have half a pound left."

Eliza tilted her head, studying her a moment. "Okay," she said slowly. "I have the day off, so I can take you. If you're *sure* you want to go. I just have to drop this sack of flour at Maggie's first."

Cassie exhaled in relief. "Thank you. I owe you one."

"Don't thank me yet," Eliza said mysteriously, sweeping past her toward the single register.

Wavering only an instant, Cassie followed, relishing the tiny twinge of excitement setting her nerves on edge. She couldn't remember the last time she'd experienced a true adventure. Now, nearly every day was filled with something new and unexplored.

※

W hen Eliza parked in a patch of dirt off the main road and pointed toward a driveway crowded by overgrown weeds, Cassie's bravery faltered. Deciduous trees clothed in mistletoe drooped over the eerie entrance like ghouls guarding an evil sorcerer's castle.

"Welcome to Frank Barrie's place. Home to Poppy Creek's very own Grinch." Eliza drew out each syllable for dramatic emphasis.

"When you said his place was creepy, you weren't exaggerating." Cassie shivered even though they were cocooned in the warmth of Eliza's car.

"We used to come out here as kids, daring each other to get as close to the house as possible. Luke's brother, Colt, made it the furthest. That's when he saw Frank roasting coffee in his barn."

"Did Luke's brother get caught?"

Eliza's lips quirked at the memory. "Almost. I'd never seen Colt run so fast in his life. And he was Poppy Creek High's star athlete!" Leaning across the console, Eliza lowered her voice just above a whisper. "Rumor has it, Frank used to be in the military and still has a stockpile of rifles. Back here in the woods, the only trespassing law is *shoot on sight.*"

Cassie's heart pounded in her ears, but she forced a shaky smile. "You're teasing."

Eliza shrugged. "Believe that if it makes you feel better." Pushing the door open, she glanced over her shoulder and asked, "Are you *sure* you want to do this?"

Cassie nodded, ignoring her clammy palms as she struggled with the release button on her seat belt. "You don't have to come with me."

"Are you kidding? I'm the Black Widow to your Captain Marvel." Eliza climbed out of the driver's seat and stretched her five-foot-four frame as tall as it would reach. "How should we do this? I take the front, and you go around the back?"

Cassie shook her head in bemusement. "We're not ambushing the man. Think of us as reverse Girl Scouts. Instead of selling something, we're looking to buy."

Eliza's shoulders drooped with a disappointed sigh. "Fine, but I was already channeling Scarlett Johansson."

Cassie giggled, her footsteps feeling lighter as they made their way down the gravel drive, sidestepping potholes.

As Frank's home came into view, Cassie's breath caught in her throat. The weather-beaten farmhouse had seen better days. Moss-green paint, now chipped and peeling, hid behind invasive ivy that seemed to swallow the house whole. Crooked shutters dangled from window frames haphazardly, and the palatial front porch looked so barren and forlorn with only a single rocking chair to fill the expansive space, Cassie's heart nearly broke.

"Yikes." Eliza whistled under her breath. "I haven't been out here in years, but I don't remember it looking *this* bad. I'd suggest knocking on the front door, but it might fall over."

As Cassie deliberated their next move, a familiar aroma flooded her senses—the thick, heady fragrance of freshly roasted coffee. She looked past the roofline to see puffy billows of smoke rising from somewhere behind the house.

Following the scent, they rounded the corner of the dilapidated building, stumbling into one another as they halted abruptly.

47

Cassie watched, awestruck, as a lithe, elderly man released the lever of a ten-pound capacity air roaster and a rush of dark, crackling coffee beans spilled from the machine into a perforated cylindrical drum. After securing a lid on the drum, the man wheeled it out of the barn and into the open air. Turning a crank, the metal cylinder began to spin on its axis, aromatic smoke escaping through the perforations, accumulating in a thick cloud that rose into the somber gray sky.

"Do you know what we're witnessing?" Cassie whispered, unable to tear her gaze from the man she assumed was Frank Barrie.

As the speed of the drum slowed from a rapid spin to a gentle tumble, Frank removed the lid and tilted the drum toward the ground, pouring the coffee beans into a large steel pan, which he deftly lifted and carried a few paces into the barn where he set it on a long wooden table.

"No clue," Eliza murmured in a hushed tone.

Cassie didn't respond right away, barely able to believe her own eyes. She'd visited dozens of artisan roasters in her lifetime, several of whom attempted to mimic the world-renowned Mariposa Method of coffee roasting. But none had ever been able to master it quite like Frank Barrie, who executed each step of the process effortlessly, as though they were as second nature as breathing. Cassie, like any die-hard coffee enthusiast, had studied the method, reading the groundbreaking book by the enigmatic inventor, Richard Stanton, from cover to cover several times. But never in a million years did she expect someone in Poppy Creek to know about it. Let alone a strange recluse like Frank Barrie.

Cassie noted the way his thin yet muscular forearms flexed under the labor as he scooped the beans into five-gallon glass mason jars. The man had to be at least in his early eighties. His silver hair and deep-set wrinkles depicted a hard life as well as his advanced years. Still, Frank Barrie was a handsome man in spite of his gruff exterior.

For a moment, the scene played out before her as though she were watching a documentary. Then, as she was about to clue in Eliza on what she knew, Frank glanced up, his dark eyes narrowing as his thick peppery eyebrows lowered over them.

They'd been spotted.

Cassie heard Eliza's sharp intake of breath by her side.

"Get off my property," Frank growled, taking a threatening step toward them.

Knees trembling, Cassie stood her ground, swallowing the fear that rose in her throat. "I'm sorry, we're not here to bother you, but—"

"Then don't," he barked, stomping toward the back porch.

Cassie felt Eliza's hand wrap around her forearm, squeezing hard.

For reasons beyond Cassie's comprehension, she couldn't give up yet. "I was wondering if—"

Her words were interrupted by a loud slam as Frank disappeared inside, jerking the door shut behind him.

Eliza tugged on Cassie's arm, her voice strained as she murmured, "Let's go. He might be back with some buckshot."

Cassie followed Eliza's hurried footsteps to the car, but something compelled her to glance back.

Fortunately, Frank hadn't followed them with military-level artillery, but a sudden movement in the front window caught her eye.

The faded brocade curtains were drawn hastily.

What exactly was Frank Barrie hiding?

❄

Luke glanced at the grandfather clock in the corner of his office, a move which didn't go unnoticed by his friend Jack Gardner.

"Man, you've got it bad." Jack's cornflower-blue eyes crinkled in the corners as he rumbled with laughter.

Clearing his throat, Luke focused his attention on the licensing agreement spread out in front of them. "You don't know what you're talking about."

"Classic rebuttal." Jack snorted, crossing his arms in front of his broad chest as he leaned against the back of the club chair. "You haven't stopped looking at the clock since I got here. I'd be offended, except I'm sure my company isn't as desirable as a certain brunette I've seen around town."

Luke's stomach clenched. So, Jack had noticed Cassie, too, huh? Well, of course he had. What man in town hadn't? Luke drew in a calming breath. It wasn't a competition. There was no future with Cassie, anyway. She'd be leaving town in a few weeks. All feelings that may or may not be culminating were moot.

"I can see the wheels turning in that lawyer brain of yours," Jack said with a knowing grin. "You're convincing yourself there's no point in pursuing a relationship with her." Leaning forward, Jack rested his bulky forearms on the desk. "But you'd be wrong."

Luke suppressed a groan. There were definite disadvantages to growing up in a small town where people have known you your entire life. Mind reading, for one. "Should we focus on this licensing agreement for your barbecue sauce?"

Jack grabbed a pen off the desk and twirled it between his calloused fingers. "Okay, counselor. Let's hear your argument against the defendant. Why can't you date Cassie Hayward?"

This time Luke didn't hold back his groan and paired it with a blatant eye roll. "You sound ridiculous. You know that, right?"

Jack ignored him. "Please approach the bench, counselor. And state your case."

Luke sighed. Loudly. "For one, she doesn't even live here."

Jack waved his hand dismissively, still spinning the pen. "Minor details. Is she taken?"

Heat spread across Luke's body as he recalled Cassie's

words from the previous night. *I don't have a boyfriend, by the way.*

"Aha!" Jack slammed the pen on the desk, startling Luke out of his reverie. "She's single! I knew it."

Luke opened his mouth to ask how he could tell, but Jack beat him to it.

"You got this goofy grin on your face." Jack chuckled, then resumed his pen twirling. "Carry on, counselor."

Luke cleared his throat again, gathering his thoughts. "Truthfully, I don't have time to date right now."

The pen slipped from Jack's fingers, clattering to the pinewood floor. "I should have you dragged away in contempt of court. That's the lamest excuse I've ever heard."

"Just so you know," Luke told him, "you're not using any of the legalese correctly."

"Whatever," Jack quipped. "Stop avoiding the subject. You may be busy, but that's not a good reason to be a coward. If you like her, ask her out. You can figure the rest out later."

Luke opened his mouth to protest, but Jack stood abruptly, the legs of the chair scraping against the floor. "I'm your last client of the day. So, when I call your office from the diner in a few minutes, I'd better hear from Dolores that you're on your way to a certain white cottage."

Rising to stand opposite his friend, Luke couldn't help a grin. "Maybe *you* should have been a lawyer. You're bullheaded enough."

"The world's got enough lawyers," Jack said, returning the pen to the desk. "But good barbecue... Now, *there's* a serious shortage. But thanks for admitting I'm right."

Luke shook his head, chuckling under his breath as Jack strode out of his office. He had to hand it to his friend... he presented a strong case.

Maybe he *should* put his concerns aside and see what happens.

CHAPTER 7

Cassie's palm rested on the open page of December 3 on the Christmas Calendar, but her thoughts were far from the day's activity. How could she concentrate on decorating the Christmas tree when she could still smell the intoxicating aroma of freshly roasted coffee from earlier that morning?

She craved a cup of the velvety beans she'd watched tumble from the roasting machine, knowing they would taste like heaven itself. What did Frank Barrie do with all of that coffee if he didn't sell it somewhere in town?

Cassie's thoughts were interrupted by a jarring knock on the front door. Her eyelashes fluttered as she took a few moments to settle back into reality. Who would be visiting at... she glanced at the time on her phone... seven o'clock in the evening? Her heart undulated as Luke's magnetic smile sprang to mind.

Quickly running her fingers through her loose curls, she headed for the source of the impatient hammering.

A smile already formed on her lips, Cassie swung open the front door, ready to welcome her guest. But her greeting fell short in her surprise, stalling on the tip of her tongue.

Ben beamed at her, both fists poised midair.

"Sorry," Eliza said sheepishly from directly behind her son. "I asked Ben to knock since my hands are full."

Cassie's focus drifted past Ben's boyish grin to Eliza, who gripped a wooden crate filled with baking supplies.

"We're here to bake cookies!" Ben chirped brightly.

"And help decorate the tree. If you haven't already." Luke bounded up the front steps, stopping beside Eliza. His sapphire-blue sweater brought out the subtle jeweled-undertones in his eyes and for a moment, Cassie was too distracted to speak.

"Can we come inside before our shoes freeze to your front porch?" Eliza teased, shifting the heavy crate in her arms.

"Of course!" Cassie stepped to the side, avoiding Luke's gaze as he brushed past her, flooding her senses with a heady scent of cedar and cloves.

Taking a deep breath, she pushed the door closed until she heard the latch click, admonishing herself to get a grip. So what if Luke smelled better than a gingerbread latte? Cassie wasn't the type to swoon. At least, not anymore.

"I see you haven't started yet." Luke's attention flickered from the bare fir tree centered in front of the enormous bay window to the boxes of ornaments stacked on the floor.

"I was sidetracked," Cassie admitted.

"I took her to Frank Barrie's place," Eliza shouted from the kitchen.

Cassie and Luke joined her around the island, where she unloaded her box of baking supplies. Ben sat at the antique butterfly table, flipping through the Christmas Calendar, oblivious to their conversation.

"Why would you take her there?" A protective edge crept into Luke's tone, causing Cassie's heartbeat to quicken involuntarily.

Eliza rolled her eyes. "Calm down. We're perfectly fine." She set a ball of chilled cookie dough wrapped in cellophane on the counter. "Cassie wanted to see if she could buy some of Frank's coffee beans."

"You should have told me." Luke still sounded a little on edge. "I would have gone with you."

"For my sake? Or Cassie's?" Eliza's dark eyes glinted mischievously, and Luke looked decidedly uncomfortable.

Coming to his rescue, Cassie asked, "How come you and Maggie haven't tried to buy some for the bakery?"

Eliza shrugged, sprinkling a handful of flour on the butcher block. "We're not really set up to serve coffee. I mean, we have the air pot, but we barely pay any attention to it." She plopped the cookie dough onto the dusted surface, pausing in thought. "Although, if we could figure out how to use that behemoth in the basement, it may be worthwhile to invest in some quality coffee."

"What's in the basement?" Cassie settled herself on the wooden stool, propping her arms on the edge of the counter, not caring that her red sweater now had white elbow patches, thanks to Eliza's generous dose of flour.

Luke perched on the stool next to her, grazing her thigh with his.

At his touch, Cassie's senses heightened to everything around her, including the faintly sweet aroma of the sugar cookie dough Eliza flattened with her rolling pin.

"When Mom bought the building over thirty years ago, the previous owner left a bunch of stuff in the basement," Luke explained, seemingly unaware of the effect he had on her. "One of the items was an old espresso machine."

Cassie straightened, immediately intrigued. "How old?"

"Not sure," Luke admitted. "Antique, for sure. It's huge. Made out of hammered copper."

"Can I see it sometime?" Cassie tried to curb the enthusiasm from her voice but clearly failed.

Luke chuckled. "You sure love your coffee, don't you?"

"Do you think you'd know how to use it?" Eliza asked.

"Possibly. I used to be a barista, so I know my way around an espresso machine."

"What do you do for work now?" Luke asked.

Cassie swallowed, tracing a line through the flour with her fingertip. "I'm in between jobs at the moment." She chose not to mention she'd been fired from her previous job because the manager of the coffee shop didn't like her "know-it-all" attitude. Was it *her* fault he didn't know the difference between Guatemala Antigua and Fraijanes?

"I'm sorry." Eliza set down the rolling pin to preheat the oven. "Has it been long?"

Long enough. Cassie shifted on the barstool, careful not to bump knees with Luke. "I'm confident I'll get a call any day now. I have a few résumés circulating."

Circulating into the trash, most likely. The truth was, Cassie knew too much to be a barista since the managers felt threatened by her skill and knowledge, but she didn't have the college degree to warrant a management position. She'd have to find something soon, though. Even if she sold her grandmother's cottage above market value, she couldn't live off the money forever.

Cassie could feel Luke's gaze on her, but she fixed her attention on the snowman she'd doodled in the flour. She couldn't bear to see even a hint of pity in his eyes.

"I wish we had a coffee shop in Poppy Creek," Eliza said regretfully. "But I bet we could find you a job doing something else. What do you love besides coffee?"

Cassie blinked, caught off guard by Eliza's question. What else did she love? Her mother, though Cassie sometimes wished she didn't. Of course, she knew that wasn't what Eliza meant.

Pressing her lips together, Cassie forced a smile. "Thanks. That's sweet of you. But I won't be staying in town. I'll be heading back to San Francisco right after Christmas."

An unreadable glance flickered between Eliza and Luke.

Luke cleared his throat. "Why don't Ben and I string the lights on the tree while you ladies put the first batch of cookies in the oven?"

"You've got yourself a deal." Eliza dumped a tray of cookie cutters onto the counter, the metal cutouts of stockings and snowflakes clattering against each other.

"We'll call you when it's time to add the ornaments." Luke slid off the barstool and turned to Ben. "Hey, bud, ready to decorate the tree?"

With a rambunctious cheer that doubled as a yes, Ben deserted the Christmas Calendar on the table and scampered into the living room, followed by Luke.

"Here, you start cutting out the dough." Eliza handed Cassie a cookie cutter shaped like a reindeer head before rummaging through her assortment of supplies. "There's one more thing I need to do."

Cassie stole sideways glances at Eliza while she dutifully made floating head cookies.

"Aha! Here it is." Eliza pulled a small ziplock bag from the crate. Grabbing a dining chair, she dragged it beneath the doorway that separated the kitchen from the living room.

Cassie set down the cookie cutter, curious what would happen next.

"While you've done a lovely job decorating," Eliza said, climbing on top of the chair, "I thought there might be one small detail you'd forget."

Eyes wide, Cassie watched Eliza tack a sprig of mistletoe to the doorframe.

"There! Now everything is perfect." Eliza hopped off the chair and brushed her hands together, looking quite pleased with her little addition.

Cassie gulped. *Great.* Now she had to add one more thing to her list of worries. No way could she let herself get caught underneath the mistletoe.

Not with anyone.

But especially not with Luke Davis.

❅

A smile tugged at the corners of Luke's mouth as he watched Cassie gape at the towering fir tree draped in twinkling lights, brilliant hues of red, green, blue, and gold reflecting off the bay window and dispersing around the room like rainbow fragments.

She held an angel ornament tentatively in her hands, her bottom lip drawn between her teeth. If the thought weren't so far-fetched, Luke would assume she'd never decorated a tree before.

Slipping his phone out of his back pocket, he scrolled through his holiday music playlist and the lively rendition of Brenda Lee's "Rockin' Around the Christmas Tree" joined the sound of pine logs crackling in the fireplace.

"There." Luke leaned his phone against the nativity set on the coffee table. "Now the mood is set for you to hang the first ornament."

Cassie's uncertain gaze flitted in his direction, then back to the tree. "How do I know where to put it?"

Ben sprang from his cross-legged position on the floor, two nutcracker ornaments in hand. "Watch me! Watch me!" Without a moment's thought, he crammed both nutcrackers on the nearest branch. They hung back-to-back, as though about to count off a duel.

Cassie giggled. "Well, if it's *that* simple…" On her tiptoes, she secured the angel to a branch directly above her. Stepping back, she placed both hands on her hips and cocked her head to the side. "Not bad."

"Nice job!" Luke grinned. "Only ninety-nine more ornaments to go."

"So, basically, we're going to be here all night," Cassie teased.

Warmth spread across Luke's chest, and he tugged at his collar. The idea *wasn't* unappealing.

"Look, Cassie." Ben tapped her arm. "I picked out this ornament for Grandma Edith all by myself." He dangled a pair of silver bells by a red satin cord. As he flicked his wrist, the bells chimed in unison, soft and ethereal.

Eliza joined them, setting a plate of warm sugar cookies on the coffee table. The sweet scent of their golden, buttery crusts mingled with the sharp, tangy fragrance of evergreen. "Ben found it in our friend Penny's antiques shop a few years ago and remembered Edith's favorite Christmas song was 'Silver Bells.'"

Luke noticed a shadow cross Cassie's features and wondered if talking about her grandmother brought her sadness. Growing up in Poppy Creek his entire life, he couldn't imagine what it felt like to be disconnected from your roots. And your family. Changing the subject, he directed a question at Ben. "Why don't you hang it on the tree and pick another ornament for Cassie?"

Ben skipped to the tree and hung the silver bells directly above the nutcrackers, apparently going for the clustered effect. Next, he handed Cassie an ornament shaped like a heart with the silhouette of a man and woman painted on the smooth porcelain.

Cassie lightly touched the couple, appearing lost in her thoughts.

Something in her wistful expression tugged at Luke's heartstrings. And, feeling restless, he reached for a cookie, even though the furthest thing from his mind was food.

"Edith got that ornament for their first anniversary," Eliza explained, her voice filled with warmth. "She must have told me the story a thousand times. It started a tradition where each year she'd collect another ornament that represented something important. Either a milestone from that year or some new hobby or interest. She said each Christmas, unwrapping the ornaments was like unpacking a time capsule."

"That's sweet," Cassie murmured, looping the gold string around a sturdy branch. Turning to Eliza, she bit her bottom lip, as if debating her next words. "Ben referred to Edith as his grandma... There's no relation, is there?"

Eliza smiled from her perch on the arm of the couch. "No, that's just something Ben does. If he feels like someone is family, then they are."

"So, when he calls Luke 'Uncle Luke' that doesn't mean you and Luke's brother..."

"Me and *Colt?*" Eliza sputtered, nearly toppling off the couch.

"I'm sorry!" Cassie flushed with embarrassment. "I didn't mean to offend you."

Luke doubled over in laughter at the look of dismay on Eliza's face. Then, noticing Cassie's discomfort, he softened. "Don't worry, Cassie. Eliza is only rattled because she had an unrequited crush on my little brother for most of her childhood."

"I did not!" Eliza crossed her arms in protest.

"Sure," Luke drawled, rolling his eyes playfully. "It was only the most obvious crush I've ever seen."

Eliza stalked over and snatched the half-eaten cookie from his hand.

"Hey!" Luke cried, swiping for it unsuccessfully.

Glaring, Eliza waved the confection in his face. "Fibbers don't get cookies."

Luke shrugged, still grinning. "Luckily I know where to find the main supply." He strode into the kitchen, chuckling under his breath.

As Luke selected a new cookie from the dozen or so cooling on the rack, he wondered if he'd get a moment alone with Cassie. He'd been mulling over Jack's words all day, growing more certain he wanted to see if their friendship could become something more. Swallowing his nerves with a bite of the sugary treat, he made a pact with himself that he'd try to steal a moment before the night ended.

Heading back into the living room, Luke overheard Eliza ask Cassie to check on the batch of cookies in the oven. Something in Eliza's tone sounded odd. There was an eager, almost mischievous lilt to it.

The precise moment Luke crossed the threshold of the kitchen, Cassie collided with him in the doorway. Instinctively, he placed his hands around her waist to steady her, the same time her palms met his chest.

"Sorry!" she gasped, then froze. Her eyes widened, darting skyward.

That's when Luke saw it.

The mistletoe hanging directly above their heads.

CHAPTER 8

Cassie burrowed beneath the thick layer of quilts, unwilling to face the reality of a new day. Her cheeks still stung from the embarrassment of colliding with Luke under that exasperating sprig of mistletoe. Fortunately, they were interrupted by a glass ornament shattering across the parquet floor.

As Cassie recalled the moment, a twinge of disappointment lurked behind her relief. But she forced the thought aside. She had no business wondering what Luke's lips would feel like gently pressed against her own. Especially since she'd sworn off dating. Not that her subconscious cared about her ban on romance, filling her dreams with all kinds of outlandish scenarios. Who kissed in the back of a sleigh? She didn't even think they existed anymore.

Before her brain could come up with something even more outlandish—like making the sleigh airborne—Derek texted again, waking her in the middle of the night, prompting Cassie to shut off her phone. He'd even resorted to following up his "I miss you" message with a string of sad-face emojis. As if an emoticon could make her forget last Christmas. As if *anything* could make her forget.

In desperate need of a distraction, Cassie threw back the covers, prepared to undertake whatever task the Christmas Calendar allocated for the day. Impersonating one of Santa's jolly helpers would be preferable to agonizing over an almost-kiss. Especially since every fiber of her being insisted a kiss with Luke Davis would be earth-shattering.

Cassie sat up in bed, disoriented by the bright light filtering through the gossamer curtains. Now that she wasn't buried beneath several quilts, the air felt noticeably colder. Squinting as her eyes adjusted to the brilliant glow, she wrapped a blanket around her shoulders and padded to the window. Thick flurries of snow danced across the frosted glass, shrouding the sky for as far as she could see.

Cassie's heart fluttered in her chest. Her very first snowstorm!

Clothed in soft, gray long johns, Cassie pulled knee-high socks over her bare feet and skipped down the staircase as eager as a child on Christmas morning.

The glittering Christmas tree greeted her as she leaped over the last step and sailed into the living room, sliding across the polished floor in her stockinged feet. The night before, she'd been so mesmerized by the tree's beauty, she hadn't been able to unplug it before going to bed. Now, as it sparkled in the bright, ethereal glow of the snowstorm, Cassie found herself even more entranced. Who knew something as simple as a topiary draped in lights and colorful baubles could evoke such an emotional response?

Tearing her gaze from the dazzling tree, Cassie checked the fire, grateful for the sturdy oak log Luke had added to the coals before bidding her goodnight. A few bronze embers still smoldered in a pile of ash and cinder.

After stoking the fire with another log, filling the cottage with the comforting, smoky scent of scorched timber, Cassie began her morning ritual—steeping a fresh pot of coffee in the

French press and checking the day's activity on the Christmas Calendar.

December 4: Bake a Mince Pie.

Leaning her weight against the edge of the kitchen island, Cassie groaned. Putting aside the fact that a mince pie sounded disgusting, Cassie doubted she had the necessary ingredients. Her last trip to Mac's had produced little more than the basics, minus a can of ground coffee—*bleh!* Sure, her grandmother's pantry was well stocked but hardly well enough for something as obscure as a mince pie.

And only a fool would consider venturing outside in a snowstorm of this magnitude.

❄

A fter his third knock, panic rose in Luke's chest. What if Cassie went out in the storm?

Luke glanced over his shoulder. In a matter of minutes, his red pickup had become nearly invisible. He knew he should've gotten there sooner! But it had taken him almost an hour to dig his truck out of the snowdrift.

Luke tried the doorknob, his pulse spiking when the handle wouldn't turn. He hammered his fist one more time, watching the wreath quiver from the force.

This time the door slowly creaked open.

Cassie stared up at him, surprise sprawled across her face. "Luke?"

Luke swooped inside, slamming the door against the freezing snow flurries. "Are you okay? I got here as soon as I could. You haven't tried to go outside, have you?"

Cocking her head, Cassie blinked in confusion. "Why would I go outside? It's practically a blizzard out there."

Luke opened his mouth to answer but faltered as the reality of the situation settled. A huge clump of snow dislodged from his coat, plopping onto the clean hardwood floor. He must look like Frosty melting on the Fourth of July. Clearly, Cassie was smart enough to stay inside in the middle of a snowstorm, not that he could say the same for himself. "I, uh, tried to call. But your phone was dead. So, I thought..." His voice trailed off as he caught Cassie trying to hide a smile.

"You thought the naive city girl had decided to take a jaunty stroll in the storm of the century?" she teased.

Grinning sheepishly, Luke removed his snow-spackled coat. "Okay, I admit my concerns were... a little hasty."

Cassie's eyes softened. "But it was sweet of you to come to my rescue."

Luke's heartbeat stilled as they stared at each other in the foyer, water droplets from the melting snow pinging against the floor. He wanted to say something, *anything*, to prolong the moment, but he couldn't think past how adorable she looked with her long johns, knee-high socks, and tousled hair. But he couldn't very well say *that*, could he?

"Well, now that you're here, you might as well get warmed up." Cassie reached for his coat and scarf, hanging them on the vintage hall stand.

Luke tugged off his beanie, quickly running his fingers through the wayward strands of dark hair. "I can't remember what's on the Christmas Calendar for today. Nothing outside, I hope."

Cassie wrinkled her nose. "I have to bake a mince pie. Although, it might as well be a pie of four and twenty blackbirds, considering I don't have the ingredients for either."

"Wow!" Luke snorted with laughter. "Pulling out the obscure nursery rhymes. I'm impressed."

"As an only child, you read a lot." Cassie flashed an endearing grin.

It wasn't lost on Luke that she wasn't wearing a lick of makeup, which let her natural beauty shine. A few freckles dusted her nose and cheeks, like a sprinkling of brown sugar, and Luke had a strong urge to run his fingertips over them. He blew out a breath, banishing the impulsive idea. "You're in luck. I happen to be a mince pie expert. I've helped my mother bake one every Christmas since I could hold a spoon."

Cassie smiled. "Your spoon-holding skills aside, how do we solve the problem of not having the right ingredients?"

After kicking off his wet boots, Luke strode into the kitchen, followed by Cassie. He headed straight for the freezer. "If you haven't already noticed, Edith was incredibly organized. And well prepared." Pulling out a jar of premade mince pie filling, he set it on the counter with a triumphant grin.

Inspecting the jar of frozen filling, Cassie arched an eyebrow. "I can't believe I'm saying this, but... isn't this cheating?"

"We still have to heat the filling, make the crust, and bake it in the oven. It counts as making a pie in my book."

"If you say so. You're the boss." Her eyes sparkled playfully, highlighting the brilliant gold flecks in the sea of green, sending a spark of awareness rippling through Luke.

Setting a double boiler on the stove, Luke swallowed. The only thing he needed to heat up tonight was the oven. They simply had to focus on baking a pie until the storm subsided enough for him to head home. The *last* thing he needed was to get stuck in an intimate, cozy cottage with the one woman who made time stand still. "So," he said, clearing his throat. "I'll work on defrosting the filling while you start the crust."

At Cassie's blank stare, Luke pointed to the Christmas Calendar. "There should be a recipe."

Cassie ran her finger down the page, scrunching her face as she scanned the instructions. "This recipe doesn't make any sense... What's the difference between a pinch and a dash?"

Luke chuckled at her perplexed expression. "Don't worry. I'll show you."

Hopping onto the barstool, Cassie watched Luke deftly assemble and measure the ingredients. "You're quite the pro."

"When your mom owns a bakery, you pick up a thing or two."

"You should have gone into the family business," Cassie teased.

Luke smiled. "Actually, I did."

"What do you mean?"

"My law practice used to be my dad's. In fact, it's still his name on the door. The L stands for Leonard."

"Gosh, I had no idea. Did you always want to follow in his footsteps?"

Luke dug his fists into the ceramic bowl, appreciating the soft, pliable feel of the dough as he shaped it by hand. "I didn't seriously consider law school until my second year of college. When my dad got cancer."

"Oh, Luke. I'm so sorry!"

Encouraged by the sincerity in her voice, Luke drew in a deep breath and continued. "It was a rough time. He eventually went into remission—long enough to see me graduate from law school. We all thought he was in the clear. But a few weeks after graduation, we learned his cancer had come back. We lost him four months later."

Without saying a word, Cassie reached across the counter and gently placed her hand on his forearm. Luke savored the gentle, comforting feel of her soft skin against his own.

Then, as if the connection between them had suddenly grown too intense, she pulled away. Averting her gaze, she tucked a strand of hair behind her ear. "He must have been very proud to have you take over his practice."

"He was." Luke's chest tightened recalling the day his dad handed him the key to the office.

"What did you want to do before you switched to law school?" Cassie asked.

Luke's hands stilled, and the sticky ball of dough fell from his grip, plopping onto the bottom of the bowl. No one had ever asked him that before. And for a moment, Luke hesitated.

He'd hardly admitted the thought to himself, let alone another human being. But for some reason, Luke wanted to tell Cassie. He wanted to tell her everything. "Do you remember the furniture in my office?"

"Of course! They're all beautiful pieces. Especially Dolores's rocking chair."

Luke's heart did a funny little dance at her words of praise, and he could only imagine the goofy grin taking over his features. "I made them."

"You made them?" she asked slowly. "Like, actually *made* them? With your own two hands?"

He chuckled. "Well, I used tools. But yes, I made them myself."

Her eyes brightened. "Luke, that's amazing! You have a gift. Seriously. People pay top dollar for craftsmanship like that. Have you ever thought about opening your own furniture business?"

Luke dumped the lump of dough onto the butcher block and began kneading. "Not really."

"Why not?" Her tone held no censure, only curiosity. But her question mirrored the same one he'd refused to ask himself for years.

"Because no one in Poppy Creek needs bespoke furniture," Luke said a little gruffer than he intended. Grappling for the right words, he exhaled, his shoulders slumping as a rush of air escaped his lungs. Finally he spoke, doing his best to keep his voice slow and even. "Poppy Creek needs me to be Leonard Davis. My dad wasn't just the guy you'd call for legal advice. He was the rock of the entire town. The one you could call at any time, for any reason. Folks around here relied on him." An image of his dad's strong features flashed before Luke's eyes, and he swallowed against the unwanted surge of emotion, jabbing his fist into the clump of dough.

"I'm sorry. I didn't realize," Cassie said softly.

"Don't be sorry. It's not you." Luke attempted a smile, only managing a crooked one at best. "It's me. It's kind of a... tough subject. So, what about you? What's your dream job?"

"The truth?"

"Preferably." Luke chuckled, feeling the tension lift from his shoulders.

Cassie paused, grazing her teeth over her bottom lip as she appeared to study him, assessing his trustworthiness. When her lips finally parted, she said, "I've always wanted to own my own coffee shop. A place where I can match people with their perfect cup of coffee." A soft light lit her eyes from within. "My favorite thing in the world is when someone doesn't know what they want, and then they take a sip of what I created for them. One sip. And their entire posture changes. Their shoulders relax. The crease in their forehead fades. It's like they've come home, and they didn't even realize they were lost."

Watching the passion illuminate Cassie's face stirred something in Luke. Something he hadn't felt in a long time. And he wanted nothing more than to lean across the counter, take her beautiful face in his hands, and kiss her. Like he'd almost done last night.

As if reading his mind, Cassie blushed. "That probably sounds ridiculous, doesn't it?"

"Not at all," Luke said, wishing his voice didn't sound so husky. "And I have no doubt your dream will come true one day."

"Thanks." The word escaped barely above a whisper, her hushed tone increasing the air of intimacy in the snug space.

Luke's heartbeat hammered so loudly he was certain Cassie could hear it. Now was his chance. He had to tell Cassie how he felt. With any luck, she'd return his feelings. But...

Luke glanced out the window. Thick snowflakes continued to tumble from the sky. If she didn't feel the same way, Luke would be trapping them inside the cottage to stew in the awkwardness. Could he really risk putting Cassie in that position?

Forcing aside his own preference, Luke asked, "How about we get this pie in the oven, and I'll show you how we spend a snow day in Poppy Creek?"

"Before I say yes," Cassie said, sliding off the stool, "please tell me it's not knitting."

Laughter rumbled through Luke's chest. "No, not knitting. Cassie Hayward, it's time for your Christmas movie marathon."

A slow, tantalizing smile spread across Cassie's lips, and Luke groaned internally. How in the world would he spend the next several hours curled up on the couch next to this irresistible woman without crossing the invisible line of friendship?

Luke certainly didn't consider himself a weak man.

But did he have *that* much strength?

He honestly wasn't sure.

CHAPTER 9

Apersistent pounding on the front door roused Cassie from a deep sleep. Groggy, she released a low moan. What *was* it with small towns and everyone showing up unannounced all the time?

It took her a moment to orient herself with her surroundings. The last thing she remembered was...

Cassie's cheeks burned at the sudden memory. She'd fallen asleep on the couch with Luke during *The Santa Clause*. Which was ironic, considering she could relate to Tim Allen's character. But halfway through the film, she'd nodded off until Luke's soft murmur, and the warmth of his breath tickling her forehead stirred her awake.

They'd parted ways at the top of the staircase, awkwardly saying goodnight before Luke disappeared into the spare room. She wasn't sure she'd be able to fall asleep with Luke a few feet down the hall. But slumber had come quickly, and she felt a strange sense of peace knowing he was nearby.

Cutting into her thoughts, the hammering on the front door grew more urgent.

"Luke? Cassie? I know you're both in there. I can see your cars buried in the snow."

Eliza!

Cassie's heart quickened as she wrestled with the tangle of covers, tumbling onto the floor in a jumble of sheets and quilts.

"Are you okay?" Luke appeared in the doorway, sleepy-eyed and disheveled, his voice deep and husky first thing in the morning.

Cassie couldn't let her eyes linger too long on the adorable cowlick in his dark hair, or the faint impressions the pillow left on his stubbled cheek. "It's Eliza!" she hissed. "She's going to think you spent the night."

Luke's chuckle came out low and raspy. "I *did* spend the night."

"You know what I mean." Finally free of the covers, Cassie jumped to her feet and pushed past him into the hall, doing her best to ignore his irresistible, musky scent.

Watching Christmas movies over slices of mince pie had already drained every ounce of self-control she possessed. The urge to lean against him as they sat side by side on the couch all evening had been stronger than she wanted to admit. Even to herself.

Throwing open the front door, Cassie was surprised to see Ben standing beside his mother, dressed head to toe in an entire department store's worth of snow gear.

"I want to hear all about *this*," Eliza said, waggling her finger between Luke and Cassie. "But it'll have to wait. School has called a snow day because of some frozen pipes, my parents are out of town, and I need someone to watch Ben while I'm at work. I tried your place first, Luke. But when you weren't home, I figured I'd check here." Eliza didn't bother hiding her smirk.

Cassie's cheeks reddened. She supposed Luke *had* been spending an inordinate amount of time at the cottage, but it didn't mean anything. Did it?

"Luke came over yesterday to check on me," Cassie blurted.

"But the storm didn't let up, so he stayed the night. In the extra bedroom."

"I see." Eliza flashed an impish grin. "I can't wait to get *all* the details." She winked before turning to Ben and planting a kiss on his forehead—the only part of his body not engulfed in layers of winter wear. "Be good. Love you."

"Love you." Ben's voice was muffled behind the thick scarf wrapped high around his neck.

As Cassie watched Eliza crunch through the snow to her Honda Accord, she asked, "Is it even safe for her to drive through the snow in that car?"

"A volunteer crew plows all the roads into town," Luke explained. Placing a hand on Ben's shoulder, he nudged the boy inside. "Come on, let's get out of the cold."

Ben waddled into the foyer before Cassie closed the door, shutting out the early morning chill.

"I have to make the rounds and check on a few people after the storm," Luke said, helping Ben escape his snow gear. "Can Ben stay with you?"

"Sure." Cassie managed a weak smile, swallowing her nerves. She'd never babysat a gerbil, let alone a child. But she liked Ben. How hard could it be?

With his outerwear now piled in a heap on the floor, Ben stood in a pair of navy corduroys and a red sweater with Rudolph appliquéd on the front, glancing from Luke to Cassie, as if waiting for a cue.

"Do you want to help Cassie with her Christmas Calendar today?" Luke asked.

Ben showcased the small gap between his two front teeth, nodding enthusiastically.

"Why don't you go check the day's activity? The Calendar is in the kitchen. Look under December 5."

Grinning from ear to ear, Ben skipped into the kitchen, leaving the adults to talk.

"You're sure you're okay with him staying?" Luke asked.

Cassie hesitated, busying herself with hanging Ben's belongings on the coat rack next to Luke's. "Yes, I'm sure. It'll be... fun." Okay, so she didn't know if it would be *fun*, exactly. But she felt a certain kinship with Ben. And to her surprise, the thought of spending an afternoon together was almost pleasant.

"Great!" Luke smiled. "Call me if you need anything."

"I will. Thanks."

An awkward pause filled the space as they stared at each other, uncertain how to say goodbye.

Luke cleared his throat and reached for his boots.

His jeans and sweater were rumpled, and Cassie briefly wondered if he'd slept in them, or... Another blush tinted her cheeks. She seemed to be blushing a lot these days, and she didn't like it one bit. No man had affected her this much since... Actually, no one ever had. Period. The realization sent nervous jitters skittering inside her stomach.

Glancing anywhere except at Luke, Cassie swept a tangled curl behind her ear. "I'll, uh, go check on Ben."

Their subsequent goodbye felt clumsy, and the second the door closed behind Luke, Cassie released a breath she hadn't realized she was holding.

Under normal circumstances, Cassie might obsess over what the new tension between them meant, but for now, she had a small child to keep alive. And who knows what he was up to unsupervised.

As Cassie entered the kitchen, Ben sat at the dining table, his legs swinging as he read the day's entry on the Christmas Calendar. Noticing Cassie, he shot an exuberant grin in her direction. "Guess what?"

"What?" She set the teakettle on the stove, desperate for a cup of coffee.

"We have to build a snowman!" Ben's excitement sent his voice soaring several octaves higher.

Cassie frowned. "Well, that seems unfair. What if it hadn't snowed yesterday? How could I complete the Calendar, then?"

Ben stared at her, his little legs still swinging beneath the chair. Clearly, he didn't concern himself with the injustice of the situation. It *had* snowed. Which was apparently good enough for him.

"Have you had breakfast yet?" Cassie asked, deciding to move on. "I thought I might make pancakes."

"Chocolate chip pancakes?" Ben scooted toward the edge of the chair, his doe eyes bright and expectant.

"Let's see." Cassie searched the pantry. "We're in luck." She held out a mason jar filled with chocolate chips, and Ben whooped, hopping down to join her.

"Mom lets me mix the batter."

Cassie chuckled. "I have a feeling you're going to be better at making pancakes than I am."

❊

After eating breakfast and washing up, Cassie helped Ben back into his snow gear, bundling herself in as many layers as she could comfortably manage. Maybe she should invest in some decent snow clothes? She immediately dismissed the idea. Her first week of the Calendar was almost over. Before she knew it, she'd be leaving Poppy Creek, heading back to San Francisco, no longer in need of a snow-suit. The realization left a surprising weight in the pit of her stomach. One she promptly ignored as she and Ben headed outside.

Building a snowman with Ben proved to be more fun than Cassie expected. Although the chilly air stung her cheeks, the exertion from rolling the huge snowballs left her plenty warm beneath her thick sweater and wool peacoat.

Several failed attempts at stacking the lumpy blobs of snow had them both doubling over in laughter, but they eventually managed to create a lopsided snowman with two walnut shells for eyes and an orange highlighter pen for a nose. To her delight, Ben said he liked it even better than a carrot. Cassie also parted with a handful of her precious coffee beans for the snowman's smile.

Stepping back, they surveyed their handiwork.

"Not bad." Cassie smiled down at Ben, whose little face glowed with pride. "But I guess he needs arms, huh? Let's look around and see if we can find some sticks buried in the snow."

As they searched, Cassie asked, "What are we going to name him? Frosty the Snowman?"

Ben shook his head. "No. This isn't Frosty."

"Who is he, then?" Cassie's gaze fell on the tip of a branch peeking out from the glittering snow. Gripping it with her damp gloves, she prepared to yank it free.

"He's my dad," Ben answered the same moment Cassie gave a firm tug.

In her surprise, she lost her balance, falling on her backside in a mound of snow.

"Yay! You found one!" Ben cheered, oblivious to the affect his comment had on her. Racing over, he plucked the stick from her hands. "Good job."

"Thanks." Cassie hoisted herself out of the snowdrift, watching Ben twist the branch into the side of the snowman. "Ben..." she said slowly.

In the several days she'd spent in Poppy Creek, no one had mentioned Ben's father before. And Cassie would be lying if she said she wasn't curious. "What's your dad's name?"

Ben shrugged. "I don't know." His tone was casual, almost breezy, as he took up the search for another appendage.

"You don't know your dad's name?" Cassie pressed, determined to make some sense out of his answer.

"Uh-uh. I've never met my dad." Once again, Ben sounded nonchalant and unconcerned, and thousands of possibilities reeled through Cassie's mind. His father could have died before he was born. Or, maybe, he'd never been in the picture at all.

A look of sadness must have crossed her features because Ben suddenly paused, worry lines creasing his forehead. "Is that... *bad?*" he asked, his voice uncertain, as if the prospect had never occurred to him before.

"No! Of course, not!" Cassie said hurriedly, hoping to put his mind at ease. "Lots of people don't know their dads. I've never met mine." The words left her mouth in a rush before she could stop them.

"Really?"

"Really." Cassie fidgeted with her scarf, wishing she'd never mentioned it.

"Do you want to meet him?" Ben lifted his chin to meet her gaze, and there was something in his soulful brown eyes that broke Cassie's heart. An unspoken longing. Maybe even a subconscious one. To not only know who your father was... but if he ever loved you. The same longing Cassie experienced when she was Ben's age. And if she were honest, still did.

Cassie parted her lips to respond, but words failed her.

The sound of her ringing cell phone broke the silence instead.

Scrambling inside her coat pocket, Cassie gratefully accepted the interruption. "One second. I have to take this."

She pressed the phone to her ear, not bothering to check the caller ID. "Hello?"

"Cassie! Finally! I thought I'd never reach you."

As the familiar baritone oozed through the speaker, Cassie nearly lost her balance. Her fingertips instinctively found their way beneath her scarf, curling around the cold metal of the silver heart charm. "Derek, I told you never to call me again."

"But I have great news." Derek's chipper tone contrasted starkly with Cassie's strangled breath.

"Stop calling me," she hissed, stepping out of Ben's earshot, grateful he seemed preoccupied trying to locate another branch. "I'm going to hang up now."

"Wait, Cassie. Two seconds. That's all I ask."

Cassie hesitated, toying with the necklace.

Derek took her silence as an invitation. "I did it, Cass. I finally bought a coffee shop! Just like we always talked about."

Drawing in a breath, Cassie closed her eyes against all the memories of late nights they'd spent dreaming about opening a coffee shop together. Derek utilizing his skills as a green coffee buyer, and Cassie lending her wealth of knowledge and experience. "That's great, Derek. Good for you." She didn't care how bitter she sounded. It had been *her* dream in the beginning. Not his.

Derek laughed, unperturbed by her tone. "I don't think you understand what I'm trying to say. I want to hire you, Cass. I want this coffee shop to be *ours*."

❄

As Luke idled the pickup in the driveway, waiting for the engine to heat up, he pulled out his cell and dialed his mom's number.

"Hi, sweetheart." His mother's cheerful tone reverberated through the speaker after the first ring.

"Hey, Mom. Just calling to check in." He wedged the phone between his chin and shoulder, checking the air vents for any sign of warmth.

Maggie chuckled softly. "You came by for dinner a few nights ago. And restocked my firewood. You don't think I went through all those logs already, do you?"

"No." Luke rubbed his hands against the bitter cold. "But it was a pretty bad storm yesterday. Just want to make sure you're okay."

"I'm fine, honey. Heading to the bakery in a few minutes.

Will you be stopping by before work? I prepped a fresh batch of cinnamon rolls last night."

Luke's stomach rumbled. "I'd love to, but I'm going to check on Dolores. I think she left the phone off the hook again. I couldn't get through."

Maggie sighed. "I keep telling her to get a cell phone. But she insists they're the scourge of humanity."

Normally Luke would have shared in a laugh over Dolores's idiosyncrasies, but his heart thrummed with nervous energy. "I gotta go, Mom. I'll see you later, okay? Love you." Ending the call, Luke tossed the phone onto the passenger seat and shifted into reverse. Something didn't sit well in the pit of his stomach.

In less than twenty minutes, Luke pulled up to a butter-yellow farmhouse framed by a white picket fence and dormant rosebushes, all coated in a thick layer of snow like icing on a cake.

Bounding up the broad steps two at a time, Luke knocked on the front door, scanning the wraparound porch for any signs of damage while he waited for Dolores to answer. A few fallen branches littered the front yard, but none near the house. Luke breathed a little easier.

He raised his fist to knock again, but the door creaked, inching open.

Dolores leaned against a walking stick, her face creased in pain. "Luke! What a pleasant surprise."

"What happened?" Luke rushed to her side, sliding an arm around her waist for support.

"Oh, it's nothing. No need to fuss over me." She tried to laugh and winced.

"Come on. Let's get you off your feet." Luke kicked the door closed with the heel of his boot and helped Dolores into the small sitting room just off the entrance.

"It's silly, really," Dolores insisted as Luke eased her into the armchair in front of the fireplace.

"Silly or not, I want to hear what happened." Luke took the

walking stick from her hand and propped it against the side table before glancing around the room for a footstool. He almost missed it buried beneath a pudgy orange fur ball.

"Sorry, Banjo." Luke shooed the large tabby cat off the ottoman before scooting it closer to Dolores.

Banjo hissed and ruffled his tail, giving Luke the evil eye before sauntering toward his plush chenille bed in front of the hearth.

"All right, DeeDee," Luke said firmly as he elevated her swollen ankle. "Tell me the whole story."

Dolores sighed. "Not much to tell. It had started snowing pretty hard, and I wanted to move my potted azalea inside. In my haste, I must have slipped on a patch of ice."

Luke cringed, imagining how painful it must have been for Dolores to get back inside all on her own. "Sit tight. I'm going to call Doc Parker to come have a look at it."

"Oh, it's fine." Dolores waved her hand dismissively. "All I need is a little rest."

"Maybe so," Luke said, striding toward the kitchen where Dolores kept her old rotary phone. "But I'm still calling Doc."

With each step he took, Luke's boots felt harder to lift off the floor. How could he have not come to check on Dolores when the snowfall first began? Guilt tore at his insides as the truth pummeled him.

He'd gone to check on Cassie instead.

Luke's heart constricted as if a C-clamp had been placed around it, tightening with each second it took for him to come to the inevitable conclusion.

He had to put all thoughts of pursuing Cassie aside.

Too many people counted on him.

CHAPTER 10

Cassie stared blankly at the Christmas Calendar, barely even registering the day's entry. Not that it made much sense, anyway.

December 6: Attend Pajama Christmas.

What on earth was Pajama Christmas? To be honest, Cassie didn't really care. Derek's words from the day before echoed in her mind, leaving little room for anything else.

I want to hire you, Cass. I want this coffee shop to be ours. He couldn't be serious, could he? Oh, she believed he bought a coffee shop. Money wasn't an issue for Derek Price. But working together? That would be impossible. Especially if he would be her boss.

Cassie poured the last of the Colombian beans into the hand grinder, her heart sinking as she gazed into the empty bag. An image of Frank Barrie spinning the metal drum, aromatic smoke swirling into the murky winter sky, sprang to mind.

After crumpling the craft bag and tossing it in the trash, Cassie grabbed her keys off the counter and strode purposefully toward the door.

When it came to coffee, Cassie Hayward didn't give up easily.

❅

U p close, the neglected farmhouse appeared to be in even more disrepair. Several of the knotted pine planks were missing from the porch, and most of the shutters seemed held in place by hope and prayer. The single rocking chair creaking softly in the bitter breeze stirred a deep-rooted emptiness in Cassie's heart she'd spent a lifetime trying to suppress.

Tentatively, she knocked on the front door.

No answer.

Maybe Frank wasn't home? There wasn't a car or truck in sight, although Cassie didn't recall seeing one on her first visit, either.

Disappointment akin to defeat settled in Cassie's stomach as she turned to leave.

Then a loud crash rang out from somewhere inside the house.

A surge of adrenaline propelled Cassie's fist to make contact with the front door, shaking loose flecks of once-white paint that floated to the ground like sullied snowflakes. "Frank? Are you okay?" When she received no answer, she tried the doorknob. It turned easily.

"Hello? Frank?" Poking her head inside, Cassie glanced around before inching across the threshold.

Her heartbeat hammered in her ears as she crept down the shadowy hallway. "Please don't be hurt," Cassie whispered, apprehension prickling her skin.

To her surprise, the inside of the house looked nothing like the outside. Though sparse and decidedly masculine, the interior was clean and functional. Maybe even pleasant. But there wasn't any sign of Frank—injured or otherwise.

After searching several rooms, Cassie found herself in Frank's study. Floor-to-ceiling bookshelves lined two walls filling the modest space with the delectable scent of aged leather and yellowed pages. The third wall comprised almost entirely of a stunning picture window that overlooked the neighboring forest of mature pines, while the fourth was home to a feather-soft chenille recliner, reading lamp, and mahogany writing desk.

The bright white screen of an open laptop called to her like a beacon. But as she drew closer, something else captured her attention. A quart-sized mason jar filled with dark, velvety coffee beans. Lifting the jar, Cassie turned it over in her hands, the beans rattling like a makeshift maraca. Why on earth did he have coffee beans sitting on his desk?

Glancing at the laptop, Cassie hesitated. She should keep looking for Frank. But the blinking cursor piqued her curiosity. One quick glance…

Leaning closer, Cassie peered at the title line.

The Mariposa Method: Second Edition.

Shock rippling through her, Cassie stumbled back a few steps, clutching the jar to her chest.

"What are you doing?"

Whirling around in fright, Cassie stood face-to-face with Frank Barrie, his arms laden with firewood.

"I…" Words failed her as she tried to process everything that was happening. "I, uh, heard a loud crash and thought you'd fallen."

Frank snorted derisively. "You thought I fell into my laptop?"

A guilty blush stung Cassie's cheeks. "I'm so sorry. I—"

"Not as sorry as you're gonna be." His narrowed gaze communicated *get out now* more clearly than any words could have.

Somehow, Cassie managed to make her legs move and propel her past Frank toward the front door. With only a few more steps until freedom, she had a horrifying thought—she was still holding the jar of coffee beans! Mustering all of her courage, she forced herself to turn around.

Frank glowered in the shadowy hall, arms still loaded with firewood, as if waiting to ensure she actually left. Even from several feet away, his steel-gray eyes bored into hers, sending chills down her spine.

Hands trembling, she held out the jar. "I'm sorry. I just realized I—"

"Take it and *go*!" The words erupted from Frank's mouth with such force and hostility, Cassie didn't hesitate before bolting out the front door.

And she didn't stop running until she was safely in her car.

❄

"You have to try it." Cassie's dazzling eyes showcased her excitement as she scooted the mug across the counter toward Luke. An aromatic wisp of steam curled into the air, instantly kickstarting his taste buds.

He raised one eyebrow. "If I *do*, does that make me an accessory to your crime?"

"If you're too chicken, I will." Eliza snatched the mug before Luke had a chance to protest, closing her eyes to savor the incredible scent before taking a sip.

Luke noticed Cassie's subtle lean across the counter and the way her lips parted in anticipation of Eliza's reaction. He couldn't help thinking about their conversation from two nights ago, and a surge of disappointment shot through him. Their connection had seemed so strong in that moment, sharing their dreams while mince pie filling simmered on the stove. But now, Luke wouldn't even be here had Eliza not insisted they take Cassie to Pajama Christmas. He was supposed to be distancing himself. But taking Cassie to one of his favorite Christmas traditions felt like the opposite of keeping her at arm's length.

"Oh, my goodness." Eliza's entire body seemed to drain itself of tension with the first sip. "This is amazing."

"Isn't it?" Cassie pressed her palms together as if she couldn't quite contain her enthusiasm. "I'm so glad you both stopped by because I *had* to share this with someone." She drew in a deep breath before announcing, "Frank Barrie is Richard Stanton!"

Her grand announcement was met with silence.

"Who?" Luke glanced at Eliza, who looked equally baffled.

"Richard Stanton," Cassie repeated. "He wrote *The Mariposa Method*. The magnum opus of the coffee world."

"Oh." Luke nodded, although his furrowed brow gave away his confusion. Frank Barrie was Richard Stanton, a famous author? It didn't make any sense. "Are you sure?"

"Positive." Cassie's entire face radiated delight. "I saw the proof myself. He's writing a second edition of *The Mariposa Method*."

"What does 'Mariposa' mean?" Eliza asked, taking another sip before handing the mug to Luke.

"It's Spanish for butterfly," Cassie explained, her voice filled with admiration. "In the book, Richard—I mean, *Frank*— equates the coffee roasting process to the transformation of a butterfly."

Luke inhaled the earthy aroma before bringing the mug to his lips. As soon as the smooth, rich liquid hit the tip of his tongue, he knew why Cassie couldn't stop raving about it. It was, by far, the best coffee he'd ever tasted. In his life.

Cassie's lips arched as she watched him. "Good, huh?"

"That's an understatement. Normally I wouldn't condone stealing. But for this..." He took another sip, savoring the way it slid down his throat, warming him from the inside out.

"I still can't believe you went to his house again. And stole his coffee." Eliza giggled, reaching for the mug.

Luke reluctantly handed it over.

"I didn't *technically* steal it. I think he was so desperate for me to leave he didn't care if I took it."

"He should have been grateful you went inside to check on him," Eliza pointed out. "What if he'd actually been hurt?"

Cassie gave a little half shrug. "In hindsight, I think he probably dropped his armload of firewood."

"But you didn't know that," Eliza pressed.

"True. But now that I've not only trespassed on his property, but stumbled upon his secret identity, I have a feeling if I had any hope of connecting with him before, it's gone now."

She sighed, looking so dejected Luke had half a mind to march over to Frank Barrie's that second and sort the whole thing out. But they were already running late.

"I'm sure we'll figure something out," he said with an encouraging smile. "But right now, we have somewhere to be."

"Right. So mysterious." Cassie smirked. "Don't get me wrong. I was relieved when you called to say you and Eliza would pick me up for Pajama Christmas, but I was really hoping you'd give me some clue as to what it is."

"Where's the fun in that?" Eliza teased, heaving her giant purse onto the counter.

"Ben isn't coming with us?" Cassie asked.

"My parents took him a little early. He likes to…" Eliza paused, then waggled her finger at Cassie. "Nope. You're not getting any hints from me."

Cassie laughed. "Okay, I give up. Should we get going, then?"

"First things first." Eliza flashed a devilish grin as she pulled a garish pair of flannel pajamas from her purse and tossed them to Cassie. "Put those on."

Cassie gaped at the gaudy pattern of snowmen, reindeer, and Santa Clauses splattered across the plaid fabric like wacky polka dots. "Do I *have* to wear this?"

"Yep," Luke and Eliza said in unison.

"What about you two?" Cassie asked.

"Oh, don't worry about us." Eliza pulled two matching sets of PJs from her bag, handing one to Luke.

Cassie grinned. "Well, I guess if I have to embarrass myself, at least I won't be doing it alone."

Luke's heart did a somersault as Cassie's gaze met his own. Something about the idea of wearing matching pajamas sent an exhilarated shiver down his spine. But he pushed the thought aside. *Distance, Luke. Distance.*

But he couldn't help it. No matter how hard he fought against the unwanted emotions, Cassie seemed to pull him toward her like a magnet.

And tonight, more than ever, it would be nearly impossible to keep his growing feelings at bay.

CHAPTER 11

C assie couldn't quite believe her eyes as they approached the town square, which had transformed into a bustling Christmas bazaar. Townspeople mingled around craft booths and dessert stands, all dressed in outlandish Christmas-themed pajamas. The night air felt crisp and cool against her cheeks, carrying the scent of caramel corn and candied chestnuts with the gentle breeze. Snow still capped the rooftops and blanketed the ground, but every glittering speck had been cleared from the center lawn, possibly from the countless space heaters and twin firepits radiating heat on either end.

As they stepped foot on the lawn, they were enveloped in a pocket of warmth, and it quickly became apparent the center of the square boasted the main attraction. A towering Christmas tree, bedecked in plaid ribbon and a plethora of handmade ornaments, waited to be lit.

"What do you think?" Luke's hazel eyes glowed with a heartfelt earnestness.

"It's a Christmas tree lighting ceremony?" Cassie asked.

"With a few additions," Eliza pointed out. "Ben loves the face painting and gingerbread house decorating."

"Not to mention the movie at the end of the night," Luke added.

"Movie?" Cassie asked, not sure how the town would manage that.

Luke pointed to several rows of lawn chairs arranged at the end of the square, surrounded by towering space heaters. "We all bury ourselves in blankets and watch *How the Grinch Stole Christmas* projected on the front of the courthouse."

"I'm impressed," Cassie said, halting abruptly as three young boys darted past them wielding sticks speared with marshmallows.

"No running with sharp objects!" Eliza shouted before mumbling, "Where are their parents?" Her eyes widened as she recognized one of the ruddy faces painted to look like Rudolph. "Wait! That's Ben!" She rolled her eyes good-naturedly. "I suppose that's what I get for having the grandparents babysit. Pandemonium." Chasing the rambunctious boys to the firepit, she called over her shoulder to Cassie and Luke, "Catch up with you two later!"

Giggling, Cassie watched Eliza scramble after them, disappearing into the boisterous, jovial crowd. Nearly every single resident of Poppy Creek seemed to be in attendance. The vibrant hum of laughter and conversation harmonized with the festive Christmas carols performed by a four-piece band. Everyone seemed so... happy. Unexpectedly, an intense yearning to belong overwhelmed Cassie's emotions.

"What's on your mind?" Luke asked. "You look like you're lost in thought."

Cassie forced a smile past the doleful realization that someday Poppy Creek would be nothing more than a distant memory. "Nothing. Just taking it all in."

Luke smiled, mirroring her appreciation. "Poppy Creek holds the event the same night every year. And no one remembers exactly how the tradition of wearing pajamas started. Although everyone has their own version they like to tell."

"Like what?" Cassie asked, intrigued by the strange tradition.

"Oh, everything from a group of moms not wanting to get their kids ready for bed after the movie to a silly dare that started a trend," Luke chuckled. "But my favorite explanation involves Mayor Hasket, who didn't retire until the ripe old age of ninety-seven. Rumor has it, his last year as mayor, he showed up in a union suit, and to save him the embarrassment, everyone went home and changed into their own pajamas."

"What's a union suit?"

Luke's eyes glinted with humor. "You know the thermal onesie with the butt flap?"

Cassie covered her mouth with her hand as a giggle escaped.

"Exactly." Luke grinned. "Ready for some hot chocolate?" He tipped his head in the direction of a small stand draped in golden lights that flickered like tiny fireflies. "Sadie Hamilton owns the sweet shop, and she makes hot chocolate so decadent, you almost have to eat it with a spoon."

Luke placed a hand on her lower back, directing her toward the booth, and even beneath her thick coat, Cassie could sense the warmth from his touch.

Abruptly Luke froze.

Cassie followed his gaze to a striking platinum blonde in thermal leggings and a long plaid nightshirt that fell mid-thigh. Her icy blue eyes drilled into Cassie, only breaking away when the volunteer at the booth diverted her attention, handing her a paper cup brimming with whipped cream. Throwing one last glare over her shoulder, the blonde stomped toward the firepit where she joined a lively group of friends.

"Who was that?" Cassie asked as they resumed their stride.

"Victoria Burke. Her parents own the Buttercup Bistro." After a moment's pause, Luke added, "We used to date."

Cassie's heartbeat slowed until it nearly stopped altogether.

For some reason the thought of Luke with the beautiful—albeit unfriendly—blonde tied a knot in the pit of her stomach.

As they stood in line for hot chocolate, Cassie knew she should let the subject drop, but she couldn't help asking, "Why did you two break up?"

Luke dug his fists into his coat pockets, and Cassie wasn't sure if his hands were cold, or if she'd hit a nerve. "Several reasons."

Cassie brushed an imaginary piece of lint from her black peacoat. *Let it be, Cassie. It doesn't matter.* But her better judgment couldn't keep her from pressing further. "So, what was the *main* reason, then?"

Luke opened his mouth to respond, but to Cassie's frustration, they'd reached their turn in line. So rather than give an answer, he placed their order instead.

Curiosity gnawed at Cassie as they stood off to the side, waiting for their hot chocolate. So much so, she couldn't concentrate on anything else. Not the beauty of the star-lit sky that looked like a thousand twinkling Christmas lights had been stretched across it. Or the tantalizing scent of rich, dark chocolate and crushed peppermint. And certainly not the buzz of merriment going on all around her.

In the short amount of time she'd known Luke, she had taken his single status for granted. It never crossed her mind he could be seeing someone. Or perhaps pining over a lost love. Now the thought caused her heart to revolt. But what right did she have to care one way or the other?

It wasn't, and never would be, any of her business.

❄

It had been three years since Luke broke off his relationship with Victoria. And living in a small town like Poppy Creek meant they'd run into each other thousands of times since then. She'd even dated someone from Primrose Valley for several months while Luke focused on work and his responsibilities around town. It didn't make sense Victoria would react so strongly to Cassie's presence. Unless Luke's feelings for Cassie weren't as tightly concealed as he thought.

"Here you go," Sadie said brightly as she handed Luke their hot chocolate. "Careful, they're hotter than a coal in a hand basket."

"Thanks, Sadie." Turning toward Cassie, he handed her one of the paper cups piled high with homemade whipped cream and a barrage of red sprinkles. They fell in step as they headed toward the second firepit at the opposite end of the square.

Luke wasn't ignoring Cassie's question. He honestly wasn't sure how to respond. Considering his current state of mind, Luke could blame their breakup on the same reasons he wanted to avoid falling any further for Cassie—no time for himself and too many obligations. But back then, the weight of his responsibilities after stepping into his father's shoes hadn't sunk in yet. No, it had been something else entirely.

"It was something my dad told me," Luke said quietly, vocalizing his train of thought.

Cassie tipped her head, cupping the piping-hot cup between her gloved hands.

"You asked why Victoria and I broke up," he explained. "It was something my dad said."

"Oh." Her face softened as she gave him an encouraging smile to continue.

Luke drew in a deep breath, relishing the frosty air as it filled his lungs. He still recalled the exact moment he had the conversation with his father, down to the sharp scent of his dad's citrus aftershave. "My mom picked up a cuckoo clock during a trip to Germany in college. Dad hated it. Even after forty years of marriage, he would jump out of his skin every time the hour hit and the cuckoo bird would spring out of its hiding place." Luke chuckled, still able to picture the look of surprise sprawled across his dad's face. "One day, I stopped by the house during a particularly bad argument with Victoria. Which happened a lot. The cuckoo clock went off, startling Dad as it always did. And he said, 'Son, I love your mother. You know *how* I know?' Before I could respond, he said, 'Every time that clock scares the bejesus out of me, I think, I'd put up with a thousand squawking cuckoo birds if it meant being married to your mom.'"

Luke paused several feet from the firepit, staring blankly at the rollicking scene of marshmallow roasting and laughter as though he were removed from it, back in their living room with his dad, conversing in front of the fire.

"That's so sweet," Cassie said softly, drawing Luke to the present.

Luke gazed down at her, her delicate features illuminated in the glow of the bright, flickering flames. Her eyes searched his, probing for the meaning behind his story.

"Yeah, it was." Luke smiled wistfully. "My dad was a man of few words. But when he spoke, people listened." The familiar ache in his chest returned. "Even though he was talking about a cuckoo clock, I knew what he meant. Loving someone means accepting the bad with the good. It means pursuing them, no matter what. Love always hopes and always perseveres. I thought I loved Victoria. But when my dad shared his story about the cuckoo clock, I knew it wasn't enough."

Suddenly self-conscious about how much he'd shared, Luke stole a sideways glance at Cassie. Was it his imagination, or were her eyes glimmering with unshed tears? He cleared his throat. "I guess epiphanies occur at all kinds of strange and unusual moments, don't they?"

He tried to laugh, but the unguarded look in Cassie's eyes made him falter. Something lingered behind the intense shade of emerald green. Understanding? Longing? He wasn't entirely sure. But he knew if he didn't look away, he would have no choice but to kiss her. He desperately needed to shift the mood. "I bet our hot chocolates have cooled off by now."

Luke watched Cassie take a sip, anticipating her reaction. But as she withdrew the cup from her lips, he couldn't help a chuckle.

"What?" she asked innocently.

"Uh, you have..." Luke gestured toward her nose where a huge glob of whipped cream sat covered in red sprinkles. "Are you cold? Your nose is a little red." He chuckled again.

Cassie's eyes widened, and she quickly swiped at the unwanted adornment.

"You should leave it," Luke teased. "The red nose looks good on you. In fact, from now on I'm going to call you Rudolph. Or *Ru* for short."

Cassie's mouth flew open in protest as Luke took a sip of his own hot chocolate. As he lowered the cup, she snickered. "Is that so?" Her eyes flashed mischievously. "In that case, I'm going to call *you* Sprinkles."

Luke rubbed his nose with the back of his hand, revealing a smear of whipped cream and red sprinkles. He had to laugh. "Touché."

Cassie joined in his laughter until the crackling of a microphone interrupted their mirth.

A hush fell over the square as Mayor Burns took his place at the foot of the Christmas tree. Luke searched the enraptured faces of the crowd, catching sight of Eliza with her parents. Ben tugged on her hand in unbridled excitement as they waited for the big moment.

The only one not clad in Christmas pajamas, Mayor Burns stood out like a lump of coal in his official-looking black suit and slicked-back dark hair. Although only in his fifties, he looked about as miserly as Scrooge himself. Pre-haunting, of course.

As Luke stood next to Cassie, waiting for the mayor to finish his long-winded speech, he took a moment to soak up the ambiance. The palpable sights, smells, and sounds. The feeling of hopefulness that settled on his chest like a thick, comforting blanket. That's what he loved most about Pajama Christmas. The intangible spirit of the season felt so real, he could almost hold it in his hands. And it's what made being with Cassie so risky. During Pajama Christmas, anything seemed possible.

Suddenly, the town square illuminated with dazzling lights as the tree erupted in vibrant color.

Oohs and aahs rippled through the crowd.

Luke glanced down at Cassie. Her entire face shone in the multicolored glow. Maybe it was how lovely she looked or how magical the moment felt or perhaps he'd never know why he did it exactly.

Before Luke could talk himself out of it, he brushed his hand against Cassie's. Their pinkies grazed, sending shivers up his arm. He held his breath, waiting for her to pull away, but she didn't stir. Heart pounding, Luke let his touch linger, relishing the intimacy of such a simple gesture.

As the band performed a poignant rendition of "O Christmas Tree," while those around him sang along, Luke allowed his heart to hope.

If only for one night.

CHAPTER 12

F ew things could distract Cassie from the scintillating memory of Luke's hand brushing against her own the night before. Few things *except* a trip to the basement of Maggie's Place. Although, as the ancient staircase leading below the bakery creaked beneath their weight, Maggie explained it wasn't really a basement at all. Rather an old mining tunnel dating back to the 1800s when gold miners settled in the area in search of the next mother lode.

Steadying herself in the darkness, Cassie placed a hand on the wall, withdrawing quickly when her palm met the sharp edges of cold stone. Instead, she stuck close behind Maggie, following in her slow, practiced footsteps.

Once at the bottom, Cassie heard a faint click, and florescent light flooded the cave.

Maggie released her grip on the metal pull cord, wiping the dust on her houndstooth apron. "I used to love coming down here." A youthful glow lit her hazel eyes as she glanced around the tiny pocket of history. "I would imagine what it must have been like for the forty-niners in search of gold. In a way, I suppose I could relate. Starting this bakery was my own quest for a new life."

Cassie smiled, inhaling the musty scent of damp earth and sediment. "Maggie, this place is incredible."

A rickety wooden table displayed long-forgotten items like rusty cast iron cookware along with pickaxes and chisels, historical artifacts left behind by previous adventure seekers. At the far end of the table, a flannel sheet covered a large, bulky object.

"Is that…" Cassie glanced over her shoulder at Maggie, who nodded, confirming her suspicion.

"I feel a little ashamed it's been sitting down here so long," Maggie admitted. "But I had no idea what to do with it."

Holding her breath in anticipation, Cassie carefully tugged the sheet. The soft fabric slipped away, revealing an antique espresso machine. Although the hammered copper had lost its sheen, it appeared to be in excellent condition. Perhaps even *working* condition.

A small gasp escaped Cassie's lips.

Maggie chuckled. "It must be something pretty special."

"It's…" Cassie gently ran her palm along the grimy surface. "Beautiful."

"I have no idea if it still works. But I'll ask Penny to come take a look at it. She runs the antiques store, Thistle & Thorn. If anyone can fix it up, she can."

"Really?" Cassie asked, barely allowing herself to hope. "Why now? After all these years?"

Maggie's eyes shimmered with motherly warmth. "Sometimes it takes the right person to inspire a change of heart."

Cassie didn't know what to say. She smiled her appreciation, holding back grateful tears. After running her hand along the cold metal one last time, she slid the sheet back in place.

Returning to the brightly lit kitchen, it took a moment for Cassie's eyes to adjust. Slowly, her gaze settled on the dingy brick walls, outdated appliances, and scratched, stainless steel countertops. Not for the first time, Cassie noticed how badly it needed a makeover. Or, at the very least, a fresh coat of paint.

"So, what do you think?" Eliza scooped warm gingerbread cookies onto a cooling rack, the spicy, sugary aroma curling into the air with the wisps of steam. "The espresso machine is pretty cool, huh?"

"It's amazing!" Cassie still hadn't found the proper words to describe the full extent of her emotions. Nothing seemed to do it justice. "I hope it still works! I'm not an expert in refurbishment, but one espresso machine works pretty much like the next. I could try my hand at it."

"Let's see what Penny thinks," Maggie said, closing the door to the basement. "It could be it simply needs a good cleaning, but Penny'll know for sure."

"Great idea!" Eliza beamed her approval. "She's a genius when it comes to old forgotten things."

A bell chimed, signaling the entrance of a new customer, and Maggie excused herself.

Sliding a fresh tray of cookies into the oven, Eliza asked, "What's on the Christmas Calendar for today?"

Cassie made a face. "I have to go sledding. Which either means my grandmother had a crystal ball, or she didn't care if I was able to complete the Calendar or not."

"Or," Eliza said, "she cared more about your *attempt* to complete it, not the completion itself. Kind of like, it's the thought that counts."

Not wanting to belabor the point, Cassie shrugged. It wasn't as if she could comment on the motivations of someone she'd never met.

"Anyway," Eliza rattled on. "It sounds fun! Ben's been begging me to take him ever since the storm." Her eyes brightened. "We should all go! Luke, too. I get off work at four today. What do you say?"

Cassie hesitated. She'd been spending an awful lot of time with Luke. *Too* much time.

Without waiting for an answer, Eliza narrowed her eyes, assessing Cassie's outfit of skinny jeans, cable-knit sweater, and black peacoat. "You *do* have proper snow clothes, right? You can't go sledding in *that*."

"Um." Cassie regarded her stylish leather boots. "Not really."

Eliza gave her the once-over. "You have a good four inches on me, so my clothes won't fit. What size shoe are you?"

"Seven and a half."

"Perfect! I wear the same size. You can borrow a pair of my boots, but we'll have to find you a snowsuit." Eliza glanced at the clock on the faded pink wall. "I take my lunch in twenty minutes. We can pop by Thistle & Thorn and see what second-hand options Penny has. While we're there, we can ask her about the espresso machine, too."

"Sounds great," Cassie lied. While she was eager to discuss the espresso machine, spending money was a bad idea. Another one of her job applications had been rejected that morning. Maybe she'd have to start applying outside the city and succumb to a disheartening commute?

Derek's offer tugged at the back of her mind, but she shoved it down deeper. Until she found herself out on the street, working for her ex-boyfriend wasn't an option. She could only hope Thistle & Thorn had reasonable prices.

The tagline of the antiques store—Curiosities and Collectibles—represented the quirky shop to a T. Every nook and cranny burst with an assortment of oddball items like vintage typewriters, a wooden butter churn, and...

Cassie lifted a beautiful silver bowl and turned it over in her hands. The way the light reflected off the shimmering surface created a mesmerizing effect.

"That's a chamber pot." A statuesque redhead uncurled herself from a velvet chaise longue and set down her worn copy of *Persuasion*.

With a shudder, Cassie hastily shoved the silver pot back on the shelf.

Eliza chuckled. "Penny, this is my friend Cassie. Cassie, this is Penny."

"Pleasure to meet you." The young woman extended her hand, wrapping her long, graceful fingers around Cassie's.

"You, too." Cassie returned her warm smile, noting the woman's eyes were almost the same coppery color as her hair.

"We're looking for some snow clothes that would fit Cassie," Eliza said.

Penny looked Cassie over, estimating her size. A slow smile spread across her lips. "I have just the thing!" Waving for them to follow, she led them toward the back of the shop where a few racks of clothing screened off a section of the expansive room. "What do you think?" Penny held up a puffy white snow jacket with a faux-fur lined hood and matching pants.

But Cassie didn't notice. She couldn't see anything except a stunning off-the-shoulder evening gown draped over an antique dress form. The delicate, emerald green lace clung in all the right places before pooling on the floor in an elegant swirl.

"Gorgeous, isn't it?" Penny asked, following her gaze. "I like to imagine it belonged to Grace Kelly or Audrey Hepburn. Want to try it on? I'm pretty sure it's your size."

"Yes! Try it on, Cass!" Eliza clapped her hands in excitement, but Cassie shook her head. No way could she afford a gown like that, even if it was secondhand. Plus, where would she wear it?

"Maybe some other time." She made herself focus on the marshmallow ensemble in Penny's hands, hoping it wasn't too expensive. "How much is the snowsuit?" Cassie cringed at the apprehensive lilt to her voice.

Penny didn't even glance at the price tag. "Five dollars."

Cassie blinked. "That's it? That can't be right."

Cassie reached for the tag, but Penny sidestepped her, taking long strides toward the cash register. "Winter wear is on sale right now, since we're halfway through the season already," she said matter-of-factly.

Cassie glanced at Eliza for backup, but Eliza merely grinned and skipped after Penny.

As Cassie followed them to the register, her heart swelled with an unfamiliar feeling of gratitude. In all her life, she'd never experienced so much kindness as she had during her week's stay in Poppy Creek.

Which meant leaving at the end of the month would be far more painful than she'd ever anticipated.

In more ways than one.

❄

As Luke sat beside Cassie on the lowered tailgate of his pickup, he tried to focus on Ben as he sailed down the snow-covered slope on his plastic toboggan. *Not* on how close Cassie's thigh was to touching his own.

Brushing his hand against hers the previous night had been a one-time thing. An impulse best left in the past. So why could he think of nothing else than scooting closer?

Luke drew in a breath, inhaling the faintest whiff of Cassie's sultry perfume with the brisk winter breeze. Golden rays of sunlight stretched across the powder blue sky, and Luke marveled all the snow hadn't melted yet. By the end of the following day, he imagined most of it would be gone.

Grasping for an excuse, Luke told himself that's how he'd been cajoled into coming along. Eliza insisted it would be the last opportunity to sled until the next snowfall and Ben had begged him to come. How could he say no to those pleading brown eyes? But if Luke were honest, it was more than that. A *lot* more. As hard as he fought against his feelings for Cassie, he couldn't pass up a chance to spend time with her. Heart thrumming, he stole a glance in her direction.

Cassie's gaze remained fixed on Ben as he flew down the hill. "Aren't you worried he'll hurt himself?" she asked Eliza.

Eliza stood off to the side, recording a video of Ben's

descent with her cell phone. She shrugged, a smile tugging the corners of her mouth. "Having a son means being worried about his safety ninety percent of the time."

"Woo-hoo!" Ben shouted when he finally reached the bottom of the hill. "Mom, did you see that?"

"I sure did!" Eliza ended the recording, beaming proudly at her son as he hopped toward them, dragging his bright red toboggan through the snow.

"Uncle Luke, do you wanna go next?" Ben asked, his round cheeks glowing.

"I sure do!" Luke set his thermos of hot chocolate on the edge of the truck before lowering himself to the ground. Already the tempting scent of Cassie's perfume faded, flooding him with both regret and relief. He wasn't sure how much longer he could sit next to her without making a move.

"I have a better idea." Eliza slipped her phone inside the zippered pocket of her neon pink jacket. "Let's race. Ben and me against you and Cassie."

Ben jumped up and down, cheering his approval.

"You're on!" Luke grinned at Cassie. "What do you say?"

Her grip tightened around her thermos. "I don't know..."

"Please, Cassie. It's super fun," Ben pleaded.

Cassie hesitated as if trying to contrive an airtight excuse.

Eliza crossed her arms, raising one eyebrow in a challenge. "I believe the Christmas Calendar said to *go* sledding, not watch other people sled."

Luke snorted with laughter. "She has a point, Ru."

Cassie leveled her gaze on him. "Okay, Sprinkles. Let's do this." She slammed her thermos on the tailgate before hopping off with a defiant *thud*.

Eliza flashed a smirk between the two of them, clearly enjoying their flirtatious exchange. "See you two at the top of the hill. Then at the bottom, when *we* win." She took off toward the slope, Ben gleefully following in her sunken footsteps.

Grinning, Luke reached for the second toboggan in the

back of the truck. "Please tell me you're secretly a gold medalist at the luge."

"Actually, I've never been sledding before."

"Never?" Luke repeated, incredulous.

"I've lived in San Francisco my entire life," Cassie said, zipping her jacket as high as it would go. "The closest thing I've seen to snow is sleet. And on the streets of San Francisco, it's basically brown sludge."

"Then you're in for a treat." Luke hoisted the toboggan over his shoulder. "Sledding is a rush."

As Luke set his toboggan at the top of the hill, several feet from Eliza's, he realized this sled run would contain an extra thrill—more physical contact with Cassie than seemed safe.

Cassie's gaze flitted to Eliza and Ben as they climbed onto their sled, Ben in front, Eliza tightly curled around him. Her eyes registered her own misgivings about the scenario.

Luke gestured toward the sled. "I'll get on first, then you can settle yourself in the front."

Cassie didn't move, toying with a strand of dark hair that had escaped her loose braid.

Breathing steadily to settle his nerves, Luke situated himself in the back of the toboggan before waving Cassie over.

She lingered a moment before climbing in front, sitting as far forward as possible.

"Uh, Cass. You're going to have to scoot all the way back to balance our weight."

Without a word, she slowly slid toward him until she was nestled in his arms.

Luke cleared his throat. "Great. Now grip the handles in front." Her scent fully enveloped him now to the point of distraction. *Get it together, Luke.* "Are you ready?"

Cassie nodded.

"Ready?" Eliza shouted, raising her hand in a thumbs-up motion.

"Ready!" Luke called back. "Count us down, Ben."

Ben's spirited voice carried effortlessly above the stillness of the late afternoon. When he squealed, *"Go,"* Luke pushed off with both hands, sending them over the edge with a *whoosh!*

A scream escaped Cassie's lips as they plummeted toward the bottom, and Luke pressed himself tighter against her without releasing his grip on the handles. Before he had a chance to ask if she was all right, her scream transformed into ripples of laughter.

Cassie leaned her head back, resting it against Luke's chest, and the sweet sound of her gleeful giggles made his heart soar. He didn't know how it was possible, but in the brief time he'd known this woman, she'd completely captivated him, heart and soul.

They continued to pick up speed as they rocketed down the slope, and to Luke's surprise, Cassie let go of the handles, throwing her hands high above her head.

"Whoa! Hold on, Cassie!" Luke shouted, immediately noticing the shift in balance.

But it was too late.

Luke lost control, and the toboggan tipped, sending them tumbling down the hill in a snowball of flailing arms and legs.

Oomf! Luke landed on his back in a snowdrift, with Cassie sprawled on top of him. Winded, it took him a moment to register the situation. "Are you okay?" he gasped.

Cassie giggled softly against his chest. "I'm fine." Propping herself up using his torso for support, she grinned down at him. "Do you think we won?"

Luke lost his breath again, but this time, it wasn't from the impact. Her eyes danced with joy, and her lips curled at the edges, ever so slightly, as if a kiss was hiding, waiting to be uncovered.

Their eyes met, and Luke heard her sharp intake of breath. Their lips were *so close.* And the kiss was right there, teasing him.

"Are you guys okay?" Ben's face peered over them, etched with concern.

"I think they're fine." Eliza smirked, not bothering to hide her delight.

Cassie quickly rolled off Luke, springing to her feet.

Luke followed less eagerly.

"That was an epic crash!" Ben gushed.

"It was," Luke agreed. But for entirely different reasons.

Every ounce of logic told him falling for Cassie was a bad idea. He didn't have time. He had other responsibilities. She'd be leaving town in a few weeks. But Luke didn't care anymore. Fighting his feelings for Cassie was a fruitless effort.

Effort he'd rather spend on convincing her to stay.

CHAPTER 13

Standing on the frenzied streets of San Francisco the following afternoon felt surreal to Cassie. As if, in only a week, Poppy Creek had rewired her brain. The sidewalks seemed more cramped; the energy more chaotic. Even her mother's favorite restaurant, Salvatore's Italian Bistro, had lost some of its luster. The sun had taken its toll on the red-and-white striped awning. And the ordinarily slick black paint of the front door looked dull and dreary.

Cassie gripped the wrought iron handle and heaved it open, slipping in among the jam-packed lunch crowd. After giving her name to the hostess, she squeezed into the only sliver of space not occupied by a hipster, tourist, or haggard assistant picking up eggplant parmesan for their boss.

Other than the lack of personal space, Cassie didn't mind the thirty minute wait to be seated. Her mother would never arrive on time for their noon lunch date, anyway. Derek used to joke, *If you want Donna Hayward to show up on time, tell her to show up an hour early.*

Cassie fingered the heart charm at her throat, feeling the tension creep up her shoulders. There was another downside to being back in San Francisco. It would be harder to keep her mind off of Derek's job offer. A small part of her—the one with a penchant for morbid curiosity—couldn't help wondering where his new coffee shop was located. Not that it mattered. It wasn't like she'd pop in for a visit.

Cassie had already been seated for fifteen minutes—enough time to down one glass of water and two breadsticks—before Donna waltzed past the hostess desk, and several impatient patrons, to their small table by the window.

"Yikes! It's a madhouse in here." Donna flopped onto the high-back chair and shrugged out of her wool coat, revealing a V-neck sweater much too tight for a lunch date with her daughter. Or anyone, for that matter. "Good thing you got here early."

Cassie offered a thin smile before taking a sip from her empty water glass. A few drops trickled down the side, providing her little comfort—or hydration. Gratitude wasn't Donna Hayward's style. Nor was motherly warmth or affection. But Cassie showed up at her beck and call, anyway. Even if it meant dropping everything to drive the three-plus hours back to the city. Although, this time, Donna's phone call had sounded urgent.

"What is it you wanted to discuss?" Cassie asked, praying her mother didn't need to borrow more money. At this point, all Cassie could offer was an IOU.

Donna pouted over the top of her menu. "No small talk for your only mother?"

Suppressing a sigh, Cassie obliged. "How was your day?"

"Fine," Donna quipped. Then, noticing the waiter approach, she flashed a dazzling smile.

Even though she was twice his age, Donna's overt beauty wasn't lost on the flustered boy, who tried very hard to keep his gaze at eye level. Not that Donna's inappropriate neckline made it easy. "Welcome to Salvatore's," he stammered. "Is this your first time with us?"

Donna tossed her long, mahogany curls over one shoulder

and batted her thickly mascaraed eyelashes. "You must be new. I'm a regular here."

"Oh." The server looked momentarily taken aback, but to his credit, recovered quickly. "I *am* new. Otherwise, I'd definitely remember you."

"Well, isn't he the sweetest?"

To a random observer, it might have appeared as if Donna were addressing Cassie. But knowing better, Cassie remained silent, allowing her mother to continue her performance.

"I'd like to order your finest red wine," Donna told him with a ceremonious flair.

"A glass or bottle?" For the first time since arriving at the table, the smitten server acknowledged Cassie's presence with a curt glance.

"Oh, what the heck? Let's order a bottle!" Donna giggled as if they were about to celebrate something monumental. Never mind Cassie had never touched a drop of alcohol in her entire life. And wasn't about to start now. Or *ever*.

"I'll be back with that in a moment. Don't go anywhere." The server grinned before turning on his heel, leaving Cassie holding her empty water glass aloft.

"They have such lovely service here, don't you think?" Donna shook out the white linen napkin and draped it across her lap.

"Is a bottle really necessary?" Anxiety churned in Cassie's stomach. Both because her mother would have no qualms about consuming the entire thing. *And* because Cassie would most likely be stuck with the bill.

Donna narrowed her green eyes. "If you must know, yes, it is. I have great news."

Cassie really needed to be hydrated to hear any more of her mother's 'great news.' Usually it had something to do with her latest flavor of the week. And the flavor of men Donna typically chose was a mixture of sardines and antifreeze. "Please don't tell me you're eloping with Jimmy."

Donna snorted. "As *if*. I'm seeing Tyler now, anyway."

Cassie tipped the water glass, desperate for the few drops of liquid clinging to the edges.

"Besides, it has nothing to do with men," Donna huffed.

That's a first. Cassie tapped the bottom of the glass, dislodging a chunk of ice.

"I've decided to enter rehab."

The ice cube sailed down the slick surface and slammed against the back of Cassie's throat. She sputtered and coughed, certain she would die right there, facedown on the red checkered tablecloth.

"Are you okay?" Donna asked, looking more embarrassed than concerned.

As the ice cube melted, it slid down her esophagus, finally giving Cassie a chance to breathe. Eyes watering, she nodded. "*What* did you say?"

"I *said* I'm signing up for rehab."

Cassie scanned the crowded restaurant. Where *was* their server? She needed water. If not to drink, then to splash on her face. Never in a million years—no matter how long she'd prayed for a miracle—did she think her mother would get help for her drinking. Cassie could even overlook the impending bottle of wine if it served as her mother's last hurrah. "Are you serious?"

Donna pursed her lips. "A congratulations would be nice."

Cassie wrung her hands in her lap, trying to make sense of what was happening. Her mother—who called a Bloody Mary a balanced meal—wanted to go to rehab. Was it court ordered? And at this point, did it even matter? For years, Cassie had longed for this moment—for her mother to finally seek help. Not only for Donna's sake but for her own. Cassie would do almost anything for a chance at a real mother-daughter relationship, without the caustic influence of Donna's addiction.

Cassie smiled, feeling tears prick the back of her eyes. "I

can't believe it. But congratulations, Mom. I'm really proud of you."

"Thank you. I even have a specific place in mind. My friend Genie told me about it. Said she got clean in thirty days."

"That's wonderful!" Cassie's heart swelled with hope. "What's it called?"

"The Snyder Sobriety Center." Donna rearranged the silverware, not meeting Cassie's eyes. "There's just one tiny problem."

Cassie's pulse undulated as though she were about to drop off the edge of a rollercoaster. "What?"

Still avoiding Cassie's gaze, Donna pressed her lips together before parting them slowly. "The program costs fifteen thousand dollars."

Cassie's heart, along with her hopes, plummeted to the floor.

"I know it's a lot of money," Donna rushed on. "But I promise I'll pay you back. I need this, Cassie. And..." She drew in a breath before adding, "I don't have anyone else to ask."

Cassie swallowed past the dry lump in her throat. Seriously, where was the waiter?

Her mother finally met her gaze, and Cassie stared into almond-shaped eyes, not unlike her own. For an instant, she could see a flicker of grief in the deep pools of green.

With a shaky breath, Cassie murmured, "I'll figure something out."

Although *what* exactly, Cassie didn't have the faintest idea.

※

Arriving back in Poppy Creek at eight o'clock in the evening after an exhausting day of driving, the last thing Cassie wanted to do was check the Christmas Calendar. But although she'd love to get her mother into rehab as soon as possible, selling the cottage may be their only hope of getting the money they needed.

Flipping open the Calendar, she scanned the entry for December 8.

Make Mulled Wine.

Cassie blinked, the edges of the page beginning to blur.

This couldn't be happening. Not today, of all days.

Her breath coming in short, strangled bursts, Cassie paced the hardwood floor, racking her brain for a solution.

But none came. If she didn't make the wine, she'd never complete the Calendar. Which meant…

Cassie squeezed her eyes shut, feeling hopelessly trapped by her circumstances.

Hands trembling, she assembled the ingredients. The spices, honey, brandy, and wine were all stocked in the pantry. As with most things pertaining to the Calendar, her grandmother seemed one step ahead of her.

Cassie simmered the medley over the stove in a copper saucepan, pretending it was anything *but* alcohol. Fortunately, once the tartness of the wine dissipated, the sweet and spicy aroma smelled almost pleasant. But as she stirred the fragrant concoction, her heartbeat thrummed erratically. Hoping to settle her nerves, Cassie scrolled through the playlists on her phone, settling on a soothing mix of jazz.

Closing her eyes once more, Cassie let the soulful notes of Etta James's "Have Yourself A Merry Little Christmas" wash over her. Leaning forward over the stove, she drew in a calming breath, inhaling the tingling scent of cinnamon, nutmeg, and cloves. *It will be fine, Cassie. One sip. That's all. Then you can move on.* But even as she tried to convince herself, her shoulders began to shake. Tears trickled down her cheeks and into the saucepan, like raindrops sprinkling across a still lake.

❄

So far, Plan: Convince Cassie to Stay wasn't going well. All of Luke's calls went straight to voicemail. And the two times he'd been by the cottage, Cassie's car wasn't there. No one in town knew where she was, either.

In one final attempt, Luke knocked on the front door, caramel corn and a DVD of *White Christmas* in hand. At least her car was in the driveway this time.

When he didn't receive an answer after waiting several minutes, he turned to go. But soft music emanating from somewhere near the back of the house made Luke pause.

Suddenly hopeful, Luke rounded the exterior of the cottage, his eagerness spurring him up the back steps with unnecessary speed. Knocking in rhythm to the song, Luke peered through the window in the doorframe, squinting past the thin layer of frost forming on the glass.

The blurry figure inside made no move to answer the door, and Luke's hand stilled, concern rippling through him. Using the sleeve of his jacket, he wiped some of the moisture from the window, and as Cassie's hunched form came into view, his heart lurched.

Cassie cradled her face in her palms as she leaned over the stove, her shoulders trembling.

Luke didn't deliberate. His hand instinctively coiled around the doorknob, and finding it turned easily, he pushed his way inside.

In three steady strides, Luke had dumped his belongings on the counter and enveloped Cassie in his arms. For several moments, he didn't move or speak; he simply held her close, letting her tears dampen the soft wool of his coat.

When her sobs began to subside, he tilted her head back, brushing a damp curl from her cheek. "Cass, what happened?"

Her lip quivered as she met his gaze, tears pooling in her beautiful green eyes. Without a word, she pointed to the Christmas Calendar.

Luke hated to let her go, but the urge to find the cause of her distress drove him to the Calendar. He scanned the page, looking for something that might have triggered Cassie's tears. Other than a recipe for mulled wine, he didn't see anything unusual. He glanced up, searching her face. "I'm not sure what I'm looking for…"

She sniffled, swiping at her red-rimmed eyes with the back of her hand. "I have to make mulled wine." Hiccup. "But I don't… I can't…"

Her breathing came in short, ragged breaths, and Luke could sense another sob building in her chest. Closing the Calendar, he rushed to her side. "Hey, it's okay. You made it. It's done." One arm wrapped tightly around her, Luke used the other to switch off the burner. The spicy, syrupy mixture had started to bubble and spurt, splattering against the stove top.

"But…" Cassie stammered. "Don't I have to…" She shuddered before she finished her sentence, but Luke knew what she meant.

"The Calendar says to *make* mulled wine. It doesn't say anything about drinking it." Luke immediately felt Cassie's shoulders relax.

She hiccupped again, a faint smile playing about her lips. "Leave it to a lawyer to find the loophole."

Luke chuckled softly. Now that the crisis appeared to be over, he savored the blissful feeling of holding Cassie in his arms. "Do you want to talk about it?" he asked gently.

"You mean about why I'm such a mess?" She smiled through her tears.

Without thinking, he brushed one away, gently grazing her cheek with his thumb. Their eyes met, and Luke saw such tenderness in her expression, he had to swallow against the temptation to kiss away her tears. "Let's sit down."

Settled side by side on the couch, wrapped in a thick quilt made soft and supple from several decades of use, Cassie shared, "I've never had alcohol before. Not even beer or hard cider." She glanced down, toying with a loose thread. "Growing up, my mom was..." Her features strained as if saying the words out loud brought her physical pain.

"An alcoholic?" Luke supplied kindly.

Cassie nodded. "She still is. Although, when I met her for lunch today, she expressed interest in rehab."

"Cass, that's amazing!" Luke squeezed her hand.

Cassie smiled, although it didn't quite reach her eyes. "It sounds funny, but my mom is actually the reason I love coffee so much."

Luke cocked his head to the side, trying to work out the connection.

"After one of her... episodes," Cassie said, staring down at their fingers intertwined in her lap, "coffee was the only thing that would sober her up. And on *really* bad days, when she refused regular coffee, I'd have to get creative to entice her." A soft, wistful expression blanketed her features. "She liked a variation of Turkish coffee the best. I'd grind the beans really fine, then boil them in sugar water until they settled in the bottom of the pan. Then I'd pour the sweetened coffee into a mug with heavy cream. She'd gulp it down in buckets."

"How young were you when this started?" Luke asked, not sure he could bear the answer. The thought of Cassie as a child, dealing with something so grown up, tore at his heart.

She shrugged, tucking a dark curl behind her ear. "For as long as I can remember, really."

Her bottom lip trembled again, and Luke draped his arm over her shoulders, pulling her against him. "Hey. What do you say we make a pot of coffee and watch another Christmas movie? I brought popcorn."

"Won't the caffeine keep you up all night?' Cassie asked, although her voice already sounded brighter.

"What kind of holiday season would it be without pulling an all-nighter once or twice?" Luke teased, coaxing a genuine smile from her lips.

"Okay," she said, straightening. "I'd like that."

"I'll grab the DVD and start the coffee."

Striding into the kitchen, Luke went straight for the saucepan. Dumping the mixture down the sink, he rinsed away every trace of the offending liquid.

Learning about Cassie's past made him feel more connected to her, stirring a desire deep in his core to protect her at all costs.

Plus, he was now more determined than ever to make this a Christmas she'd never forget.

CHAPTER 14

Despite her emotional and physical exhaustion from the previous day, Cassie woke with a smile on her lips. Ending the evening on the couch with a cup of coffee in hand and Luke by her side had been exactly what she needed.

Cassie remembered dozing off at the end of the film, then being lifted gently in Luke's arms and carried upstairs. At the time, she'd been too tired to protest. But, truthfully, she wasn't sure she would have, even if she'd had the energy. Something felt oddly *right* about nestling against his chest, wrapped in the security of his embrace. Given her childhood, she wasn't sure she'd ever truly felt cared for until she met Luke.

After she heard the front door latch behind him, Cassie had wriggled out of her jeans and sweater, burrowing into the warmth of the flannel sheets. She'd drifted to sleep almost instantly, returning to a recurring, and somewhat disconcerting, dream—a tender kiss shared with Luke beneath softly falling snowflakes.

Stretching beneath the covers, Cassie sighed as she recalled the dream, almost wishing she could float back to sleep and revisit the magical, albeit *imaginary*, moment. Because imaginary was all it could ever be between them, as she constantly reminded herself. But, after the ordeal with the Christmas Calendar yesterday, getting more sleep wasn't an option. She didn't want to put off checking the day's activity. Better to know what she was up against as soon as possible.

Flipping open the Calendar, she read the entry for December 9.

Carry Out a Random Act of Kindness.

Cassie's brow crinkled as she reread the line. *That's odd.* Usually the tasks were clearly outlined, not nebulous. A random act of kindness could mean anything. How would she choose?

Her chest tightening with uncertainty, Cassie filled the teakettle with water and set it on the stove. Narrowing down the endless possibilities to one option wouldn't be easy. And how would she select the benefactor of said act of kindness? Eeny, meeny, miny, moe?

As Cassie set to work grinding a handful of coffee beans, one name forced its way front and center in her mind. But she quickly brushed it aside.

Uh-uh. No way!

The teakettle whistled, and Cassie slowly poured the bubbling water over the grounds in the bottom of the French press, inhaling the rich, earthy scent as it wafted toward her with the barrage of steam. As she mentally ticked off her options, waiting for the coffee to steep, the stubborn name refused to vacate the forefront of her thoughts.

"Okay, fine," Cassie grumbled aloud, compressing the plunger with a firm shove. "Frank Barrie it is."

❄

Cassie tapped her foot against the slivered pine slat of Frank's front porch, clutching a jar—well, *his* jar—now filled with generous squares of chocolate fudge, courtesy of

Maggie's Place. What man could refuse fudge? Surely, not even the curmudgeon of Poppy Creek.

Chewing all the mint-flavored Chapstick off her bottom lip, Cassie waited anxiously for Frank to answer her persistent knock. Considering their previous encounters, she resigned herself to the likelihood that he'd ignore her entirely. As she debated leaving the jar of edible kindness by the haggard front door, it slowly creaked open.

Frank peered through the narrow slit between the door and its frame, his sharp gray eyes widening in surprise.

Cassie's stomach flip-flopped as she struggled to clear the lump of nerves from her throat. "Hello, Mr. Barrie. I don't think I've ever properly introduced myself. I'm Cassie Hayward." She summoned a genuine smile. "And I brought you something."

The door groaned on its hinges as Frank pushed it open a few more inches. "What did you say your name was?"

"Cassie Hayward," she repeated, her voice a little less shaky this time. "I brought a small thank-you for the coffee." Cassie held out her humble offering but Frank made no move to accept it.

Losing her meager supply of confidence, she rambled, "I'm sure you already know this, but it was the best coffee I've ever had."

"And how would I know that?" One peppery eyebrow shot straight up.

"Because, well," Cassie stammered, wishing she could crawl through one of the many cracks in the front porch, "you're the coffee master. Yoda, if you will."

To her shock, Frank tipped his head back and laughed. Actually *laughed*. "Yoda, huh? I prefer Obi-Wan Kenobi myself. Less green and wrinkly."

His eyes twinkled, astounding Cassie to the point of dislodging her jaw from its proper position. *Did Frank Barrie have a sense of humor?*

"Well…" Cassie trailed off, now completely at a loss for words. "I guess I'll leave this here and get out of your hair." She glanced around for an appropriate place to set the jar since Frank still hadn't accepted her gift. But other than the rickety old rocking chair, the front porch was painfully barren. It seemed rude to place it on the floor, now that he was standing in front of her, but what else could she do? She hovered awkwardly.

"Since you seem to know who I am," Frank said, his voice flat, "I suppose you fancy yourself something of a coffee expert?"

Heat spread across Cassie's cheeks. He sure knew how to make a girl uncomfortable. "I guess you could say that."

"Let's see how good you are, then." Frank swung the door open a few more centimeters, wide enough for Cassie to squeeze inside.

Cassie blinked, certain she must be imagining things.

"What's the matter? Feet glued to the floor?" Frank grunted.

Flustered, Cassie scrambled across the threshold.

As she followed Frank down the dimly lit hallway, she suddenly became self-conscious of her feet. Was she walking too fast? Too slow? Should she match his stride? Or trail behind? Finally, they made it to the kitchen, and Cassie exhaled in relief. Never in all her life had placing one foot in front of the other been so stressful.

Frank's kitchen was… *pure heaven.* Cassie couldn't think of a better way to describe it. While simplistic in decor, with unstained pine cabinets and white tiled countertops, the kitchen boasted enough coffee-related paraphernalia to start a slew of coffee shops. Cassie even spotted a mini Cavaliere espresso machine, she was sure cost over four thousand dollars.

"Sit," Frank barked, nodding to the tiny round dining table and mismatched chairs.

Obediently, Cassie sat and watched, in complete awe, as

Frank proceeded to hand grind tan-colored coffee beans and scoop them into a pour-over filter, before switching on an electric kettle. Each move was swift and deliberate, as though he'd performed the same dance a hundred times.

In less than five minutes, Frank scooted a piping-hot cup of coffee in front of Cassie. The steam curled in an aromatic wisp, tickling her nose.

Cassie stared at the tawny liquid, wondering what she should do next. Did he expect her to drink it in front of him? Or was he going to prepare a second serving for himself? The thought of sharing a cup of coffee with the illustrious Richard Stanton sent tingles of excitement coursing through her.

"Tell me what you think." Frank crossed his arms in front of his chest, waiting for her to take a sip.

Cassie hesitated. *Oh, no!* It was a test. Maybe even a trap.

Taking a deep breath to steady her rattling nerves, Cassie wrapped her hands around the stout mug and lifted it to chin level. She closed her eyes, inhaling the sharp, tangy aroma, aware he was watching her every move.

Tentatively, she took a sip, allowing the hot liquid to remain on her tongue a moment before swishing it around her mouth. Her taste buds instantly registered several flavor notes, but...

Uh-oh.

Cassie suppressed a groan. This wasn't going to bode well for her.

Slowly, she opened her eyes and set the mug back on the table.

"Well?" Frank narrowed his gaze. "What do you think?"

Cassie's heart pounded against her rib cage as if shouting, Warning! Warning! It's definitely a trap! "Um..." she stalled, uncertain how to talk herself out of this mess. Telling him the truth wasn't an option.

He cocked one bushy eyebrow. "Out with it. How does it taste?"

Cassie's pulse jumped erratically as she tried to remember

how to breathe. *In and out. In and out.* Maybe telling him the truth wouldn't be so bad? Without meeting his gaze, Cassie said, "It tastes... okay."

Surreptitiously, she stole a glance in his direction. No smoke billowed out of his ears yet, so she pressed on, a bit bolder this time. "It's a little sour. With grassy undertones. And the finish is... shallow." Fearful, she sucked in a breath, waiting for Frank to implode.

He stared at her evenly. "And how would you fix it?"

"I would... roast the beans longer, taking the color a smidge darker."

Frank's expression remained stoic, void of any clue regarding what he thought of her assessment.

As the seconds ticked by, Cassie counted each pulsing throb against her temple, doing her best to remain calm. While in reality, she was ready to sacrifice her last pot of coffee to know what Frank was thinking at that precise moment.

Without a word, Frank snatched the mug off the table and strode to the sink, dumping the contents down the drain.

Was he angry? Neither his posture or expression gave any hint of the emotions brewing inside. But a niggling feeling told her Frank already knew the answer to his question. So, why was he testing her?

"Make sure you close the door behind you on the way out," he grunted.

One thing was loud and clear—she was being dismissed.

On wobbly legs, Cassie stood.

Frank kept his back to her as he rinsed the mug at the sink.

Leaving the jar of fudge on the table, dutifully fulfilling the day's task, Cassie shuffled to the door.

"Here."

Turning, Cassie barely caught the bag of coffee beans Frank tossed in her direction.

"Tell me what you think of those." Without so much as a farewell, Frank twisted his back to her again.

"Okay." Cassie clutched the crinkly craft bag to her chest. "Goodbye."

She thought she heard Frank mumble something, but couldn't quite make it out.

Completely bewildered by the entire exchange, Cassie turned and found her way down the corridor and out the front door.

Standing on the ramshackle porch, she ran her fingers through her hair.

Had Frank Barrie just given her an assignment? And if he had... *why?*

Was it possible that drawing her into his world was Frank's own act of kindness?

Or was that simply wishful thinking?

Much like Cassie's dream.

※

Luke drilled a screw into the two-by-four, securing it in place before pushing back his goggles to inspect his work. Satisfied with the alignment, he blew hard, scattering sawdust across the concrete parking lot of Poppy Creek Elementary where they'd set up their work station.

"Hey!" Reed Hollis swatted at the fine powder settling on his jeans before returning his attention to the jumble of wooden boards at his feet. "How's this supposed to go again?"

Jack Gardner shook his head in bemusement. "You're building an A-frame for the stable, genius. It looks like an *A*."

Reed narrowed his eyes at his childhood friend. "And what exactly are *you* making?"

Jack glanced down at his own discombobulated pile of wood. "A manger?" he said, more as a question than an answer.

Reed snorted. "That's what I thought. You aren't any more skilled at carpentry than I am."

"Don't be so sure, Flower Boy." Jack squatted, reaching for

two pieces of wood, pretending like he knew exactly what to do with them. "These manly hands can build circles around you."

Reed, the owner of Poppy Creek's only nursery and flower shop, threw his head back in laughter. "Right, Betty Crocker. You cook for a living. Not exactly the manliest job in the world. Besides, I'd like to see *you* prune a hundred rosebushes. The first thorn, you'd cry like a baby."

Jack mumbled something sarcastic under his breath, which instigated Reed into "accidentally" knocking over the arrangement of boards Jack had stacked like Jenga pieces.

Luke sighed, sinking his head into his palm. Asking his best friends to help him make the sets for the school's Christmas pageant seemed like a good idea at the time. But now, he wasn't so sure. He pulled rolled-up papers out of the back pocket of his worn jeans. "I have instructions for you, lunkheads." Luke handed them over with a good-natured swat.

"Hey!" Jack protested with a chuckle. Then, glancing at the plans, he said, "I think I can manage this."

"They're upside down." Luke groaned. Jack could make the best pulled pork and baby back ribs in town. But a skilled carpenter he was not.

"I know that," Jack lied before flashing a grin at Reed. "At least Luke's in charge of building the actual stage."

"True." Reed chuckled. "I wouldn't want to put any kids at risk by having one of us give it a try."

"Speaking of taking risks..." Jack waggled his thick eyebrows at Luke. "Have you asked Cassie out yet?"

"*Right...*" Reed matched Jack's impish grin. "How's that going? Should I be renting my tux yet?"

"Are you *sure* you guys want to give me a hard time about this?" Luke turned the drill back on for a menacing effect.

Jack held up his hands in surrender. "Okay, okay. Calm down, Sprinkles."

Heat shot up Luke's neck. "How did you—"

"Eliza told me. You know she can't keep a secret to save her life." Jack's blue eyes twinkled playfully. "And before you turn your drill of death on me, I think it's great. You know what they say. First comes the nickname..."

"Then they take your last name!" Reed finished in a singsong voice.

Luke rolled his eyes. "What are you, five?"

His friends grinned like clowns. No, not *like* clowns. They *were* clowns. Who just so happened to be the best friends a guy could ask for—*most* of the time.

"In all seriousness, though." Jack finally composed himself. "How's it going with Cassie?"

Luke hesitated, one hand poised on his safety goggles, ready to resume work. But the truth was, he wouldn't mind a bit of advice. "It's going well. Great, actually. I'm learning a lot about her. In some ways, it feels like we've known each other forever."

Luke caught a quick glance between Jack and Reed and narrowed his eyes. "Whatever juvenile comment is stirring in your blockhead brains, save it. I'm being serious."

"We know you are," Jack said solemnly. "We weren't going to make fun of you. Truth is, we're jealous."

Caught off guard, Luke blinked. "Really?"

"Darn straight!" Reed told him. "We've all been hopeless bachelors for years. Now you've found Cassie and—"

"We've never seen you happier," Jack finished.

"And we're happy for you, you twitterpated traitor." Reed slugged Luke in the arm, but his dark eyes were warm and affable.

Luke's chest swelled with appreciation for his well-meaning, if somewhat maddening, friends. "Thanks, guys. But it's not exactly a done deal. Cassie could still leave at the end of the month."

"So, what's your plan?" Jack asked.

Luke paused. What *was* his plan exactly? "She has a lot on

her mind at the moment. But eventually I plan to tell her how I feel and see if she feels the same way."

"'Eventually'?" Jack and Reed said in unison, each raising their eyebrows in question.

"I'd tell her sooner rather than later," Jack said.

Reed nodded his agreement. "Yeah, why wait?"

The question hung in the air between them, and Luke twisted the toe of his boot into the concrete.

Luke had known Cassie for little more than a week.

Was it too soon to admit he was falling in love with her?

And that, maybe, he'd already fallen?

CHAPTER 15

C assie coiled a strand of hair around her finger as she read the day's entry in the Christmas Calendar.

December 10: Go Ice Skating.

Images of her and Luke hand in hand as they sailed across a frozen lake floated through her mind.

Quickly, Cassie slammed the book closed, shutting out all thoughts of Luke. *What in the world was happening to her?* She'd gone one day without seeing him, and already she felt as though she were going through withdrawal symptoms.

Cassie winced. Bad analogy. The hefty price tag for her mother's rehab remained an ever-present burden, like a sack full of coal draped around her shoulders. Yet, in the two days since their luncheon, no solution had presented itself.

Leaning across the kitchen island, she buried her face in her hands, allowing herself a moment to wallow in defeat. Maybe she needed to start applying for jobs outside the coffee industry? Retail always seemed to be hiring. Or waitressing. She shuddered, pushing herself up from the counter.

A little more than two weeks of the Christmas Calendar was all she had left. Then, however long it took to sell the cottage. She hated her mother had to wait that long. The sooner Donna got help, the better.

Cassie opened the real estate app on her phone, scrolling through properties for sale in nearby towns. The several digits that comprised the average listing price used to fill her with extravagant daydreams. But now... conflicting emotions wrestled in her stomach. On the one hand, selling the cottage meant leaving Poppy Creek. On the other, even the lowest comp price was enough money to pay for Donna's rehab and have some left over to... *to what?* Open her own coffee shop? The possibility sent goosebumps tingling across her arms.

Crossing the kitchen, Cassie swung open the pantry door and reached for Frank's bag of coffee. She hadn't been able to touch a single bean, wary of the implications. Frank had asked for her thoughts. But what if, like the last cup, she didn't like it? She'd told him the truth once, but a second time? Cassie wasn't sure she had the gumption.

Unfolding the tin ties that held the bag closed, Cassie snuck a peek inside for nearly the hundredth time since yesterday afternoon. The sweet, earthy aroma flooded her senses, causing her mouth to water. Cassie tilted the bag toward the light, peering closer, noting the beans looked plump and satiny, the exact color of decadent dark chocolate. Her pulse quickened, filling Cassie with a familiar, breathless excitement.

"Come on, Cassie," she murmured aloud. "You may not know much, but you *do* know coffee."

She paced the kitchen floor, tapping one finger against her lips as she debated the best brewing method. Typically, she preferred the French press. But on this particular occasion, Cassie decided to follow official cupping protocol. Since Frank entrusted her with this task, she wanted to carry it out to the best of her abilities. Even if the steps of the process would undoubtedly conjure up unpleasant memories.

Cassie drew in a deep, calming breath as she filled the copper teakettle with tap water and placed it on the stove. A few remaining droplets of water trickled from the faucet, pinging against the porcelain sink. Cassie closed her eyes, still able to hear the pitter-patter of raindrops as they danced across the large picture window of the coffee shop that fateful evening in March.

Cassie hadn't been sure what to expect when she'd attended her first cupping demonstration at the grand opening of a new coffee shop on Market Street. But she certainly hadn't expected the handsome and charming coffee buyer performing the demonstration to smooth talk her into a date.

Derek Price was unlike any man she'd ever met. Not only had he known more about Cassie's favorite subject than Cassie herself, but he'd captivated her with outlandish tales of his adventures on coffee plantations around the world. So much so, their first date had lasted over four hours.

The coffee beans crackled inside the grinder as Cassie cranked the handle, releasing a nutty, pungent aroma. Instantly, her memories transported her to the night of their very first kiss.

Playfully, Derek had decided to appraise Cassie's palate, blindfolding her for a taste test. She'd correctly guessed three different coffee varieties before Derek surprised her by gently pressing his lips against hers. At the time, the gesture seemed incredibly romantic. Now, Cassie wondered if she'd been blindfolded throughout their entire relationship.

The kettle screeched, wrenching Cassie back to the present. Slowly, she poured hot water over the coffee grounds waiting in the bottom of the mug. Then she set the timer on her phone for four minutes, observing the water change color as it reacted with the fragrant granules.

Cassie watched the seconds tick by on her phone, pondering how time had such a powerful effect. The coffee needed to interact with the water for precisely four minutes to reveal its desired properties. Time had taken the opposite toll on Cassie's relationship with Derek. Nine months was all it had taken for that chemical reaction to blow up in her face. In the most soul-crushing way possible.

The alarm buzzed, scooting her phone across the counter with the vibration. Jabbing her finger on the end button, Cassie dismissed the timer... and all thoughts of Derek.

With nervous anticipation, Cassie lifted a silver teaspoon and gently plunged it into the mug, breaking the crust of the coffee before withdrawing the spoon. As the foam ran down the sloping curve onto the handle, Cassie inhaled the aroma, observing the various fragrance notes, exactly as Derek had taught her.

Cringing, she squeezed her eyes shut again, desperate to push the memories back into the deep recesses of her mind. The last thing she wanted was for Derek to taint this experience. He'd already ruined Christmas for her. She wouldn't let him have *this*, too.

Steadying her hand, she lifted the mug to her lips, sipping in a slow, deliberate motion so the sample hit her taste buds in the correct order. A harmony of sweetness and complexity overwhelmed her senses in the best possible way, and Cassie had to keep herself from guzzling the entire mug of liquid heaven in one gulp.

Having no idea how thorough of an answer Frank expected, Cassie followed the next steps of the cupping process to the letter, making notes in her phone as to the coffee's acidity, body, balance, flavor, and aftertaste.

With each step, Cassie's joy bubbled up inside until it spread across her face in an exuberant smile.

She had no idea what would come of the assignment—if anything—but for now, Cassie would allow herself to dream.

❄

Luke smiled behind the dainty porcelain cup brimming with peppermint tea, grateful to see Dolores bustling about her kitchen with considerable ease.

"You're sweet to check on me, but my ankle is good as new." She set a matching sugar bowl and creamer next to the antique teapot before sinking into the chair beside Luke. "I only use this walking stick because it reminds me of Arthur." Her smile grew soft and wistful as she gazed at the intricately carved handle.

"One of his finest pieces." Luke set the teacup down and reached out a hand. "May I?"

Dolores passed it to him before serving herself, filling the cozy, farm-style kitchen with the refreshing scent of mint.

Luke ran his hand over the smooth manzanita, admiring the streaks of bronze, copper, and gold in the wood grain.

"You're every bit as good as he was, you know." Dolores blew on the piping-hot liquid, the steam fogging up her glasses.

Luke's throat tightened, and he reached for the tea again, taking a comforting sip. "Did Arthur ever tell you about the first time he taught me to whittle?"

Dolores shook her head, her silver curls bouncing with the motion. "If he did, my unreliable brain has since forgotten."

"You may not believe this, but I got called into his office my first day of high school," Luke admitted with a wry smile. "I didn't know what to expect, but I'd heard rumors about crazy old Principal Whittaker."

Laugh lines crinkled Dolores's features. "He *did* have some unconventional methods."

"You could say that." Luke chuckled. "I'd gotten into a fight with another freshman eager to establish himself as the school bully. But Arthur didn't even ask me about it."

"I suspect he already knew who the real troublemaker was." She winked over the gold-etched rim of her teacup. "Did he give you a good scolding, anyway?"

"I thought he was going to, but…" Luke shook his head, still baffled by the memory. "Arthur kicked his dusty boots on top of his desk and leaned back with a hunk of manzanita in one hand and a carving knife in the other. I tell ya, my eyes bugged out of my head when I saw the glint of that knife."

Dolores giggled. "Sounds like my Arthur, all right. What did he say?"

"He said, 'You know what's great about working with wood? You can make it anything you want it to be, but it's still a chunk of wood.'"

Pausing mid-sip, Dolores cocked her head, a puzzled expression on her round face. "What was that old fool rambling on about?"

"I think he was trying to say you can't change your circumstances, but you *are* responsible for what you make of them."

Tears sprung to Dolores's eyes, and she stared intently at the elegant rosebud pattern on her teacup, blinking them away.

"Of course, I didn't realize that until later," Luke said softly, tracing the carving with his calloused fingertip. "But he'd planted the seed."

Dolores smiled through her tears, pulling an embroidered handkerchief from the pocket of her afghan. "He was a pretty smart old fool, wasn't he?" Dabbing her eyes, she added, "Wait. Didn't you say he *taught* you how to whittle?"

Luke leaned the walking stick against the edge of the table and reached into his back pocket. He withdrew a small Swiss Army knife and handed it to Dolores.

She turned it over in her palm, her lips parted in surprise. "Arthur's pocket knife? He told me he lost this on a fishing trip."

Grinning, Luke squeezed her other hand. "I'm sure it was the only fib he ever told you, DeeDee. He probably would have gotten in a lot of trouble for giving one of his students a knife on school property."

"He gave it to you that day?" This information seemed to soften her.

"Right after school. He handed me the pocket knife and my own branch of manzanita, quickly showing me the basics."

"Did he give you any guidance on what to make?"

"Nope. He said what I made of it was entirely up to me."

Eyes brimming with fresh tears, Dolores held out the pocket knife, waiting for Luke to stretch out his hand. She placed it in his palm, gently curling his fingers around it before cupping his hand with her own. "He'd be really proud of you, you know."

Luke nodded, unable to speak past his emotions.

"Have you made anything recently?" she asked, returning to her tea.

"Actually, I have been working on something." Luke's thoughts drifted to the surprise he planned for Cassie, reminding himself why he was there in the first place. "Dee-Dee, how long did Arthur wait before he said he loved you?"

Dolores laughed. "*Wait?* Arthur never waited for anything."

"What do you mean?"

Dolores set her teacup back on its coordinating saucer, the china clinking delicately as she gathered her thoughts. "The first time I met Arthur, I was on a date with another man."

"Really?"

"His best friend in the navy, truth be told. Dennis Flanders. They were both home on leave, and they picked up my girlfriend Sally and I for ice skating. Sally was supposed to be Arthur's date, but he spent the entire evening skating with me."

"I bet Dennis loved that," Luke interjected with a laugh.

"Poor Dennis gave up pretty quickly, switching his attention to Sally. Which suited Arthur and I just fine." For a moment, her gaze fluttered past Luke, and he could almost see the memories dance across her shimmering blue eyes. "At the end of the night, Arthur marched right up to me and said as soon as he returned home from the war, he was going to marry me."

Luke slapped his palm against the table, rattling the china dishes. "You're kidding! What did you say to *that?*"

"I said he'd better try his darndest to stay alive, then. 'Cause no girl wanted to lose her fiancé overseas."

Luke leaned back against the chair, shaking his head in amazement. "How did you two know so quickly?"

"It's different for everyone, of course. Arthur said he fell in love when he saw me fall on the ice fifty times and get right back up to try again." She laughed at herself. "I'd never been ice skating before, but Arthur wasn't the only determined one."

"And you?"

"I knew any man who'd be that bold on my behalf was a man worth keeping." Dolores met his gaze with warmth and affection. "You're a lot like my Arthur, you know." Placing a hand over her heart, she tapped her fingers. "Here. Where it counts."

Luke swallowed, feeling tears prick his own eyes.

That's the kind of story he wanted with Cassie, except their own unique version. But he knew it would never happen if he didn't follow Arthur's lead.

Tonight, he would have to be bold.

CHAPTER 16

Cassie didn't wait for Luke to say hello before grabbing his hand and tugging him through the doorway. "You *have* to try this!" She pulled him into the kitchen, bubbling with excitement.

"Hello to you, too," Luke chuckled.

"I know we're meeting Eliza and Ben at the ice rink, but you have to taste this first." Rocking back and forth on her tiptoes, Cassie held out a mug brimming with freshly brewed coffee, nearly sloshing it over the rim in her eagerness.

"Don't tell me you raided more of Frank's coffee supply," Luke teased, bringing the mug to his lips.

Cassie placed one hand on her hip, rolling her eyes playfully. "Once again, I didn't *technically* steal it. And this time he gave it to me."

"When?" Steam wafted toward Luke's face, carrying a rich, heady aroma that seemed to instantly catch his attention. "Wow, this smells good!"

"Doesn't it?" Cassie couldn't contain her delight, grinning like an overly enthusiastic elf. "I took him a jar of Eliza's fudge yesterday, and he invited me inside."

Her revelation caught Luke off guard, causing him to sputter in surprise as hot liquid shot up his nose.

"Are you okay?" Cassie asked.

"Fine, thanks. Just singed my sinuses." Luke swiped at the coffee dribble on his chin. "Cantankerous and reclusive *Frank Barrie* invited you inside? What did he want?"

"He wanted my opinion on one of his blends. Well, *two*, actually. I tried one at Frank's. And he sent me home with the one you're drinking right now."

"That's strange." Luke tried a second sip. And if his expression was any indication, the sultry flavors lingered on his tongue long after he'd swallowed. "This tastes incredible! Even better than the first cup I tried the night of Pajama Christmas."

"I know!" Cassie beamed, pleased he had a similar reaction to her own. "I've been thinking about this all day. You know how I mentioned Frank's writing a second edition of his book?"

Luke nodded, taking another sip.

"What if…" Cassie drew in a breath, wondering if her thought would sound crazy when she finally said it out loud. "What if Frank is working on new blends for his book? And he wants *my* help?"

"That would be great…" Luke trailed off, his brow knit together. "But why do you think he'd ask for your help?"

With a heavy sigh, Cassie slouched against the edge of the counter. "Yeah, that's the one thing I can't figure out, either."

Luke set the mug down and reached for her hand, giving it a squeeze. "Hey, if Frank's half as smart as you say he is, he can probably tell natural talent when he sees it. I don't even know why I asked."

"Thanks." Cassie waited for him to release her hand, but he didn't move a muscle, except to apply another gentle squeeze.

His touch sent a shiver up her arm, and she slowly lifted her gaze to meet his. The heat simmering in his hazel eyes startled her, and she subconsciously parted her lips.

"Cass..." His voice barely above a whisper, Luke leaned across the counter.

Cassie didn't dare answer—or breathe—and simply tilted her chin.

But the sharp trill of her cell phone wrenched them from the moment.

Luke's eyes mirrored her surprise as he scanned the kitchen for the source of the interruption.

Heart hammering, Cassie yanked her phone from her back pocket. "Hello?"

"Were you running or something?" Eliza asked. "You sound all weird and breathy."

"Uh, no. I—what is it?" Cassie mouthed, *It's Eliza*, to Luke, who nodded in understanding.

Was she imagining things or did he look disappointed? Cassie turned away from his sightline, smiling to herself.

"Where are you guys?" Eliza asked. "Luke said to meet at the rink at seven thirty and Ben's getting antsy to get out on the ice."

"We're leaving now," Cassie said. "Don't wait for us."

"Are you sure?" Eliza sounded relieved.

"Absolutely. We'll be there soon." After saying goodbye, Cassie hung up the phone, suddenly conscious of the awkward undercurrent rippling across the room. "That was Eliza," she said lamely.

"I know." Luke smiled. "Shall we get going, then?"

"Sure." Slipping her phone back in her pocket, Cassie grabbed her insulated thermos. Pouring the remaining coffee inside, she said, "Can't waste stuff this good."

"Definitely not." Luke flashed the kind of grin that made Cassie feel a little light-headed.

While she screwed the lid on tight, the butterflies in Cassie's stomach drifted about in a forlorn flutter, as if mourning an opportunity lost. As much as she tried to fight the longing, there wasn't any way around the truth.

Bad idea or not, Cassie wanted Luke to kiss her. And preferably, tonight.

❄

Cassie adjusted the collar of her peacoat, pulling it tighter around her neck as they approached the ice rink. "It's an actual rink." Her breath escaped in a filmy white cloud as she rubbed her gloved hands against the cold.

Luke chuckled. "Were you expecting a frozen lake?"

"Truthfully, yes."

"It doesn't usually get cold enough to freeze an entire lake suitable for skating." Luke hesitated, stealing a glance in her direction. "Are you disappointed?"

Cassie warmed at the tentative edge to his voice. "How could I be disappointed with something this beautiful?"

While not a lake, the man-made rink was nestled in the center of a field, surrounded by the neighboring forest. Snow-capped mountaintops towered in the distance, silhouetted by the silvery moon and multitude of stars. Large old-fashioned bulbs stretched above the rink, casting a shimmering glow across the ice, where skaters swirled and spun like dancers on a stage.

"Do you know how to skate?" Luke asked, standing in line at the makeshift rental booth.

"I used to rollerblade. Which is basically the same thing."

"I admire your confidence," Luke said with a laugh.

Once they laced up their skates, Cassie hobbled toward the edge of the rink, close behind Luke. She noticed his furtive glances over one shoulder, as though he were ready to catch her at any moment. "I'm fine," she assured him. "These skates are easy to balance on."

He didn't look convinced, grasping the railing while offering Cassie his free hand. "It's slippery on the ice."

Out on the rink, Ben caught sight of them and hollered,

"Uncle Luke! Cassie!" He waved as he zipped past, the fringe of his scarf fluttering behind him like a cape.

"My goodness, he's fast!" Cassie said in awe.

"He's been skating since birth," Eliza said, skidding to a stop. "Have you been ice skating before?"

"She's rollerbladed," Luke offered, joining Eliza on the ice. He made the transition from dry land look effortless.

"I see." Eliza smirked. "This should be fun, then."

Cassie's bottom lip puckered as she eased herself across the divide. "I don't know what you're both so worried about." She pushed off the wall, smoothly sailing a few feet before slowing to a stop. "See? I'm fi—" Her balance faltered, along with her words. Arms flailing fruitlessly, she plopped—bottom first— onto the cold, hard ice.

In an instant, both Luke and Eliza were by Cassie's side, lifting her back on her feet.

"You were saying?" Eliza teased.

"Ha-ha," Cassie mumbled, wiping the flecks of shaved ice from her gloves. But she couldn't help a laugh at herself. "Okay, so it's harder than it looks."

"Are you okay?" Luke asked, steadying her with one arm around her waist.

Cassie nodded. "Yes. And I'm determined to learn, no matter how many times I fall."

"That's the spirit!" Eliza cheered, patting Cassie's shoulder. "I'll leave you in Luke's capable hands while I go check on Ben. He's probably looped past us a dozen times by now."

Eliza flashed a wink at Luke before she sped off. But when Cassie glanced up to see if he noticed, she found him staring at her with a spine-tingling expression. And if she hadn't been holding on to his arm, she would have toppled over a second time.

❄

137

L uke marveled at the events of the evening thus far. Except for the double date, the night mirrored Arthur and Dolores's meet-cute right down to Cassie falling on her backside. And then, those incredible words of determination spilled from her lips, reminding him—for the millionth time— why he'd fallen hopelessly in love with her.

"Should we try that again?" Cassie asked, steadying herself on his arm.

Luke suppressed the urge to confess his feelings right then and there. "Absolutely. We'll start slow, almost like a shuffle. Then we'll transition to a gentle glide. Sound good?"

Cassie nodded, tucking her arm through his, gripping it tightly.

Luke smiled, savoring her nearness and the scent of her perfume, which had become a fragrance that was at once familiar and alluring.

As Luke guided Cassie around the rink, he did his best to remain present in the moment. But his thoughts kept drifting to when and where he would make his move. Definitely not on the crowded ice. Somehow, he'd have to steal her away to somewhere more private. If only he could—

"Luke, look out!"

Startled, Luke glanced up to see a child paused in the middle of their path. Swerving quickly, Luke dragged Cassie with him. They swayed and staggered for several seconds, struggling to remain upright. When they finally stopped teeter-ing, Cassie's hands were draped around Luke's neck while he grasped her waist.

Suddenly, it didn't matter that dozens of people swirled around them, their skates swishing across the ice. Even the cacophony of their shouts and laughter faded into the background.

To Luke, Cassie was the only other person in existence.

Brushing a loose curl from her cheek, he let his touch

linger, and her sharp intake of breath sent ripples of heat through his body.

As he searched her face looking for a sign, her eyelashes fluttered and her lips parted ever so slightly.

Finally seizing his opportunity, Luke lowered his mouth to hers. But before he could taste her lips, Ben's voice shattered the thin veil of intimacy surrounding them.

As if he'd been yanked from a dream, it took Luke a moment to focus on Ben's blurred figure as it sped toward them, sliding to a stop.

"Here ya go." Ben grinned as he thrust a cell phone toward Cassie. "I found it on the ice in the spot where you fell."

"Th-thank you." Cassie sounded as frazzled as Luke felt.

Luke glanced around, scanning the rink for Eliza. When he spotted her near the edge chatting with Penny Heart, he felt a surge of irrational irritation that she hadn't stopped Ben from rushing over and ruining the moment.

Ben didn't seem to notice he'd interrupted something monumental. "I know it's yours because the message has your name in it." Ben grinned as if proud of his deduction.

Without glancing at the text, Cassie stuffed her phone back inside her coat pocket.

"I didn't know all of the words," Ben admitted. "But I know it's about a job. Are you getting a new job, Cassie?"

Luke's gaze darted to Cassie's face.

Her cheeks were tinged pink, and Luke could tell it was from far more than the cold.

CHAPTER 17

Please call me back.
I've decided to sweeten the deal.
Forget the job offer.
Let's be partners. 50-50.
I need you, Cassie.

Cassie read Derek's text for the hundredth time, but she still couldn't believe it. Fifty-fifty partners? It didn't make any sense. Why would Derek want to share his business with her? Between his lucrative job as a coffee buyer and his trust fund, he didn't need her financial contribution. Even if she had enough money to make one. So, why give her equity? What exactly did he want in exchange?

The questions swirled in her mind as her finger hovered over the delete button.

Before Cassie could make a decision, the shrill cry of her cell phone interrupted her thoughts, nearly causing her to tumble out of bed in surprise.

Derek's message disappeared as Eliza's glowing, pink-cheeked face flashed across the screen.

Cassie smiled, recalling the moment Eliza had snatched her

phone the afternoon they went sledding, programming her number with the title of *New Bestie*.

Cassie hadn't bothered telling Eliza she didn't need the "new" modifier, since Cassie didn't have a best friend. Or *any* friends, really. Sure, she made friendly acquaintances all the time. She'd even grabbed coffee once or twice with a few coworkers. But an honest-to-goodness friend—the kind you confided in and trusted explicitly? They seemed as mythical as Saint Nick himself. Or, at least, they had before Poppy Creek.

"Cassie!" Eliza's cheerful warmth resonated through the speakers. "Sorry if I'm waking you, but I didn't think you'd want to miss this."

"Miss what?"

"Penny's here. *And...*" Eliza dragged out the syllable for dramatic effect. "The espresso machine is working!"

Cassie couldn't get dressed fast enough, even slipping on mismatched socks in her haste. She flew down the staircase, pausing only when she remembered she hadn't checked the Christmas Calendar for the day.

Racing into the kitchen, she flipped through the pages until she reached December 11, crossing her fingers the activity would be quick and easy.

Make Eggnog.

Relief flooded her. Definitely quick and easy! And decidedly more pleasant than making mulled wine.

Snapping the book closed, Cassie spun on her heel.

She'd check off the task later.

As she dashed past the pantry, she halted abruptly. Yanking the door open, she snatched the bag of Frank's coffee beans before resuming her sprint.

❄

Heart fluttering in anticipation, Cassie pushed through the entrance of Maggie's Place, welcoming the aroma of freshly baked cinnamon rolls.

"Good morning, sweetheart." Maggie stepped from behind the cash register to envelop Cassie in a hug. "We have a surprise for you." One arm draped around Cassie's waist, Maggie led her to the end of the long display counter.

Nestled in the back corner sat the gleaming copper espresso machine, flanked by Eliza and Penny, arms splayed like Vanna White.

"Ta-da!" they cheered in unison.

Cassie's breath caught as she took in the sight. Not only was the machine operational, Maggie had designated an entire space for it, arranging a stack of white ceramic mugs and an assortment of other items Cassie would need, including portafilters and tamps.

Following her gaze, Maggie said, "We found those in an old tin canister labeled Coffee in the basement. I'd forgotten all about them." She smiled warmly, her hazel eyes shimmering with delight. "What do you think? Is this enough space?"

"Enough space for what?" Cassie's voice hummed with equal parts anticipation and hesitancy.

"For you to serve lattes!" Eliza blurted, unable to hold back her excitement. "And whatever else you do with this thing."

Cassie gaped at Eliza, then Maggie. "Wait... what exactly are you saying?"

Maggie grinned. "If you're interested, we'd love to have you serve specialty coffee drinks here at the bakery. For a few hours in the morning, to start. I can't pay you much, but I'll purchase all the supplies. And, of course, all the pastries you can eat." She laughed brightly, Eliza and Penny joining in.

But Cassie couldn't make a sound past the lump in her throat. After a pause, she murmured hoarsely, "I... don't know what to say."

"Say yes!" Eliza encouraged.

"But…" Cassie trailed off, barely able to string two thoughts together. "What coffee would I use?"

"We'll have to figure that out," Maggie admitted. "But I'm sure we'll come up with something."

"Our sister town, Primrose Valley, is bigger than we are," Eliza pointed out. "Maybe we can find something there?"

Cassie's heart swelled at their use of "we."

"I travel to all of the surrounding towns looking for stuff for my shop," Penny added. "I can ask around for you."

"Perfect!" Eliza hugged herself as if she might burst with happiness any second. "But for now, do you have any of Frank's coffee left?"

Reaching into her purse, Cassie took the opportunity to blink back her impending tears. Overwhelmed with emotion, she wasn't sure if she wanted to laugh, cry, or hug all three of them at once. Never in all her life had she been so fully embraced and accepted by anyone, let alone an entire town.

Sniffling, she withdrew the bag of Frank's latest blend.

"Yay!" Eliza applauded as though Cassie had just pulled a rabbit out of a hat.

"What are you going to make first?" Penny asked.

A smile spread across Cassie's face as an idea came to her. "I think I'll make an eggnog latte."

❄

Luke couldn't stop grinning as he gazed at Cassie across the dining room table. When his mother told him she'd invited Cassie to join their weekly family dinner, Luke had been thrilled. But when Maggie also told him about her job offer, Luke felt more elated than the first time he used a power saw. The only problem was, he hadn't been able to think about anything else all day. He wanted—no, *needed*—to know if Cassie planned to stay in Poppy Creek.

"You should have seen the line out the door!" Maggie beamed with pride as she raved about Cassie for the third or fourth time that evening. "People were tripping over themselves to get one of Cassie's eggnog lattes."

Luke stole another glance at Cassie, noting the soft pink flush across her cheeks. She'd remained quiet throughout most of dinner, but she seemed happy, which gave Luke hope.

"You might be exaggerating a little, Maggie." Cassie smiled, glowing under the praise.

"Nonsense! I've never seen the bakery more crowded with eager customers. And I hope it was only the first successful morning of many more to come."

Cassie's smile wavered. "Your offer is incredibly generous, but I—"

Maggie held up her hand. "You don't have to decide right this minute." Rising to her feet, she added, "If you two wouldn't mind clearing the table, I'll slice the mulberry pie and we can eat dessert in front of the fire."

Luke stood and began stacking the plates as his mother disappeared into the kitchen, but he wasn't willing to let the topic drop just yet. Over the sound of clinking dishware, he asked, "So, what *do* you think about working at the bakery?"

Cassie's lips parted, but before she could answer, the shockingly loud call of a cuckoo bird reverberated throughout the house.

They both jolted in surprise, and Luke almost dropped his armload of dishes.

Cassie threw her head back and laughed until tears ran down her cheeks.

Luke couldn't help a chuckle himself.

Catching her breath, Cassie flashed a sheepish grin. "Saved by the bird."

❄

After generous slices of mouth-watering mulberry pie, Maggie brought out two mugs of piping-hot apple cider and handed them to Luke and Cassie on the couch.

"You're not having any?" Cassie asked, accepting the ceramic mug shaped like a snowman.

"It's long past my bedtime," Maggie said with a twinkling smile. "But you kids stay up and enjoy the rest of the evening."

Luke wanted to leap from the couch and engulf his mother in a grateful hug. But he kept his cool in front of Cassie, taking a casual sip of cider instead.

After bidding them goodnight, Maggie shuffled down the hall, leaving Luke and Cassie alone with little more than the crackling fire and ticking cuckoo clock to fill the heavy silence.

Cassie stared into her mug as if searching for conversation topics in the amber liquid.

Luke wondered if her rosy blush meant she saw right through his mother's ploy to give them time alone. Either way, Luke cleared his throat, intent on not squandering the opportunity. "So, what do you think of Mom's offer? Do you think you'll take it?"

Keeping her head lowered, Cassie ran her finger along the rim of the mug. "I'm not sure."

"Didn't you say there's not much keeping you in San Francisco? In Poppy Creek you'd have a home, a job, and people who care about you."

"It's not that simple."

Luke searched her face, feeling his chest tighten. All of the puzzle pieces were coming neatly together. Why couldn't Cassie see it?

"Why not?" he pressed. "What's getting in the way? Is it the mysterious job offer Ben mentioned last night?" The question left a sour taste in his mouth and he tightened his grip on the mug, waiting for Cassie to dismiss the suggestion.

But she merely shrugged, setting her cider on the coffee table. "Maybe."

Luke winced and swallowed hard. He could sense her slipping away. Setting down his own mug, he took a deep breath, trying to calm his agitated pulse. "Can you tell me about it?"

For a brief moment, her gaze flickered to meet his. But just as quickly she looked away. "Not tonight. It's getting late. I should head home." Without waiting for a response, she rose from the couch and strode toward the door.

Springing to his feet, Luke followed her. "You called the cottage *home*, Cassie. Doesn't that mean something?"

"It's an expression, Luke. It doesn't mean anything." Avoiding his gaze, Cassie shrugged on her coat.

"That's not true and you know it."

"We'll talk about this later, okay?" Cassie flung open the front door, letting in a rush of cold air.

Watching her step outside into the soft moonlight, panic settled in Luke's chest. He couldn't lose her. Not without telling her how he felt.

Not bothering to grab his coat, Luke ran after her, bounding down the porch steps two at a time. "Let's talk about it now. What is it, Cass? Is it the money?"

As soon as the words left his mouth, Luke wanted to take them back. They sounded harsh and judgmental. Not at all how he meant them.

Halfway to her car, Cassie whirled around, her eyes blazing in the dim light. "And what if it *is* about the money? Is that so wrong?"

"No, it's not," Luke said hastily, pausing a few feet in front of her. "I just meant..."

Cassie narrowed her eyes, but he could see the hurt hiding behind her indignation.

Luke closed the gap between them. "I'm sorry. I don't know what I'm saying. The truth is I *really* want you to stay."

"Why?" Her voice was barely above a whisper. "Why do you care?"

Their toes nearly touching, Luke gazed into her stunning green eyes—the ones that made him feel like the best version of himself, as though she could see all the good in him and all the greatness he could become.

Lost in her gaze, he couldn't move, soaking up every ounce of magic before it slipped away. Thick, feathery snowflakes began to drift from the sky, swirling around them like they were standing in a snow globe, a perfect moment captured in time.

"I care," Luke said, his breath mingling with hers, "because I'm falling in love with you, Cassie."

In the span of a single heartbeat, Cassie's hands slid around Luke's neck as he encircled her waist with his own.

When their lips met, all the emotions Luke had been trying to control since the instant he laid eyes on her erupted in their kiss, a burst of passion and tenderness that nearly knocked him over.

Snowflakes collected on his exposed neck, sending shivers down his spine, but Luke didn't care. The warmth of Cassie's lips permeated all the way to his soul. And he would have stood in the snow, tangled up in her kiss, until spring.

As their kiss deepened, Cassie abruptly broke away. Her eyes wide and startled, she stepped back, covering her mouth with her hand.

"Ru..." Luke reached for her, but she shook her head, blinking back tears.

"I—I have to go." Without looking back, Cassie fled to her car, disappearing in the swirl of snowflakes.

As Luke watched her slip from sight, his heart wrenched inside his chest, as if he might have just lost a piece of himself... for good.

CHAPTER 18

Cassie lay awake in bed as slender rays of sunlight filtered through the frosted windowpane. Although she hadn't been able to sleep a wink, she wasn't tired. Too many thoughts circulated in her mind.

Gently, Cassie pressed a fingertip to her lips, still able to feel the warmth and pressure of Luke's mouth on hers—still able to taste him.

The inexplicable kiss had been everything she'd imagined it would be, plus so much more. The moment their lips met, everything else fell away. And for the first time, Cassie saw her future with clarity. She wanted to stay in Poppy Creek... with Luke. But as quickly as the realization overcame her, the fears crept in. Could she risk her heart again? And what about the promise to her mother?

I'm falling in love with you, Cassie.

Luke's words were like an anchor securing her to a safe shore. And if she were honest, she wasn't just falling in love with him. She'd already fallen. But she didn't have a clue what to do about it.

Cassie padded softly down the staircase, greeted by the

sight of her Christmas tree reflecting vibrant colors across the bay window. The robust branches still permeated the house with the fresh, tangy scent of fir needles. Closing her eyes, Cassie took a moment to inhale the cleansing aroma.

With comfortable familiarity, Cassie moved through her morning routine, stocking the fireplace with another log, brewing a pot of coffee, and flipping to the day's activity in the Christmas Calendar.

December 12: Read A Christmas Carol.

Cradling her favorite mug, Cassie glanced out the kitchen window. A thin layer of snow coated the ground, creating the perfect atmosphere to curl up and read by the fire. Plus, Cassie looked forward to getting out of her own head for a few hours.

After topping off her mug, Cassie surveyed the small book-case in the corner of the living room. Musty leather-bound classics lined the shelves, offering their colorful spines for her perusal. Tracing the etched titles with her fingertip, Cassie's gaze fell on a thin cherry-red spine with gold lettering. Carefully, she slid it from its resting place.

Tucked beneath a heavy quilt, a cup of coffee in hand, Cassie cracked opened *A Christmas Carol*, not knowing what to expect. She'd heard the basic storyline—cantankerous old man who hates Christmas is visited by strange ghosts. But she wasn't prepared for the experience that unfolded.

From page one, Cassie was completely engrossed in Charles Dickens's world of hope, kindness, and redemption. And by the end, she'd long finished her coffee and dampened the corner of the quilt with her tears.

One line in particular stayed with her, even as she turned the very last page.

"No space of regret can make amends for one life's opportunity misused."

The sentiment sank deep into her heart, touching her soul.

Had Cassie been given an opportunity in Poppy Creek? A chance to change her life and become part of something greater than herself. Part of a community who loved and cared for one another. Even part of… a family.

A tear slid down her cheek, seeping into the page. Cassie quickly dabbed the blemish with the edge of her sleeve before gently closing the book.

Unlike Scrooge, Cassie didn't have a ghost to show her the future. But she didn't need one. She knew in her heart that if she didn't try everything in her power to stay in Poppy Creek, with Luke, she would regret it for the rest of her life.

❄

L uke stared at the tiny blocks of wood waiting to be pieced together. Usually working in his shop brought him a sense of calm. But right now, Luke didn't think anything could dispel the ache in his chest.

He'd thought about calling Cassie all day. Even driving over to the cottage to talk. But what would he say? He'd already poured out his heart. A part of him had been so sure she felt the same way. But when she broke their kiss, running away without an explanation, she'd broken his heart, too.

He peered at the shapes again, wondering why he should even bother to finish her surprise. But then, he knew the answer to that. While he wasn't sure what he should do next, he had to do something. *Anything.* Even if it meant…

The grating sound of the barn-style door sliding open startled Luke from his thoughts. To his surprise, his mother entered the shop carrying a casserole dish wrapped in foil.

"Hey, Mom. I wasn't expecting to see you tonight. Is everything okay?"

Ignoring his question, Maggie took in the workshop, her eyes widening as they passed over several pieces of furniture in various stages before completion. "It's been a while since I've visited." She set the casserole dish on his workbench before running a hand along the rough surface of the unfinished rocking chair. "This is beautiful."

"Thanks." Luke smiled, particularly pleased with that piece.

"I knew you enjoyed this hobby, but I didn't realize..." Maggie paused, once again taking in the scope of the space. Turning to face her son, her features softened. "Luke, do you ever wish that you had more time to—"

"Mom," Luke cut in quickly. "Is something wrong? I didn't miss your phone call, did I?" Luke reached for his back pocket in search of his cell phone. His mother rarely came to his house, preferring to have Luke visit her. Luke suspected she enjoyed being surrounded by all of the memories.

"No, nothing's wrong," Maggie assured him. "I wanted to drop off some leftovers from last night. And ask how things went with Cassie after I went to bed."

Luke sighed. "Things could have gone better." Dragging out a stool, he perched on the edge, gesturing for Maggie to take the rocking chair. It still needed a little work, but it was functional. Plus, it sat closest to the space heater.

"What happened?" Maggie rocked slowly, concern creasing her forehead.

"I asked her to stay in Poppy Creek once the Calendar is over," Luke said simply, not ready to divulge everything. Especially not their kiss.

"And what did she say?"

"That she hasn't decided what she wants to do yet."

"Did you tell her that you're in love with her?"

Luke's head shot up as color rushed to his cheeks.

Maggie laughed. "Don't look so surprised. We've all known for a while now."

"Who's 'we'?"

"Myself. Dolores. Eliza. Jack—"

"Okay, okay!" Luke groaned. "I get the picture. The problem is I don't think Cassie feels the same way."

"Did you ask her?"

"More or less."

Maggie planted her feet against the sawdust-covered floor before gently pushing off again. "Did you know the first time your father asked me out I said no?"

Luke frowned. "No, that's not right. I remember the story of how you met. At the Fall Flower Festival. Dad plucked a rose off the winning float and gave it to you with some cheesy line about how you were the prettiest rose in the parade."

"That's true." Maggie smiled fondly. "But that wasn't the first time he asked me out. It was actually the third. We just like that story better."

"Okay... So, what's the real story, then?"

Maggie rested her head against the back of the chair, her hazel eyes soft and dreamy. "The first time your father asked me out was a Sunday after church. The second time was on Valentine's Day three months later." She chuckled at the memory. "He bought every box of chocolate at Mac's just so he could fill one box entirely with the caramel-centered ones. My favorite."

"Impressive. Why'd you turn him down? Especially after that."

"No good reason, really," Maggie admitted. "I'd just returned from my trip to Europe, and I had the itch to travel the world. Your father was fresh out of law school and was anxious to set up the first practice in Poppy Creek. Seems foolish now, but I thought we were too different to make a real go of it."

"What changed your mind?" Resting both elbows on his knees, Luke leaned forward, soaking up every word.

Maggie's eyes glittered with wistful tears. "That story about the parade... there's a part we leave out."

"You mean you lied about your lie?" Luke teased.

Maggie's lips twitched. "I suppose you could say that." She planted her feet once more, but this time she remained motionless. "When your father plucked that rose off the float, he got cut by a thorn. Pretty bad. In fact, the blood trickled all the way down his hand, staining his best trousers."

Luke cringed. "I can see why you left that part out."

Maggie released a regretful sigh. "We shouldn't have. Truth is it was one of the most romantic things your father ever did for me."

"What? Bleed all over himself?" Luke asked with a laugh.

"When that thorn stuck your father's hand, he didn't even flinch," Maggie said proudly. "He stared me right in the eye, got down on one knee, and held out that rose with an invitation to dinner that night."

"Wait." Luke held up his hand. "You turned him down after he gave you an entire box of your favorite chocolate, but you said yes to a rose covered in blood?"

Maggie's shoulders shook with laughter. "It wasn't *covered*. Besides, you know what I saw? I saw a man who pursued me, even through pain." Her features sobered as she met Luke's gaze. "Marriage might be a bed of roses, but sometimes those roses have thorns. And when times get tough, you want someone by your side who will fight *with* you and *for* you. When you have that, differences seem a whole lot smaller." Tears glistened in her eyes, and she sniffled a few times before adding, "And you know what? Your father was the biggest champion of my dreams. From taking me to Paris on our honeymoon to buying the bakery."

Luke swallowed past the tightness in his throat. He'd always admired his parents for their love, devotion, and ability to find joy even in the most difficult circumstances. But now he had an even deeper appreciation for their love story. "So, you're saying I shouldn't give up?"

"I'm saying, some things take time."

"Like, third time's the charm?" Luke grinned, adding a little levity before they both wound up in tears.

"Sometimes." Maggie smiled softly.

They sat in silence for a long moment, the low hum of the space heater and the gentle swishing of the rocking chair filling the space between them.

"I think a season of change is coming," Maggie murmured, breaking the stillness. "For all of us."

CHAPTER 19

As Cassie poured herself another cup of coffee, she realized she hadn't stopped smiling all morning. Since reading *A Christmas Carol* the previous day, the impact of her epiphany had been settling in, creating a seismic shift in her heart and mind. Staying in Poppy Creek would change so much more than her address. It would change her entire life! And the one area where it scared and excited Cassie the most was her relationship with Luke. What would it mean for them? And what would he say when she told him the news?

Cassie's smile faltered as her hand shot to the necklace at her throat. She spun the heart charm, tightening the delicate chain as her mind raced with possibilities. What if Luke no longer had feelings for her? Or what if he couldn't forgive her for running away the night they'd kissed?

Releasing the charm, Cassie took a long sip of coffee, allowing the soothing liquid to calm her racing pulse as it tingled against her taste buds. Before she told Luke—and any of her hopes *or* fears became a reality—Cassie needed a plan. She'd still have to sell the cottage to put her mother through rehab. Which meant Cassie needed to find a new place to live as soon as possible.

Finishing off her third cup of coffee, Cassie scrolled through property listings on her phone. She wasn't surprised to find Poppy Creek didn't have a single apartment complex. But rental properties in general were practically nonexistent. She'd have to broaden her search to surrounding towns, which wasn't ideal. Especially if she'd be working at Maggie's Place.

Cassie glanced at the time, and her heart skittered in anticipation. At that exact moment, Maggie would be flipping the sign in the bakery's front window to Open.

Swallowing the last drop of coffee, Cassie rinsed her favorite mug in the sink and set it on a dish towel to dry. As she reached for her car keys on the kitchen island, she caught sight of the Christmas Calendar. She quickly thumbed the pages to the day's date.

December 13: Have a Snowball Fight.

Cassie's gaze darted to the window. All of yesterday's snow had melted into puddles. Panic gripped her chest as she circled back to the Calendar, double-checking the day's entry.

The words remained unchanged.

How could this be happening? Up until that moment, the activities had been perfectly aligned with the weather, as if her grandmother were orchestrating the forecast from a perch in the clouds. But this time the Calendar was off by an entire day.

Cassie's knees weakened and she leaned against the counter, her pulse increasing as quickly as her doubts. After all she'd been through, could this one mishap ruin everything?

She needed to talk to Luke. He might know what to do. But what would she say? She owed him an apology. And an explanation. She couldn't go to him for help before she fixed things between them. But how exactly would she do that?

Cassie massaged her fingertips against her temple, taking deep breaths to calm herself down. Maybe the Calendar would work itself out? After all, there was still time for it to snow again.

Strangers things had happened in Poppy Creek than snow-fall two days in a row.

All Cassie needed to do was give the Calendar more time.

And maybe time would help her figure out what to say to Luke.

❄

As Cassie walked the few feet from her car to Maggie's Place, she kept one eye on the sky. Nothing but miles of periwinkle blue dotted with frothy white clouds. Still, Cassie told herself not to panic. She still had plenty of time.

"Good morning, dear," Maggie greeted her with a rosy smile. "Aren't you bright and early today."

Cassie didn't even wait for Maggie to finish sliding the last cinnamon roll into the case before skipping around the counter and enveloping her in a hug.

Maggie laughed. "And in a bright and chipper mood, too."

Pulling back, Cassie beamed at the older woman who'd become more of a mother to her in a short amount of time than her own flesh and blood. "Maggie, is your job offer still available?"

"Of course!" Maggie's eyes widened. "Are you saying—"

Cassie threw her arms around her again. "Yes!"

As Maggie squeezed her back, Cassie closed her eyes, inhaling the scent of cinnamon and sugar, suddenly overcome with emotion. "Thank you, thank you," she murmured, close to tears.

"What's going on?" Eliza burst through the kitchen door with a fresh batch of gingerbread scones. "Why are you crying? Did—" Realization flashed in Eliza's dark eyes and she carelessly tossed the baking sheet onto the counter as she cried, "You're taking the job!"

Pulling back, Cassie swiped her damp cheeks. "I am."

Eliza squealed and tackled Cassie in a bear hug.

157

Giggling, Cassie squeezed her back. "I still have a few things to figure out. So, I probably won't be able to officially start until after Christmas."

"I can't believe you're staying!" Eliza cheered, hopping up in down in her excitement. "This is the best news *ever*."

"It certainly is." Maggie's eyes sparkled with happy tears. "We should celebrate."

Just then the bell jingled, signaling their first customer of the day. Maggie excused herself after hugging Cassie one more time.

"Have you told Luke?" Eliza whispered, pulling Cassie off to the side.

Blushing, Cassie stared at the scuffed hardwood floor. "Not yet."

"Then let's go find him! I bet he's at his office already."

"Wait," Cassie said quickly, placing a hand on her arm. "Not yet."

"Why not?"

"I, uh, have a few things to take care of first."

"Like what?" Eliza planted one hand on her hip, both eyebrows raised.

"Well, I'd like to get a few things in order first. Like talking to Frank about serving his coffee."

"Really?" Eliza's eyes lit up as though she'd already forgotten all about telling Luke. "Do you think he'll say yes?"

"Maybe. I hope so." Cassie hadn't thought it all the way through yet, but she felt hopeful. "I also have to figure out what I'm going to do about the Christmas Calendar."

"What do you mean?"

As Cassie glanced toward the front window, her stomach twisted. Rays of sunlight danced across the tabletops, reflecting off the crystal vases filled with holly leaves and red carnations. "I'm trying not to panic yet, but today's activity is a snowball fight. And we're fresh out of snow."

Eliza frowned. "Yikes. That's not good."

"To put it mildly," Cassie agreed.

Eliza steepled her fingers and pressed them to her lips, her eyes scrunched shut in concentration.

Cassie waited patiently until Eliza's eyes popped open and she grinned mischievously. "I have a feeling this afternoon's forecast will show heavy snowfall."

"But how—" Cassie started as Eliza grabbed her hand.

"Come on. I'll show you my idea."

❄

Luke shifted Ben's Captain America backpack to his other shoulder, grateful Ben's school let out early, necessitating Luke pick him up for Eliza. Besides giving them "guy time," hanging out with Ben provided a momentary distraction.

Luke needed to clear the air with Cassie soon. Even though he still had no idea what to say. But aside from his own feelings, he had a job to do. And he couldn't let another day pass without finding out if she'd completed the necessary activities on the Christmas Calendar.

What Luke needed was some sort of peace offering—a way to move past the awkwardness of the kiss. Then, with a little more time, he could try again.

Luke smiled, recalling his parents' unconventional love story.

Some things take time...

His mother's words had looped in his mind ever since their conversation. Luke didn't mind being patient. But come Christmas Day, he'd be out of time.

"So, are you ready for the pageant in a few days?" Luke asked, diverting his own complicated thoughts. "Did you memorize all your lines?"

Ben nodded, kicking a pinecone across the grass. "Nanna's been practicing with me. She said acting is in my blood. Gross."

He made such a comical face, Luke laughed. "She means

you're a natural. Your grandma was a big-time actress before moving to Poppy Creek."

"I know," Ben said matter-of-factly. "She tells me all the time."

Luke stifled another chuckle. Before he could ask Ben to share some of his lines, Ben shouted, "Look! It's Mom and Cassie!"

Following the direction of Ben's outstretched finger, Luke spotted Eliza and Cassie waiting for them in the middle of the town square.

Luke froze mid-stride, the mere sight of Cassie turning his insides to mush. What were they doing out here? Squinting, Luke tried to make out the objects they were holding.

"Send us your youngest," Eliza bellowed in a dramatic, warrior-like tone.

Ben giggled. "That's me! That's me!" He raised his hand, waving it over his head before racing toward his mother.

Luke watched, completely baffled, as Eliza whispered something in Ben's ear. Then she pointed at two lumpy objects nestled in the grass, which Ben quickly scooped up in both arms.

As he trotted back toward Luke, the mystery items came into focus. Two sacks of flour made from tightly woven cotton fabric, each with bold lettering that read Samuel Ball's Snow White Flour.

"This one's yours." Snickering, Ben handed Luke a sack of flour.

"What's it for?"

Ben giggled again, but didn't say anything as he untied the string cinching his sack closed.

Still confused, Luke called out, "Eliza, what in the world is—"

But before he had a chance to finish his question, Eliza roared, "Charge!" and she and Cassie bolted across the field. In a matter of seconds, they were bombarded with fistfuls of flour.

Ben squealed, tearing across the lawn with Eliza in quick pursuit.

Cassie's laughter mingled with the billowy cloud of white powder, and as the dust settled, Luke caught sight of her brilliant smile.

"You'd better get it together, Sprinkles. Or you're going to lose this snowball fight," she teased, holding up a handful of flour. Her green eyes sparkled with mischief, but something in her purposeful gaze communicated so much more than her words.

And in that moment, Luke realized the playful fight was actually a white flag.

CHAPTER 20

When Frank opened the front door, he nearly fell over in surprise.

Cassie grinned, realizing she must be quite the sight, covered head to toe in flour. She'd done her best to brush most of it off, but she still looked like a loaf of artisan bread.

Without mentioning her odd appearance, Frank pushed the door open a few more inches, grumbling, "About time you showed up."

"I'm sorry it took so long," Cassie said, forgoing the excuses. "But I think you'll be pleased with what I have to say."

Frank held up a finger, indicating she should wait. Then, waving for her to follow, he led her down the hallway to his study. He shuffled to his desk and eased into the fancy, ergonomic chair while Cassie hovered by his side.

The laptop flickered to life as Frank put on a pair of reading glasses. "I'd ask you to sit down, but you appear to be coated in more flour than fried chicken."

Cassie giggled. "It's a long story."

Frank narrowed his gaze over the rim of his glasses, clearly not amused. *Or* interested. "What did you think of the coffee I gave you?"

So, he was going to get right to the point, was he? Well, so could she. "Frank, is this for your book? The second edition, I mean." Cassie held her breath, fully expecting him to sidestep her question.

But to her surprise, he pushed back his glasses and rubbed his eyes, mumbling, "Apparently, one best seller isn't enough. The publisher wants more. And they want me to include specific blends this time. Seems no one can think for themselves these days."

Cassie offered a sympathetic smile, her hunch confirmed. "For what it's worth, I think a second edition is a great idea. And you should definitely include the blend you gave me. It was the best coffee I've ever had, by far."

After readjusting his glasses, Frank poised his fingers over the keyboard. "What flavor notes did you notice?"

Beaming proudly, Cassie pulled up the Notes app on her phone and set it on the desk. "I followed a basic cupping method and jotted down each score."

Surprise, then something vaguely resembling admiration, flickered across Frank's face. But he quickly reset his features in his trademark stony expression. "Good."

The click-clack of the keyboard filled the silence as Frank transferred the information from her phone into an open document.

Cassie chewed her bottom lip, the question she'd been dying to ask gnawing at her stomach. She drew in a deep breath. "Frank... I've been wondering... Why ask me? About the coffee, I mean. It's not like you need a second opinion. You're Richard Stanton, after all. The number one authority on all things coffee."

His fingertips froze over the keys, his strained features highlighted in the blueish glow of the computer screen. After a moment, he reached into the top right drawer of his desk and withdrew a tiny orange pill bottle. He handed it to her, then resumed typing.

Confused, Cassie turned it over in her hand, the pills rattling inside the plastic container as she tried to make sense of what he'd given her. She didn't recognize the name on the label or anything else about the prescription. Although it appeared to be some sort of heart medication.

When she finally scanned the fine print stipulating the side effects, she winced.

May affect sense of taste.

Cassie's gaze flew to Frank's face, which remained unreadable. "I'm so sorry," she whispered, her heart aching for him.

"I'm not dying," he snapped before softening slightly. "It comes and goes. But..." His voice trailed off and Cassie noticed the droop in his shoulders.

Cassie—perhaps more so than anyone—knew exactly what it would mean for Frank to lose his sense of taste, a coffee roaster's most coveted tool. An exceptional palate was a gift. One that could elevate you far beyond the rest of the industry.

Fighting back compassionate tears, Cassie forced a smile. "My taste buds are at your disposal anytime."

Giving her a skeptical side-eye, he asked, "Have you ever roasted before?"

"Once. But it was a drum roaster."

Frank snorted. "Whatever knucklehead invented that monstrosity should never be allowed to touch another coffee bean in his life."

"They're that bad?" Cassie asked, amused by his intense reaction.

"Let me ask you something," Frank said with a stern glare. "Would you cook a ten-pound turkey on a frying pan?"

Cassie frowned. "No..."

"Of course, you wouldn't! The bottom would get scorched, leaving the rest of it raw. You need the circulating heat of an oven. Any fool knows that."

Cassie suppressed a laugh. "So, a drum roaster is the frying pan and the air roaster is the oven?"

"Now you've got it!" Frank slapped his palm on the desk, nodding his approval. "Come on. Let's go see if you can cook a turkey."

❄

Cassie couldn't believe she was roasting coffee with Richard Stanton—her coffee hero—in his quirky barn turned roastery.

Frank walked her through the entire process, from letting her select three different varieties of green beans—Sumatra, Costa Rica, and Kenya—to carrying out each step of the roasting process until they had ten pounds of Cassie's blend cooling in a tall mason jar.

"The glass lets the coffee sweat out unwanted moisture," Frank explained.

Cassie grinned, not dreaming of interrupting him, even though she'd read his book a dozen times. There was something special about hearing it from the mouth of the master.

"Frank, what do you do with all of this coffee?" Cassie asked, taking in the row of jars filled from a previous roast. "You can't possibly drink it all yourself."

Frank immediately stiffened. "What I do with it is my own business," he snapped, silencing Cassie on the spot.

Unscrewing the lid, he scooped some of the piping-hot beans into a smaller quart-sized mason jar. "I'll send this home with you, and you can taste it once it cools down. The flavors still need time to develop." He shoved the jar in her hands. "For now, go jot down the precise blend and temperature in the notebook in my study. In case you got lucky and it tastes halfway decent." His lips quirked ever so slightly, belaying the harshness of his words.

Thrilled to be given the responsibility, Cassie tucked the warm jar under her arm and scurried into the house.

Shuffling through the various papers littering the desk,

Cassie searched for Frank's notebook to no avail. Unwilling to give up, she pulled open the top drawer, where two leather-bound books rested side by side. *Aha!* It had to be one of those! Lifting the largest of the two, she untied the thick leather cord and flipped it open.

An aged photograph fluttered to the floor.

As her fingers curled around the faded edges, Cassie's heartbeat stilled.

Frank's youthful, smiling face beamed out at her beside a pretty auburn-haired girl flashing a diamond engagement ring.

Cassie gasped, sinking into the chair as her knees gave out.

The almond-shaped green eyes staring back at her were more than vaguely familiar.

They belonged to her grandmother.

❄

C assie tightened her grip on the steering wheel, her heart still pounding from the startling discovery. Frank Barrie was engaged to her grandmother! Nothing seemed further from the realm of possibility.

When she'd heard Frank's footsteps echo down the hall-way, she'd quickly slipped the photograph between the pages, shoving the book back inside the drawer. Her heart wrenched with guilt. She didn't want to hide anything from Frank. But she also wasn't sure she could face the repercussions. Their relationship had come so far, barely surviving one secret. How would he feel if he found out she'd uncovered another one?

Somehow, Cassie managed to conceal her newfound knowledge. When they'd concluded their work, Cassie bid Frank goodbye and slipped away to her car.

Pulse still racing, Cassie fidgeted with her phone, debating her next move. Acting on instinct, she found herself dialing Eliza's number.

"Hey, Cass! What's up?" Eliza asked over Christmas music blaring in the background.

Cassie hesitated, suddenly realizing the peculiarity of her request. "Can you... give me Luke's address?"

A long silence followed, and Cassie could imagine the huge grin plastered across Eliza's face.

She instantly regretted not calling Luke instead. But hearing his deep, spine-tingling voice would have made Cassie lose her nerve.

"Sure," Eliza said with an impish lilt to her voice.

Blushing even in the privacy of her car, Cassie punched the address into her GPS. "Thanks, Eliza." Before her inquisitive friend could pepper her with questions, Cassie hung up the phone.

As she headed back to the main road, Cassie's cautious inner voice implored her to turn around and go home. Showing up on Luke's doorstep unannounced was a risky idea. Especially as the sun dipped below the horizon. But in a moment when Cassie needed advice, she instantly thought of Luke. Not only could she trust him with Frank's secret, but she'd come to value his input... more so than anyone else's in her life.

Suddenly, Cassie had an overwhelming urge to see Luke's home—and the insights it would provide into the man himself. And the closer she got to her destination, the more her curiosity grew.

Rounding the final bend in the road, Cassie nearly slammed on the brakes as a breathtaking, two-story home came into view. A blend of wood and stone, the lodge-style estate stood on several acres of sprawling land, bordered by a thick forest of pines. An enormous A-frame picture window showcased a dazzling Christmas tree at least nine feet tall. Large, colored bulbs outlined nearly every inch of the house, which was pretty enough to be on a Hallmark card.

After ringing the doorbell—which Luke had somehow

programmed to play "Jingle Bells"—Cassie drew in a shaky breath, doubts running through her mind. She should have called first. What if he wasn't home?

Admonishing herself for her impulsivity, Cassie whirled around and bounded down the front steps. But as she headed for her car, the whirring of a saw cut through the stillness of the brisk, wintry air. Her pulse matching the speed of a spinning blade, Cassie rounded the corner of the house and crunched along the gravel path, anxiously closing the distance between her and the sound.

Light streamed through the open barn door, casting curious shadows on the ground. As Cassie inched closer and peered inside, her breath caught in her throat.

Luke leaned over a table saw, the sleeves of his flannel shirt pushed up to his elbows. Even from a distance, Cassie could see the muscles in his forearms flex as he guided the plank of wood toward the rotating blade.

Cassie swallowed, her mouth suddenly dry. Alarmed by the rush of emotions rippling through her, she backed away, rear-ending a pile of wood. The logs toppled over, clattering to the ground.

Startled, Luke glanced up, pushing his safety goggles on top of his forehead as he clicked off the saw. "Hello?" He squinted in her direction, where she stood partially shrouded in darkness.

The hairs on Cassie's arms tingled at the hopeful catch in Luke's voice as he asked, "Cassie, is that you?"

CHAPTER 21

L uke blinked a few times to make sure he wasn't dreaming. Could it really be her?

Timidly, Cassie stepped from the shadows into the warmth of the barn. "Hi." She tucked a curl behind her ear, blushing slightly as she met his gaze.

Luke's heart sputtered to a stop. Something about having the woman he loved here in his workshop made breathing impossible. It took him a moment to string the right words together. "Wow, this is a nice surprise."

"I should have called," Cassie blurted, then flushed an even deeper shade of pink.

"Why?" Luke asked, flashing a teasing grin. "If you haven't noticed, no one calls ahead in Poppy Creek."

The corners of Cassie's lips curved in a small smile. "That's true."

"What brings you by?" Luke pulled out two stools from beneath his drafting table, dragging them in front of the space heater.

But Cassie's gaze traveled past them to the unfinished rocking chair. "Luke, this is beautiful." As though drawn to it, she reached out a hand, running it along the unpolished surface.

"Thanks." Luke felt a similar sense of pride when his mother had praised the same chair the night before. But coming from Cassie, the words sent a different sensation coursing through him—one that ran so much deeper. "I have a few more hours of work left before it's finished, but it's coming along."

"Is it for sale?"

"I don't know what I'm going to do with it, to be honest. I just enjoy the process."

Cassie turned to face him, a softness in her eyes. "I think I know what you mean."

Resisting the urge to pull her into his arms, Luke offered, "If you want, I can teach you a little woodworking. I'll even let you use the table saw."

Cassie grinned. "Is it anything like a chain saw?"

"Pretty close." Luke chuckled, fondly recalling the night they'd cut down Cassie's Christmas tree. "You'll want to remove your coat and scarf first. I try not to wear anything too bulky or loose. Nothing that could get caught in the blade."

As Cassie slipped off her outerwear, revealing the softest looking beige sweater Luke had ever seen, he asked, "Before I forget, was there something specific that brought you by?" Anything to distract him from how completely huggable she looked.

"Yes! Something huge, actually."

Luke's stomach churned, and he prayed it was good news. "Should I be sitting down?" he asked, hoping humor would calm his flash of nerves.

"That's not a bad idea," Cassie said, then drew in a breath.

Luke waited, perched on the edge of the stool.

"Frank Barrie…" She paused and glanced at the ceiling as if the words to follow would fall from the sky.

Luke scooted even closer to the edge, barely able to contain his curiosity.

When Cassie met his gaze again, the words escaped her lips in a rush. "Frank Barrie was engaged to my grandmother!"

"What?" Luke lurched forward, catching himself before he fell off the stool.

Cassie laughed softly. "That's basically how I reacted, too."

"How did you find out? Did he tell you?" Luke still couldn't believe it.

"It was sort of... an accident. I stumbled across an old engagement photo."

"Wow," Luke breathed, running a hand through his hair. "I had no idea."

"I don't think anyone did," Cassie said.

"Does Frank know you found out?"

"No. And I'm not sure how to tell him." Distress settled across Cassie's features. "We've come so far. I feel like he's finally trusting me. I'm afraid if I tell him, he'll get angry and..."

"Not want to see you anymore?" Luke finished gently.

Cassie's eyes clouded with sadness.

Leaping from the stool, Luke wrapped an arm around her shoulders. "Hey, don't worry. Once you explain it to him, I'm sure he'll understand." He ran his hand up and down her arm for comfort. "And I have no doubt you'll find the perfect moment to tell him."

"Thank you." Cassie smiled up at him.

Luke's breath hitched in his throat as their eyes locked.

Suddenly, he was all too aware of the sensation of his fingertips against her feather-soft sweater. And the heat from her body so close to his. He cleared his throat, but before he could voice any of his thoughts, Cassie asked, "Should we get to work on that rocking chair?"

"Uh, yeah," Luke stammered. Sliding his arm from around her shoulders, he passed her a pair of safety goggles.

"This feels vaguely familiar." Cassie smirked.

"Yep! But it'll be even better. Trust me."

After Luke walked her through all the steps, including

safety tips, he moved off to the side, where he could watch from a close enough distance to intervene if she needed help.

Her features set in determination, Cassie eased the walnut plank toward the spinning blade. But as she leaned forward, a glint of metal caught Luke's eye.

Quickly, he leaped forward and flipped off the switch, and the machine rumbled to a stop.

"What's wrong?" Cassie asked, yanking off the goggles.

"Your necklace." Luke strode to her side. "You don't want anything dangling near the blade."

Taking the charm in his fingertips, he moved to tuck it behind the collar of her sweater, but the engraving caught his eye. "Cass…" he began, peering closer. "What do the initials MC stand for?"

❄

Cassie tugged the wool blanket around her shoulders as Luke placed another log on the campfire, the embers sparking into the inky black sky.

When he appeared satisfied with the strength of the flames, Luke settled on the Adirondack-style bench next to her.

Cassie held the blanket open, allowing Luke to sidle in next to her, instantly feeling the heat surge between them.

"Warm enough?" he asked, tucking the edges around her.

"Yes, thanks." Cassie toyed with the silver heart charm at her throat—the reason for Luke's effort. When she'd said it was a long story, he'd insisted on making her more comfortable first. And, almost as if he'd known she'd be more at ease outside, he'd set to work adding kindling to the large built-in firepit made from mortared stones.

Nestled beside him, Cassie marveled at how in tune they'd become. He seemed to know what she needed almost before she did.

"So." Luke's gaze traveled to the necklace. "Now that we're settled, what does MC stand for?"

"It stands for Megan Conway," Cassie said simply, staring into the coppery flames.

"Who's Megan Conway?"

Running her finger along the smooth edge of the charm, Cassie blinked back hot tears. "I don't know. We never met."

Luke placed a hand on her knee. "I'm sorry, Cass. But I still don't understand."

Cassie squeezed her eyes shut, and a single tear escaped and slid down her cheek.

Gently, Luke brushed it aside, sending tremors coursing through her. He pulled the blanket tighter around her shoulders, drawing her closer against him.

"Derek, my ex, gave me this necklace our first Christmas together," Cassie explained past the lump in her throat. "It was the first time anyone had given me a Christmas present beyond the occasional Secret Santa gift exchange at work. It was special. Something he'd picked out just for me." Her voice trembled, and she had to pause, sucking in a breath to steady her emotions.

"Your mother never gave you a Christmas present?" Luke asked, tracing a comforting circle on her upper arm with his thumb.

"Mom never really *did* Christmas," Cassie admitted. "So, when I opened my gift from Derek and saw this beautiful necklace..." Her voice broke off.

Luke didn't pressure her to continue, merely tightening his embrace.

Cassie leaned into him, gathering comfort from his closeness. "It took me a minute to realize the wrong initials were engraved on the charm. Derek tried to play it off, saying the jeweler made a mistake. But he sounded so nervous, so unlike himself, I didn't believe him."

Cassie felt Luke's fingers clench against her arm, and the

small display of outrage on her behalf was like a balm to her broken heart. There wasn't a doubt in Cassie's mind that Luke was different than Derek, or, really, any man she'd ever met. And as the bitterness from her past slowly loosened its grip around her heart, she said, "Derek finally told me the truth, admitting he'd been seeing someone else and bought us the same present, mixing them up by mistake."

"I'm so sorry, Cassie." Luke's voice strained with empathy.

"It's okay," she murmured, not meaning Derek's actions, but rather her own state of mind. Nuzzling her head against his chest, Cassie savored how safe and protected she felt in his arms… how *loved*.

"Can I ask you something?" he said quietly.

"Anything."

"Why do you still wear the necklace?"

Cassie didn't respond for several seconds, the sound of the crackling embers filling the silence between them. How could she explain something so deeply personal? Explaining that a flimsy silver necklace felt like the strongest piece of armor in the world didn't make any sense. Not to anyone but her.

Finally, she answered in a voice barely above a whisper. "It's… a reminder."

"Of what?"

"That hope causes nothing but heartache." The words slipped from her lips easily and yet… they didn't quite seem true anymore.

For a moment, Luke said nothing. He continued to run his thumb along her arm in comforting circles, staring intently into the fire. When he finally spoke, his words rang with a gentle truth. "You know, I've always thought hope *cured* heartache."

As Cassie listened to the sound of Luke's strong, steady heartbeat, a slow smile spread across her lips. "You know," she echoed softly, "I think you're right."

CHAPTER 22

After sharing her past with Luke, Cassie was even more assured in her decision to turn down Derek's job offer. While the temptation to own a piece of her lifelong dream was strong, it wasn't strong enough to tie herself to Derek. Besides, by staying in Poppy Creek, a different dream was coming true —one far more meaningful.

Cassie spent the morning making specialty coffees at Maggie's, using the beans from her last roast with Frank. Once again, a line formed out the door for Cassie's unique and tantalizing concoctions. While she didn't have any ownership in the bakery itself, she felt a sense of pride in what she created. And the smiles on people's faces when she crafted something special just for them gave her a sense of purpose. Whether it was making a gingersnap latte for Dolores or a candied lavender mocha for Penny. She'd even invented a spicy chai latte for Jack, incorporating smoked paprika and cardamom from his signature BBQ sauce.

After several hours at the espresso machine, Cassie felt so exhilarated she didn't want it to end. But she'd exhausted her supply of coffee, which meant several disappointed customers had to leave with their pastries sans latte.

"All done for the day?" Maggie asked.

Her tone carried a hint of weariness. And considering she'd been on her feet all morning glued to the cash register, Cassie couldn't blame her for being tired.

"I'm all out of coffee, but I'd love to stick around for a bit. Maybe I could fill in for you for a while?"

"Oh, no. I couldn't ask you to—"

"You didn't ask," Cassie interjected with a smile. "I offered. Honestly, I'd love to help out. I think Eliza and I can manage for the rest of the day."

"Manage what?" Eliza swooped in with a tray of colossal sugar cookies frosted to resemble brightly colored ornaments.

"Cassie graciously offered to fill in for me, but I—"

"That's a great idea!" Eliza cut in, refilling the dwindling cookie display. "You deserve a break. You haven't had one since..." She scrunched her nose in thought. "When did you open this place? Thirty years ago?"

Maggie laughed. "Thirty-one. And I suppose you have a point. It *has* been a while. But are you sure?"

"Of course!" Eliza beamed. "I'm done baking for the day, so that just leaves the prep for tomorrow. I can show Cassie how to use the register."

"Oh, I've used plenty of registers bef—" Cassie stopped short when her gaze settled on the bronzed antique register. It had more buttons and gears than the espresso machine! "Never mind." She grinned sheepishly. "You'd better show me. But I'm a quick learner. Honestly, Maggie, we'll be fine. *Better* than fine. And considering I'll be working here after Christmas, I should learn, anyway."

"Exactly!" Eliza practically shooed Maggie out the door.

"Okay, then." Maggie slowly tugged the polka dot apron over her head. "It will be nice to have a little time off." Her hazel eyes glimmered as she appeared to ponder the possibilities. "I have a few presents to wrap, Debbie Macomber's latest book on my nightstand, and a couple last-minute Christmas cards I still need to send."

"Oh!" Cassie's hand flew to her heart. "I almost forgot! I'm so glad you reminded me, Maggie. Today's activity is Send Someone a Christmas Card. Do you know where I can buy one?"

"Don't be silly," Maggie said. "You'll come by my place tonight and use one of mine. I have dozens of beautiful cards itching to bring a smile to someone's face."

"That would be lovely. Thank you." Cassie decided not to mention she planned to send the card to her mother. And knowing Donna, her smile would be of the upside down variety. But maybe some of the Christmas spirit Cassie found in Poppy Creek would find its way into her mother's heart, too.

Kissing both girls on the cheek, Maggie said goodbye and sailed out of the bakery with an unmistakable skip in her step.

Grinning after her, Eliza squeezed Cassie's hand. "I'm so glad you suggested this! She works way too hard. And she's seemed tired lately. A break will do her some good."

"Happy to help." Cassie swiveled on her heels, excitement fluttering in her stomach as she scanned the shop. "Where should I start?"

"First," Eliza said, placing both hands on Cassie's shoulders, spinning her around, "I'll show you the register. Half the keys stick and it won't calculate the change for you."

Cassie let out a good-natured groan. "What have I gotten myself into?"

"You'll get the hang of it. Just don't accidentally short Frida Connelly on her change. She's a retired math teacher, and she counts it every time."

Eliza laughed, and the infectious lilt teased a giggle from Cassie's lips, too. Since the moment she met Eliza, the spunky blonde won her over with her endearing honesty and well-meaning meddling. And Cassie could tell that working together was going to be more fun than quality control at Santa's workshop.

Cassie had experienced so much joy in Poppy Creek, she simply couldn't understand why her mother had ever left.

❄

As Cassie sat at the white wicker dining set situated in Maggie's cheery kitchen nook, she sifted through a stack of glittery Christmas cards, enjoying the scent of cinnamon and sugar filling the homey space.

"I can't believe you took a break from the bakery to come home and bake," Cassie teased.

The corners of Maggie's eyes crinkled as she laughed. "I'm so busy managing the operations side of the business, I hardly get to bake for myself anymore." Maggie rolled the plump ball of dough in a shallow dish of cinnamon and sugar. "And that vanilla cinnamon latte you made me earlier left me craving a fresh batch of snickerdoodles."

Cassie's mouth watered as her gaze drifted toward the oven. "They *do* smell delicious."

"The first batch will be ready by the time you're finished with that Christmas card." Maggie smiled, nodding toward the stack Cassie had only sifted halfway through. "And who's the lucky recipient?"

Cassie fidgeted with a particularly gaudy card with hearts and flowers bursting from Santa's sack, which appeared to be crafted from an actual swatch of red velvet. "My mom," she murmured, running a finger over the soft fabric.

"How lovely. I'm sure it will make her day."

"Maybe. If she even opens it. She usually avoids any hint of holiday mail as though an elf might pop out and sing a telegram."

Maggie chuckled. "Do you think your mother will visit you in Poppy Creek for Christmas?"

"Not a chance." Cassie sighed, thumbing through the stack of cards absentmindedly. "Unfortunately, I don't think you could pay my mother to come back here."

Frowning, Maggie rolled another clump of dough in the palm of her hand, making a perfect circle. "That's too bad."

A niggling thought tugged at the back of Cassie's mind. One she'd debated asking Maggie half a dozen times, but could never quite bring herself to form the words. "Maggie..."

"Hmm?" Maggie concentrated on lining all the cookies in a perfect row on the baking sheet.

"Did you..." Cassie paused and swallowed past the uncomfortable lump in her throat. "Did you know my mother?" There. The question was out. She couldn't take it back now.

A ball of dough slipped from Maggie's fingers, bounced against the edge of the cookie sheet, and flattened on the tile floor.

As Cassie watched Maggie scoop it up with a spatula and toss it in the trash, her heart beat in an anxious rhythm, awaiting Maggie's response.

Maggie returned to the mixing bowl and began rolling a replacement when she finally answered. "I knew *of* your mother. I was a bit older, so our social circles didn't cross paths all that often."

"What was she like? As a kid, I mean."

"Well, as a youngster, she seemed adventurous and precocious. Always getting into trouble. She wanted to do anything the boys could do, but better. Whether it was climbing the tree higher or riding her bike faster." Maggie chuckled, shaking her head. "Your poor grandmother. She was a bundle of nerves worrying after your mom."

"And my grandfather?"

"Oh, he thought it was wonderful. He'd take your mother fishing and teach her how to shoot a pellet gun. In some ways, it was like he had a son *and* a daughter. That is, until..."

"Until what?" Cassie had completely forgotten about the

179

Christmas cards and scooted toward the edge of the chair, the wicker creaking as she shifted her weight.

"Until she grew up," Maggie said softly. "Seemingly overnight, she developed into a young woman. An incredibly beautiful one, at that. And her tastes for adventure went off in a... different direction."

"Boys?" Cassie asked, already confident of the answer.

"Among... other things," Maggie answered tactfully.

It didn't take much imagination for Cassie to guess what Maggie meant. She'd long suspected her mother's drinking endeavors had started early. "That must have been difficult for her parents."

"It was. They did their best. But your mother..." Maggie trailed off, the cookies long forgotten.

"Had a mind of her own?" Cassie finished.

"Things only got worse when your grandfather passed away."

"How old was my mom?"

"Barely seventeen."

Cassie's throat tightened. Never having met her own father, she could only imagine the pain of losing someone you loved. "How awful."

"Your poor mother seemed to completely lose herself after that. She got pregnant a few months later. Which nearly broke your grandmother's heart."

"Was she angry?"

"More scared, I think. Of course, I can only guess. I wasn't privy to all of this information when it happened. I heard rumors. But I suspect the fact that she'd just lost her husband, her own health was fragile, and your mother was still a child, all factored into your grandmother's decision to..." Maggie hesitated.

"To what?" Cassie sat so close to the edge of the chair she might as well have been sitting on the floor.

Maggie closed her eyes, her features strained. When she finally opened them, her eyes sparkled with tears. "She asked your mother to give you up for adoption."

All the air drained from Cassie's lungs, and she collapsed against the back of the chair.

"Oh, honey." Wiping her hands on her apron, Maggie rushed over and sank into the chair beside her. Placing her palms over Cassie's hands, she gave them a reassuring squeeze. "Your grandmother loved you dearly. I'm certain she did."

A tear slid down Cassie's cheek as she forced a thin-lipped smile. During her time in Poppy Creek, she'd come to believe her grandmother loved her, even though she'd never been a part of her life. But now, Cassie didn't know what to think.

"When people are afraid," Maggie said slowly, "they tend to do things they wouldn't normally do. And I think your grandmother was terrified she and your mother couldn't give you the life you deserved."

Cassie nodded, although her heart physically ached. The life she deserved? What did that even mean? All she wanted was a family—someone who loved her. What more did she need?

"I'm so sorry," Maggie whispered, her own tears falling freely. "Perhaps I shouldn't have told you."

Cassie interlocked her fingers with Maggie's, squeezing back. "I'm glad you did. Truly. It helps to finally have some answers, even though I still don't understand why my mother left Poppy Creek."

"No one knows. The suspicion is that your grandmother gave her an ultimatum and your mother refused. A few months after you were born, your mother disappeared, taking you with her."

"It just doesn't make sense." Cassie released Maggie's hands, pressing her fingertips to her throbbing temple. "Why *didn't* my mom give me up for adoption? She doesn't exactly relish the role of motherhood."

"I'm sure it was because she loves you and didn't want to give you up," Maggie said simply.

Cassie frowned, but an inkling of hope pricked her heart. Could that really be true? Cassie wanted to believe it. But something deep in her gut told her there had to be more to the story.

"Do you know who my father is?" she asked.

"I wish I did, but I'm afraid I have no idea. No one else in town seems to know, either. Your mother never told you?"

"No, she didn't." Cassie's lips trembled slightly as conflicting emotions—pain, disappointment, hope—washed over her.

"Well, I'll tell you one thing I *do* know," Maggie said, rising to her feet.

Cassie glanced up expectantly.

"The first batch of cookies should be done. And nothing brightens a mood better than a warm-from-the-oven snickerdoodle."

Cassie smiled as Maggie slipped on a pair of plaid oven mitts and yanked open the oven door. The mouthwatering aroma of sugar and spice spilled into the kitchen.

While Maggie busied herself with sliding the cookies onto a cooling rack, Cassie turned her attention to the stack of Christmas cards. The one resting on top depicted a charming cottage covered in shimmering snow with the words *Home for the Holidays* scrawled across the top in red swirly letters.

Fanning the card open, Cassie pressed the crease into the table.

Before her conversation with Maggie, Cassie had planned to send a simple holiday greeting.

But now the words she penned carried an extra level of meaning.

. . .

D*ear Mom,*

Merry Christmas.
Wishing you a heart full
of hope this holiday season.
Love always,
Your daughter

CHAPTER 23

When Cassie stepped into the cottage that evening after leaving Maggie's, she didn't bother to turn on the lights. Standing in the darkness, she watched the multicolored glow from the Christmas tree dance across the vintage wallpaper.

Closing her eyes, she inhaled the same comforting scents of lavender and lemon wood polish she'd noticed the first day she arrived. The aroma she'd come to associate with a woman she'd never met, but whom she'd come to love dearly nonetheless. The same woman she'd recently learned may never have wanted her—a thought Cassie couldn't quite reconcile in her heart.

As she flicked on the switch, light flooded the living room, illuminating familiar sights she'd grown to cherish. The comfy couch where she and Luke had sat side by side watching Christmas movies. The cozy armchair where she'd read *A Christmas Carol*. So many memories had turned this cottage into a home. But there was still one room in the house where she'd yet to venture.

The brass doorknob to her grandmother's room turned easily, and the creaking hinges gave way as if they were expecting her. Cassie's heartbeat thrummed in her ears as she crept across the threshold.

Shut off from the rest of the house, the frigid chill in the room sent a shiver down Cassie's spine. A small potbelly stove sat dormant in the corner, unused since her grandmother's passing.

Two brocade armchairs faced the stove and a four-poster bed rested against the opposite wall. But what caught Cassie's attention was an antique dresser adorned with a collection of silver picture frames.

Inching closer, Cassie lifted the first frame, rubbing her thumb along the tarnished edges as she studied the black-and-white photograph of a young couple on their wedding day. Their blissful, smiling faces shone even beneath the dust-laden glass. Cassie noticed, with interest, that her grandmother's vibrant, youthful features didn't appear much older than in the photograph she'd discovered in Frank's office.

The next handful of frames displayed the same couple as they aged over the span of several decades. But as Cassie's fingertips grazed the final frame, she pulled back in surprise. A young Donna Hayward gazed into the distance, her large green eyes hollow, the rims smudged with inky black eyeliner. In her thin arms, she cradled an infant with a telltale patch of chestnut curls visible above the folds of a pink crochet blanket.

To Cassie's knowledge, she was looking at the only photograph of herself as a child.

A burning sensation filled the back of Cassie's throat as she blinked at the image. Hot tears threatened to spill down her cheeks, and she quickly flipped the photograph facedown on the dresser, overcome with emotion. First the revelation in Maggie's kitchen and now this...

Cassie didn't know what to do with herself. So, she did the only logical thing that came to mind—she tore through the rest of her grandmother's belongings in search of more answers.

Combing through the dresser drawers yielded nothing

useful. Neither did the antique steamer trunk of extra quilts at the foot of the bed. It wasn't until Cassie dislodged something wedged in the bottom drawer of her grandmother's nightstand that her skin prickled with hope.

A plain manila envelope, crinkled and smelling faintly of potpourri and menthol.

Hands trembling, Cassie carried the envelope to the edge of the bed, the springs groaning in protest as she perched on the worn, floral quilt. In one quick motion, Cassie spilled the contents of the envelope onto the bed.

A jumble of glossy Polaroids and typed letters stared up at her.

As a familiar face came into view, Cassie's breath stalled in her throat. Unable to believe her own eyes, she frantically rummaged through the pile, growing dizzier by the second as the same features appeared over and over again.

Every single face in the collection of photographs was hers.

❄

Cassie paced the faded wool rug, trying to make sense of the items on her grandmother's bed. She'd gone through the photographs and letters from the private investigator a dozen times, still unable to fully accept the reality of the situation. But Cassie should have known her grandmother had hired someone to track her down. How else would Edith have found her?

Yet the fact that Edith hired an investigator wasn't what upset Cassie. It was the cold, hard truths staring her in the face that Cassie found truly unsettling. Words like *unemployed, alone, jaded, depressed,* jumped out from the investigator's reports, each one a dart to Cassie's pride. She didn't relish the idea of being followed by a stranger, let alone judged by one. Cassie felt exposed, humiliated, and...

Cassie's pace slowed as a thought gripped her, and she sank

into the armchair, cupping her face with both hands. Her shoulders began to shake as a sob rose in her chest.

Since the moment she'd sat in Luke's office, stunned by the news of the clause in her grandmother's will, Cassie had wanted to know why. *Why* had Edith added the clause? Was it a game? A joke? A senile woman's peculiarity?

As realization curled around her heart, Cassie cried both from gratefulness and from grief. Grateful that her grandmother had saved her from a life of emptiness. And grieved that she'd never had a chance to know her. Maybe at one time Edith thought Cassie would be better off with another family. But after seeing the kind of life Cassie led, Edith found a way to bring her into the type of family Cassie had always hoped for—the one she'd found in Poppy Creek.

While she still didn't know the significance of the Calendar itself, Cassie felt certain it wasn't merely the frivolous whim of a dying woman.

It was a gift.

※

L uke wasn't sure what to expect when he received Cassie's cryptic text that simply read *Come to the cottage ASAP.*

But when Cassie threw open the door, flushed and wide-eyed, Luke felt a pang of concern. "What happened?"

Stepping aside for Luke to enter, Cassie flashed a small, sheepish smile. "I got… a little carried away."

Luke's jaw dropped as he took in the chaos of the living room. Every single drawer and cupboard had been opened, their contents scattered about the room. As far as he knew, there'd never been a burglary in Poppy Creek. But this haphazard scene sure looked like one. "Are you okay? What happened?" he repeated.

"I found something." Cassie grabbed Luke's hand and led him to the coffee table.

His heart flipped—both from her touch and anticipation. "What exactly were you looking for?"

"Anything and everything," Cassie told him. "I found the... Gosh, I don't even know what you call it. A dossier? A file?" Cassie scrunched up her face in thought, then shrugged. "Let's call it a report. I found a report the PI sent my grandmother about me. And it got me thinking... what else could I find?"

Luke frowned. "He sent her a report? I thought she'd just hired him to find your address."

"Yeah, well. Turns out it was a bit more extensive than that. But that's not why I asked you to come over." Kneeling, she pulled him down beside her. "Look at this." Cassie lifted a small velvet box from the coffee table. As she slowly cracked open the lid, a folded note fluttered onto the table, revealing a stunning antique engagement ring. A flawless oval-cut diamond sparkled in the center, bordered by vibrant-hued emeralds. "Isn't it the most gorgeous ring you've ever seen?" Reverently, Cassie slipped it onto her ring finger, allowing the diamond to catch the light.

Luke couldn't respond. The sight of the ring on Cassie's finger completely stole his breath.

Then, as if breaking a spell, she slid it off her finger with a sigh. "It's the same ring my grandmother was wearing in the photo I found in Frank's office. And that's not all." She tucked the ring back in the box and picked up the folded piece of paper. "Guess whose name is on the note?"

But Luke could barely concentrate on Frank's name scrawled in sloping cursive.

All he could think about was the way Cassie looked with that ring on her finger.

CHAPTER 24

Cassie smiled to herself as she hung the evergreen wreath on the crooked rusty nail jutting out of Frank's front door. She'd chosen a simple swirl of fresh greenery with a few pinecones sprinkled throughout. No bow. Zero frills. At the very least, even if he didn't appreciate the festivity, he might leave it up for the pleasant aroma.

Closing her eyes, Cassie took a moment to enjoy the delightful scent herself. When she opened them again, Frank's suspicious gaze greeted her.

"What's that?" he grunted.

"It's a Christmas wreath." Cassie breezed past him into the hall, realizing her unease around Frank had all but evaporated.

Frank grumbled under his breath, but shut the door, leaving the wreath in its place.

"Have you tried my blend yet?" Cassie asked, loosening her scarf as the warmth emanating from the large brick fireplace enveloped her.

"It wasn't half bad," Frank said with a glimmer in his eye.

"Half bad?" In mock protest, Cassie placed both hands on her hips. "It was nearly perfect, thank you very much! But I was thinking we could try using the same beans and take the temperature to four hundred degrees this time."

"You want to go lighter?" Frank furrowed his brow, but after a few moments, the tension released. "That could work. It would balance out the earthiness of the Sumatra." His eyes brightened with eagerness as he ambled down the hall toward the back porch.

Stomach fluttering, Cassie followed closely behind. She loved seeing the excitement in his step. Without knowing the details of his ailment, she assumed he had good days and bad.

Today seemed like a good day.

Once again, Frank let Cassie take the lead with the roast. When they returned to the kitchen afterward, he made a pot of coffee using Cassie's original blend from a few days earlier while the new version cooled. Although he kept his back to her as he shuffled about the kitchen, Cassie could have sworn she heard him whistling.

Taking the seat opposite her, Frank slid a mug across the table.

Cassie gripped it with both hands, inhaling the aromatic steam as it curled above the rim. "Frank, can I ask you something?"

"I joined the navy so we could live in a free country." His lips twitched before he took a sip from his mug.

Cassie smiled, feeling a little more hopeful after his attempt at humor. "I'm going caroling tonight with a few friends and some folks from town. I'd like you to come with us."

The humor drained from Frank's features and Cassie rushed on. "We're meeting at the little chapel at the top of the hill before walking to Main Street. Seven o'clock. I can pick you up if you don't drive."

"I drive," Frank muttered. "But why would I want to do something like that?"

"Because it's fun." Cassie hoped her tone conveyed enough enthusiasm.

Frank narrowed his eyes. "And that's the reason you're going?"

Cassie shifted under his scrutinizing gaze. She supposed that were half-true. The other half was a little more complicated. But maybe he'd just given her the opportunity she'd been waiting for.

"That's part of it," she said slowly.

"And the other part?"

Cassie's grip tightened around the mug. She'd gone over this conversation a thousand times in her head, but now that she faced it, she didn't know what to say. "Do you... know why I'm here?" she asked, hoping to lay a foundation for the conversation to follow.

"To pester an old man?" he teased.

Cassie couldn't help a slight grin. "I meant in Poppy Creek."

Frank shrugged and took another sip of coffee.

"I'm here because I inherited my grandmother's house. Her name was Edith Hayward." Holding her breath, she waited for his response. But except for an almost imperceptible twitch in his jaw, she saw nothing. "But it wasn't as simple as I thought," Cassie continued. "She added a clause in her will. To inherit the house, I have to carry out a different festive task each day until Christmas." This news elicited a flicker of surprise and Cassie pressed on. "Today I have to go caroling. Turns out, there's an organized group that goes on the same evening every year. My grandmother used to be one of them. I'm told she had a beautiful voice."

"Like a nightingale," Frank murmured. His eyes widened in shock as though the words had escaped without his consent. The legs of the chair scraped against the hardwood floor as he stood abruptly. Turning his back to her, he refilled his mug from the Moka pot resting on the stove.

From behind, Cassie caught his shoulders tremble slightly. But when he turned around, his expression remained unreadable.

After easing himself into the chair, he took a long sip.

Cassie reached inside her pocket and withdrew the velvet box. "I found something among my grandmother's belongings last night." She set it in the center of the table and nudged it toward him. "There's a note inside. For you."

His steely gaze darted to hers, panic settling in his features.

"Don't worry," Cassie assured him. "I didn't read it. But I did see what's inside the box."

Frank still hadn't made a move toward it, his knuckles whitening as he gripped his mug.

"Frank," Cassie said gently. "What happened between you and my grandmother?"

Cassie waited in patient silence as Frank stared intently into his coffee as though he'd lost something.

When he finally spoke, he sounded miles away. "You two are a lot alike, you know. Passionate. Strong-willed. Full of life and adventure." He traced the rim of the mug with his finger, pausing at a small chip. "Your grandmother liked to pave her own way in life. It was one of the things I loved about her." He paused, the creases in his brow deepening.

Cassie leaned forward, enrapt with every word.

"But then I was deployed overseas, and I called off the engagement."

"Why?"

Frank shut his eyes against the painful memory, and when they finally drifted open, they gleamed with unshed tears. "Fear can make a person do foolish things."

"Fear of dying?"

With a look of sadness, he shook his head. "Fear of pain."

With bated breath, Cassie waited for Frank to explain.

"Your grandmother was like an exotic creature." The creases in his forehead diminished as he gazed into the distance. "Beautiful and wild. I didn't know if…"

The faint tapping of a branch against the kitchen window finished his thought.

Cassie scooted toward the edge of the chair. "If she would wait for you?" she concluded, the pieces finally coming together in her mind.

With an anguished expression, Frank nodded. "I didn't know if I could survive the war only to die of a broken heart."

They sat in silence, the howl of the wind echoing Frank's sorrow.

As she mulled over his words, Cassie realized that, in a way, Frank had fulfilled his own prophecy. And now he lived each day with regret wrapped around him like Jacob Marley's chains.

Fear can make a person do foolish things... like not living their life.

Reaching across the table, Cassie opened the box, revealing the note tucked inside with the ring. "Neither of us can go back in time," she said softly. "But we *can* go forward."

Her own eyes shimmering with tears, Cassie placed a hand on Frank's forearm and gently squeezed. "I really hope you come tonight."

With that, Cassie left Frank alone with his thoughts.

And the note.

❄

L uke gazed at Cassie with fondness as she scanned the church parking lot.

"I don't think he's coming," Cassie said with a disappointed sigh.

"There's still time." Luke joined her in surveying the crowd of carolers.

Eliza and his mom passed out baked goods while Penny and Dolores helped Sadie serve her famous hot chocolate. Ben and a group of friends played a rambunctious game of tag, their shouts and laughter carrying into the crisp night air.

Soon, another sound joined the cacophony. The thundering rumble of a car engine.

Dumbfounded, Luke gawked as a mint-condition 1951 Chevy convertible crested the hill. The deep, glittering purple color reminded him of sunlight shimmering through a glass bottle of grape soda.

Luke admired the smooth lines and gentle curves of the stunning classic as it parked at the end of a long line of less impressive vehicles.

Frank Barrie, clothed in a long tweed coat and gray fedora, slid from the driver's seat.

"He came!" Cassie cheered with delight.

Searching the unfamiliar faces, Frank remained by his car, tall and proud like a statue of a soldier.

Cassie rushed toward him, smothering him in an unrestrained hug.

Luke grinned as Frank's eyes widened in surprise before he awkwardly patted her back.

"She's pretty special, isn't she?"

The sound of his mother's voice by his side startled Luke, but he instantly softened. "She sure is." His gaze never left Cassie as she looped her arm through Frank's and led him toward the gathering, introducing him to a few people along the way.

"To think," Maggie continued, "Frank has lived in Poppy Creek all these years, and it took an outsider to draw him from his shell."

Luke paused at the term *outsider*. Sure, Cassie had started out that way. But somehow, the description no longer fit.

"Did she tell you she's going to stay?" Maggie asked softly.

Jerking his head, Luke gaped at his mother. "How do you know? Did she tell you that?"

"She may have accepted my job offer."

Scooping his mother off the ground, Luke twirled her around. "Thank you! Thank you!"

Tilting her head back, Maggie laughed. "Don't thank *me*. We all want her to stay. Though maybe not as much as you." She patted his cheek as he set her back down. "I'm so happy for you, son."

Her hazel eyes shone, mirroring the joy in his own heart. But Luke immediately sobered. "You know, just because she's staying doesn't mean it's for me."

"Maybe not entirely," Maggie admitted. "But I see the way she looks at you. Many years may have passed since your father and I first fell in love, but I can still recognize the signs."

Luke glanced down at the pitted asphalt, feeling the familiar tightness in his throat. "I still miss him."

Maggie gave his hand a comforting squeeze. "Me, too. There are still times I forget he's gone. I'll turn to tell him something, and then reality comes rushing back. Other times, his absence is so strong, my heart hurts almost as much as the day we lost him."

Luke nodded wordlessly. The day he'd helped Cassie decorate the cottage, he'd known she was special. And the first person he'd wanted to tell was his dad.

Maggie sniffled, rubbing her eyes with the back of her hand. "Your father would be very proud of you, Luke."

"Thanks, Mom." Luke offered a faint smile, but Maggie shook her head.

"Let me finish." Gripping his hand, she met Luke's gaze with purpose. "He'd be proud because of who *you* are. As parents, we try our best to teach you what we know. But it's when you become your own person, the man God created you to be, that a parent is truly proud." She shook her head, smiling through her tears. "Lord knows I loved your father. But the world only needed one Leonard Davis. And it got the best one. Now it needs the best version of *Luke* Davis."

Overwhelmed with emotion, Luke didn't know what to say. But before he could respond, the stirring sound of "O Holy

Night" filled the clear, starlit sky as the carolers began their descent down the hill toward Main Street.

Maggie's breath caught in her throat as she clutched Luke's hand.

Beaming down at his mother, Luke wrapped an arm around her shoulders.

His heart full, Luke lifted his voice to join the others in singing his father's favorite song, glimpsing Cassie at the top of the hill.

Arm in arm with Frank, she glanced over her shoulder and caught his eye. Her lips spread into an inviting smile as she held out her hand for him.

The moonlight cast a silvery glow across her face, and Luke took a mental snapshot of the moment.

The moment he received his father's blessing.

CHAPTER 25

C assie wasn't sure if she walked or floated into Thistle & Thorn. After spending the evening caroling with Luke, Frank, and so many others who'd become dear friends, her heart felt more airborne than Santa's sleigh. And when she'd read the day's activity—Buy Someone a Christmas Present—Cassie knew exactly what she wanted. And if one place on earth would have it, it would be Penny's peculiar store.

"Hi, Cassie." Penny set the vintage camera back on the shelf, tossing the dust rag over her shoulder. "What brings you by? Did you come back for the green dress?"

"I wish." Cassie sighed, her longing gaze traveling to the goddess-worthy gown. If she could afford it, she wouldn't hesitate to claim it as her own. But as it was, buying a present for Luke would be a stretch on her dwindling bank account.

"Then what can I help you find?" Penny asked.

Running a restless hand through her hair, Cassie hesitated. She *should* tell Penny what she was looking for. Otherwise it could take all day to find it. But even though the significance of the gift would be lost on anyone but Luke, Cassie felt too shy to share. "I'll just take a look around, if that's okay?"

"Of course!" With a bright smile, Penny tugged the rag off

her shoulder, ready to resume her work. "There's a whole lot more in back that I haven't sorted through yet. Feel free to take a look if you don't find what you want out here."

"Thanks, I will." Smiling gratefully, Cassie began her search.

As she explored the eclectic shop, Cassie marveled at how Penny had managed to create an atmosphere both chaotic and calm. There didn't seem to be any clear organization and yet, everything appeared to be exactly where it belonged. Christmas carols resonated from a crackling gramophone, and the evocative scents of aged leather and spicy pipe tobacco lulled her into a dreamy state, making the minutes tick by like seconds.

After she'd looped around the store several times, only stopping to admire the gown twice, Cassie's search came up empty.

"Penny?" Cassie interrupted the tall redhead as she dusted an odd chess set of exquisite marble sculptures featuring cats on one side and dogs on the other. "You mentioned looking in the back..."

"Yes! Please do!" Penny's copper eyes shone with delight. "I love it when customers peruse the back room. It's like sending someone on a treasure hunt."

Cassie smiled. She already felt a little bit like Indiana Jones. But as she followed Penny's graceful stride, her pulse quickened with anticipation.

Ceremoniously pulling aside a heavy brocade curtain, Penny revealed an enormous back room bursting with antiques and collectables of every sort.

Immediately overwhelmed, Cassie swallowed, wondering if was too late to change her mind.

"Incredible, isn't it?" Penny gushed, clearly misreading Cassie's shock for awe. "You never know what hidden gem you'll uncover."

Finding her voice, Cassie asked, "Do you collect all of this yourself?"

"Not always. I do a fair amount of scavenging myself. But a lot of stuff is dropped off, too. Sometimes in huge shipments when someone passes away and family members don't want to bother with an estate sale. I'll give them a price, sight unseen, and they'll unload everything in here."

"You pay for it without knowing what it is?" Cassie asked. "What if it's worthless junk?"

"One man's junk is another man's treasure." Penny winked, then laughed. "Besides, that's half the fun in what I do. Sometimes, in a shipment of seemingly ordinary things, you find something extraordinary."

Cassie's heart fluttered at Penny's romanticized explanation.

"Well, I'll leave you to it. Happy hunting."

With a swish of the curtain, Penny disappeared, leaving Cassie alone in the jungle of doodads and thingamabobs.

Inhaling deeply, Cassie noticed the air smelled mustier than out front, and the bronzed glow from the antique light fixtures cast an otherworldly sheen about the room.

Thirty minutes into her exploration, Cassie began to feel a little claustrophobic. But as she turned to find her way out of the maze of objects, Cassie froze.

There, tucked away on a cluttered shelf, sat the very item she'd been searching for.

An authentic cuckoo clock.

❄

Nostalgia washed over Luke as he glanced around the office where he'd spent so much of his life. First, visiting his father at work. Then, when it became his own space.

Since his father's passing, Luke tried to keep the essence of the office the same, merely adding a few items of furniture he'd crafted himself. But the layout and design remained exactly as his father left it—homey and inviting.

Leonard Davis believed a law office should evoke calm rather than anxiety. He wanted his clients to feel as though they were entering his own living room, not a stuffy reception area. Especially if they had to discuss something painful like the death of a loved one. That meant setting up his practice in a location with enough square footage to accommodate an over-sized sofa, a few chairs, shelves filled with books and boardgames, a table for refreshments, and, of course, a large Christmas tree during the holiday season.

The private office space wasn't small, either. Luke had more than enough room for his expansive desk, two leather club chairs, and an entire wall of bookcases and filing cabinets. But his favorite feature of the room was a window seat that over-looked the courtyard. Luke would sit there for hours reading or doing his homework after school. Just thinking about selling the space left an emptiness in the pit of his stomach.

"Hey! Anybody home?" Jack's loud bellow interrupted Luke's thoughts.

Striding back into the reception area, Luke asked, "Did we have an appointment today?"

"Do we ever?" Jack laughed, heading straight for the cookie jar.

"Good point. Remind me to talk to my secretary about that."

"Ha!" Jack stuffed an entire gingersnap into his mouth, mumbling, "If you ever get one. The closest you've got is Dolores. Where is she, by the way? I kind of miss getting the evil eye from Banjo when I visit."

Luke chuckled. "She's at another one of Harriet Parker's knitting circles. Apparently, they're trying to make a hundred blankets for the homeless shelter by Christmas. What brings you by?"

Snatching another cookie, Jack strolled into Luke's office, draping himself across one of the club chairs. "Legally speak-ing, how much trouble would I be in if I decided *not* to sell my barbecue sauce to that fancy new restaurant in Primrose Valley?"

"Not much." Luke pulled Jack's file from the top drawer of the cabinet. "I added a clause in your contract that gives you ninety days to rescind."

Jack snapped his fingers. "And *that's* why I hire the best!"

"I'll be sure to send you my fee," Luke teased.

"You mean, all the ribs you can eat?"

"Exactly." Luke grinned before sinking into his chair with a sigh. "I hate to say it, but I'm going to miss this."

"Miss what?" Jack asked, devouring the second cookie.

"Bartering legal fees for barbecue." Luke rubbed the kink in his neck, avoiding Jack's gaze. "I'm thinking about a change in careers." As the words lingered in the silence, Luke stole a glance in Jack's direction.

Even Jack's week-old beard couldn't hide the huge grin on his face.

"What?" Luke asked. "Why are you grinning like that? I didn't think you'd consider this good news."

"Hey, as much as I appreciate the legal advice, I've been dying for my own Adirondack chairs. And now you'll have the time to make them. I assume you're going into the furniture business full-time."

Luke gaped at his friend, completely incredulous. "How'd you know?"

"You know, for a lawyer, you're not very smart," Jack teased. "It doesn't take a genius to figure out you're as nuts about woodworking as you are about Cassie. Well, *almost*."

"Clearly it doesn't take a genius if *you* figured it out," Luke lobbed back, and both men shared a laugh.

Sobering quickly, Luke asked, "You don't think it's a crazy idea?"

"Maybe a little." Jack shrugged. "But so are vegan hamburgers. And I get several requests a week for those things. Crazy doesn't necessarily mean bad."

Luke flashed a bemused smile, ready to ask if Jack was really considering a change in his menu.

"But seriously," Jack continued. "If you tear down a few of these walls, you'd have a great studio right here."

Startled, Luke straightened. Keeping the office and turning it into a studio to showcase his work had never crossed his mind. "You know what? That might actually be a good idea, Gardner."

"I occasionally have those."

"*Occasionally* being the operative word."

"Hey! I'm full of great ideas!" Jack protested. "It was my idea for you to go out with Cassie."

"Technically, it was Dolores's idea." Luke leaned back in his chair with a satisfied smirk.

"Okay, fine. I'm a generous man. I'll share credit with Dolores on that one." Jack steepled his fingers, his brow scrunched in thought. "But…"

Luke kicked his feet up on the desk, leaning back even further as he waited for Jack to continue.

Jack grinned, his eyes sparkling with a devilish glint. "*I* want credit for telling you to propose."

Caught off guard, Luke toppled backward, crash-landing on the floor.

CHAPTER 26

As Cassie sat cross-legged in front of the coffee table wrapping Christmas presents—the Calendar's task for December 17—everything seemed right with the world.

In just over a week, she'd own the cottage and would be able to put it on the market. Assuming it sold quickly, she could enroll her mother in rehab in a matter of months, not only getting her the help she desperately needed, but perhaps paving the way for a meaningful mother-daughter relationship.

Enveloped by soft acoustic Christmas music, Cassie soaked up the ambiance around her. A bright, crackling fire danced in the hearth. Bits of ribbon and colorful wrapping paper littered the floor like confetti celebrating the stack of presents tucked beneath the tree.

Cassie only had one gift left—Luke's cuckoo clock. She hadn't quite decided how to wrap the oddly shaped item.

Cassie's skin tingled as she envisioned Luke's face when he opened it. Surely, he would remember sharing his father's story and understand the significance. In her mind, there wasn't a more perfect way to tell Luke she loved him. And awaiting his reaction left her breathless with hopeful anticipation.

A loud hammering on the front door caused Cassie to jump in surprise.

Suspecting it might be Luke, she raced to find something to cover the cuckoo clock. But a familiar voice made her blood run cold, rooting her to the spot.

"Knock, knock! It's Santa!"

Chills skittered down Cassie's spine as she made her way to the door. And even though she knew exactly who she'd find on the other side, she still blinked in disbelief.

"Hello, *daughter* of mine," Donna slurred, slumped against the doorframe.

"Hi, Mom." Cassie recoiled as the scent of alcohol assaulted her senses. Peering over Donna's shoulder she asked, "How did you get here?"

"Ride share." Donna stumbled through the doorway, gripping a large bottle of vodka. "A group of kids on their way to a ski resort or something. Cheap fare, and I gave them my second bottle as a tip." She waved the vodka above her head, teetered, then clutched the hall table for support.

Cassie cringed, but at least was grateful Donna hadn't driven herself in her present condition. She hadn't seen her mother this far gone in a long time.

A tiny twinge of resentment pierced Cassie's heart. Considering all she had to sacrifice for Donna's rehab, her mother could at least avoid the binge of the century. But then, if Donna had self-control, they wouldn't be in this mess in the first place.

Shutting the door against the cold, Cassie helped Donna struggle out of her coat. "What brings you by, Mom? I have to admit, I'm a little surprised to see you."

"You mean that lovely Christmas card wasn't an invitation?" Donna's words dripped with sarcasm and, finally free of her coat, she took a lengthy swig from the bottle.

Her stomach twisting, Cassie watched the level of clear liquid drop rapidly.

"Imagine *my* surprise when I saw the return address."

Clutching her purse, Donna staggered into the living room. "This place looks exactly the same. Although I didn't expect to ever see it again. I assumed dear old Mom left it to a charity or something." The vodka swished in the bottle as Donna collapsed onto the couch. Carelessly, she kicked her boots off and they clattered to the floor.

"I was surprised, too," Cassie admitted, perching on the edge of the armchair. Then hesitantly, she asked, "Did Grandma leave you anything?"

Donna released a derisive snort. "Some hick lawyer called to say she left me a letter, and would I like to pick it up in person or have it mailed?"

Cassie bristled, certain the "hick" lawyer had been Luke. "And what did you say?"

"I said he could burn it for all I cared." Donna gulped down the rest of the vodka, then scanned the room as if looking for a place to dispose of her trash.

Clamoring to her feet, Cassie held out her hands. "Here, I'll take—"

But before she could finish her sentence, Donna lobbed the bottle into the fireplace. Shards of glass shattered against the hearth. The remaining drops of alcohol reacted with the flames, igniting a startling blaze that shot up the chimney.

Cassie flinched as Donna cackled. But at least the drinking would be over now.

As soon as Cassie completed her thought, Donna rummaged through her purse, withdrawing a mini bottle of rum. She immediately twisted off the cap and took a swig.

"Mom, let me make us some coffee." Cassie stepped quickly toward the kitchen, but Donna waved her hand in dismissal.

"So, *daughter*..." she slurred, emphasizing the word in a way that concerned Cassie. Had her Christmas card inadvertently provoked her mother's binge? "Have you sold this dump yet?"

Wincing, Cassie drew in a deep, calming breath. "I haven't. I don't technically own it yet."

Donna's green eyes narrowed. "Why not?"

"There was… a clause in the will." Cassie hesitated, uncertain how much she should share. Her mother wasn't exactly rational under the best of circumstances. The last thing Cassie needed was one of Donna's famous outbursts.

"What kind of clause?" Donna gulped more of the amber liquid.

Cassie swallowed, her gaze darting to the Christmas Calendar lying on the coffee table beside Luke's present.

Donna followed her gaze, her eyes widening as they fell on the gold lettering.

With a sigh, Cassie opened her mouth to explain. "That's—"

"The Christmas Calendar," Donna murmured, scooping it into her arms.

"Yes. But how did you know?"

Suddenly somber, Donna brushed her palm against the plaid binding, her gaze soft and glistening. "My dad made this the year he got sick."

Cassie held her breath, afraid to even blink for fear she'd hinder her mother from sharing further.

Donna pressed it to her chest, squeezing her eyes shut. "He wanted to savor every moment of his last Christmas." Her words carried like a mournful gust of wind, bringing Cassie close to tears.

"That must have been a special Christmas together," Cassie said softly.

Donna's eyes flew open and flashed with anger. And as though the fabric had burned her fingertips, Donna flung the Calendar onto the floor. "He died Christmas Eve."

Dread filled Cassie's chest as Donna downed the rest of the rum, tossing the empty bottle into the fireplace along with the other one. Once again, the flames erupted as the sound of broken glass clashed with the tranquil melody of Christmas music.

Cassie jerked her head away, unable to watch her mother

spiral out of control. "I'm going to make us some coffee." Turning sharply, she hurried into the kitchen and set a kettle of water on the stove.

Not wanting to leave her mother alone, Cassie prepared the coffee as swiftly as possible, pulling the kettle off the stove before the water had even boiled. After allowing the grounds to steep for two minutes, rather than four, she poured the steaming coffee over three teaspoons of sugar. The spoon shook in her hand as she gave the mixture a quick stir.

Rushing back into the living room with two brimming mugs, Cassie froze.

Donna lay passed out, facedown on the carpet, a puddle of liquid a few inches from her face.

Bleak acceptance filled Cassie's heart, as it had so many times before. Setting the mugs on the coffee table, she checked her mother's breathing. Slow and steady.

In case she threw up again, Cassie left Donna lying facedown, and draped a blanket over her sprawled body. Cassie knew her mother would feel better once she slept it off.

Quietly, Cassie cleaned up the mess on the carpet and set to work tidying the rest of the room. As she picked up scraps of wrapping paper and ribbon, a strange uneasiness stirred in the pit of her stomach.

Where was the Christmas Calendar?

The fire crackled and sparked, startling Cassie and drawing her attention.

Her hand flew to her throat.

Singed fragments of plaid fabric and blackened bits of paper wafted up the chimney in a cloud of smoke.

Along with Cassie's hopes for the future.

❄

C assie cried until her throat burned and her eyes swelled, unable to shed another tear. Every muscle in her body, including her heart, felt numb.

She wanted to be angry—outraged, even—and show her mother the door once and for all. But as she gazed at Donna, prostrate on the floor, all she felt was pity.

Her mother needed help. Desperately. The drinking was more than a reckless pastime—it was a disease. One that had a grip on Donna so tight, even the people around her couldn't breathe.

Cassie could think of only one thing to end its hold on both of them.

After getting a much-needed drink of water, Cassie picked up her phone.

"Hey, Cass." Derek's tone exuded a mixture of surprise and delight. "It's great to hear from you."

"I'm not calling to chitchat." The phone shook in Cassie's hand as she forced herself to continue. "I'm calling about your offer."

"Great! I knew you'd come around."

Cassie grimaced at his arrogant certainty. This was a mistake. Her finger hovered over the end call button, but her gaze flickered to her mother. Sucking in a breath, she closed her eyes. "I have one condition."

"Anything."

"I want a loan... of fifteen thousand dollars."

Her request was met with silence.

Then Derek's cool, assured voice filled her ear. "Sure. No problem. When do you want it?"

"Tomorrow morning. Have it wired to my bank account then we'll meet to discuss the terms of our partnership."

She held her breath, waiting for Derek to protest her unreasonable demand.

"Will do," he said. "Shoot me your banking info and I'll have it squared away in the morning. And, Cass... is everything okay?"

Her lower lip trembled, agitated that he dared to show his concern. *And* that it affected her.

Squaring her shoulders, she said briskly, "I'll call you tomorrow to arrange a time and place to meet," then hung up the phone.

As her breathing slowed, Cassie's knees weakened and she sank onto the barstool. What had she just done? She thought of Luke and her heart wrenched.

Pressing her palm to her chest, she practiced taking slow, steady breaths. It was only a loan. A temporary solution. She'd work with Derek for a little while, then find a way out. Somehow.

Bleary-eyed, Cassie dragged herself back into the living room. Donna hadn't moved an inch, but her eyelids quivered as though she were dreaming.

Sagging into the couch, Cassie pulled the quilt around herself.

She needed to sleep. Maybe things would look better in the morning?

Cassie buried her face in the throw pillow, muffling her groan. Who was she kidding? The Calendar was gone—literally a pile of ash. And to think, just that morning, she'd thumbed ahead a few pages to take a sneak peek, then snapped the book shut before she ruined all of the surprises.

Flipping onto her back, Cassie stared at the pine beams stretched across the ceiling. Hindsight really was twenty-twenty. If she'd allowed herself to peek ahead until the end, maybe she could still complete everything. Regret left a sour taste in her mouth.

Cassie squeezed her eyes shut, willing herself to fall asleep. She could only solve one problem at a time.

And first, she needed to get Donna into rehab.

CHAPTER 27

As they sat in the reception area of the Snyder Sobriety Center the following afternoon, Cassie stared at her phone. The text she'd composed to Luke glared back at her accusingly. It wasn't good enough. Not even close. But it would have to do until Cassie figured out a few more things first.

Cassie stretched out her fingers, noticing her palms were clammy. After wiping them on her jeans, she pressed send. The pathetic message telling Luke she'd be gone for a few days, but not to worry, traveled the invisible lines of communication.

Within seconds, Luke's name appeared on her screen. Cassie's heart skipped, and she breathed a sigh of relief that she'd turned her cell on vibrate before they began the tour of the facility. Glancing sideways, she checked on her mother. Donna alternated between sitting and standing, repositioning herself in different corners of the room as though she were playing musical chairs.

Rather than answer Luke's call, Cassie responded with another text.

Can't talk now. Back in SF. I'll complete today's task here. I'll explain everything soon.

Her throat thick with shame, she sent the message before stuffing the phone back inside her purse.

The truth was, she *did* plan on continuing with the few activities she remembered. Although she wasn't exactly sure why. She supposed, deep down, she wasn't willing to give up just yet. Even though the very idea was ridiculous. The Calendar was gone. And there wasn't a single thing she could do about it.

Cassie stole another glance at Donna. Her mother had remained eerily silent throughout the entire tour, which surprised Cassie. Even factoring in the world's worst hangover, Cassie expected to see at least a glimpse of Donna's usual vivacious performance. Not the timid, docile woman wringing her hands a few chairs down.

Cassie wondered if reality had hit her mother like a runaway sleigh. This clearly wasn't a vacation or a spa retreat—it was serious. Donna had seventy-two hours to change her mind. After that, she was on lockdown for thirty days. No Jimmy, Tyler—or whichever boyfriend she chose this month—could visit. And all of her belongings had to fit in a single duffel bag. No wonder Donna looked ready to bolt for the door at any moment.

"Donna Hayward?" the receptionist called out.

Cassie's features softened as her mother's eyes widened in panic.

"It'll be okay." Cassie offered a reassuring smile as they made their way toward the front desk.

"Did you enjoy the tour?" The blonde, middle-aged receptionist beamed at Cassie as though they'd just visited some world-famous museum.

"You have a lovely facility." Cassie tried not to fixate on the woman's bright magenta lipstick. Turning to Donna, she added, "Don't you think so, Mom?"

Donna responded with a tight-lipped smile.

"Don't worry," the receptionist said kindly, attaching a few papers to a clipboard. "Everyone's nervous on their first day."

She slid the clipboard across the counter. "Did you understand everything outlined during your tour?"

Donna nodded slowly.

"Excellent," the woman chirped. "This waiver is simply a confirmation. Please sign here, here, and here." She placed an X beside the appropriate boxes before handing the pen to Donna.

As Donna reached for it, Cassie noticed a slight tremble in her fingers. She racked her brain for something encouraging to say, but the receptionist spoke first.

"The full amount is due upfront. As stated, you have three days for a refund, minus a thousand-dollar deposit." She directed her comment at Donna until Cassie pulled out her wallet.

Cassie's chest tightened as she slid out her credit card. The thin piece of plastic weighed heavily in her fingertips as she passed it to the receptionist.

The entire process only lasted a few minutes, but to Cassie, each minute dragged on for an eternity. She could count every labored heartbeat as it throbbed in her temple. And her stiff hand seemed to resist as she signed the receipt.

"Perfect." The receptionist collected the clipboard from Donna and attached the receipt at the top. "You're all set. Joshua will show you to your room."

A muscular young man with a friendly smile approached, holding out his hand for Donna's bag.

Cassie sighed inwardly, waiting for one of Donna's inappropriate comments. But Donna merely handed him the duffel without saying a word.

"Right this way." Joshua nodded toward a wide corridor. The polished tile flooring gleamed beneath the custom light fixtures. And original watercolors depicting various San Franciscan landmarks dotted the muted blue walls.

But Donna didn't seem to notice any of the upscale features.

Hollow-eyed, she trailed behind, barely picking her feet off the slick floor.

Tears stung Cassie's eyes as she watched her mother shuffle down the hall, head bent. And before she could think better of it, she leaped for Donna's hand, pulling her into a hug.

Burying her face in her mother's long hair, Cassie murmured, "I love you," as she inhaled the familiar scent of strawberry-scented shampoo.

Cassie clung to her mother, not expecting Donna to hug her back. But to Cassie's surprise, the tension melted from Donna's shoulders, and before Cassie realized what was happening, Donna's arms encircled her waist.

The embrace lasted mere seconds.

But the moment would stay with Cassie forever.

Imprinted on her heart as a banner of hope.

❄

Standing on the corner of the tiny residential street, Cassie almost smiled at the row of lovely Victorian homes draped in miles of multicolored Christmas lights. But any enjoyment she would normally have experienced ticking off the day's task on the Christmas Calendar evaporated with the chill of Derek's voice.

"Hey! Sorry I'm late. It took me twenty minutes to find a parking spot." Derek rounded the side street, halting mid-stride when he caught sight of Cassie.

Her stomach lurched at the obvious sign of approval plastered across his face.

"You look great," he breathed, scanning the length of her body.

Cassie squirmed inside her peacoat. She hadn't gone to any extra trouble, wearing her cinched black coat over skinny jeans and a cream sweater. Although her red knit cap and plaid scarf could be considered festive. She flushed, recalling the first time she'd glimpsed Luke noticing her appearance. But somehow, his appreciative glance felt much different than Derek's.

"Hi," she said stiffly, tightening her collar against the cold— and Derek's unwanted gaze.

"Why exactly are we meeting here instead of the coffee shop?" His breath escaped in a puff of white as he rubbed his bare hands together for warmth.

"Because I want to look at the lights."

"Since when?"

"Since now."

Derek tilted his head, narrowing his blue eyes, but he didn't press her further. "Did the wire transfer go through okay?"

"Yes, thanks." Cassie dug her hands into her coat pockets as she started down the narrow sidewalk, trying to ignore how closely Derek fell into step beside her. He still wore the same musky cologne, and it irked her that she noticed. "I want to talk to you about that, actually. You understand it's simply a loan, right? I plan on paying you back soon."

Derek shrugged, his broad shoulders straining beneath his fitted cashmere overcoat. "Sure. Whatever."

"Not 'whatever,' Derek." Cassie paused in front of a particularly beautiful three-story Victorian draped in silvery lights. Huge falling snowflakes drifted across the front, cast from a laser projector hidden somewhere in the well-manicured yard. "This is important. Our partnership is only temporary. I'll work with you for as long as it takes to get the coffee shop open and running smoothly. And I'll help you hire the perfect manager. Someone you can trust to run the place while you're gone."

Derek opened his mouth to protest, but Cassie held up her hand. "We can both agree on a fair wage, but I don't want equity. When I've earned enough money to pay you back, I want out of the arrangement. Understood?"

Derek's lower lip protruded, as though he were about to

pout. But then his lips spread into a boyish grin. "Understood. New businesses can take a *long* time to set up."

Cassie groaned, not bothering to muffle the sound as she continued her stride.

Chuckling, Derek caught up with her. "You may not want to admit it, but working together is going to be fun."

Cassie knit her eyebrows together in response. But Derek was undeterred.

"I'm serious," he insisted. "I guarantee this will be the best decision of your life."

Incredulous, Cassie snorted. The man had a lot of nerve! She could guarantee it most certainly *wouldn't* be the best decision of her life.

She could only hope it wouldn't be her worst.

CHAPTER 28

Sliding his key into the lock, Luke took one last look at the driveway. Cassie's blue Prius was nowhere in sight, which meant she was still in San Francisco. Only two days had passed since she left, but it felt like forever.

As Luke pushed through the front door, he marveled at how quickly he'd come to view the cottage as Cassie's home. The once familiar scents of lavender and lemon oil gave way to Cassie's heady perfume and the lingering aroma of freshly brewed coffee. Her white snow jacket hung from the vintage hall stand, and Luke gently ran his hand over the puffy sleeve, his pulse quickening at the memory of their bodies sprawled in the powdery snow.

Tucking the tiny package under his arm, he stepped into the living room, surprised by how empty the space felt without Cassie's presence. He also noticed the disarray, as though she'd left in the middle of gift wrapping.

Luke smiled as he took in the stack of presents neatly arranged beneath the tree. Adding his to the pile, he straightened, ready to head home. But as he cast one last glance around the room, he decided to tidy up a little for Cassie's return.

Whistling as he set to work, Luke lifted the quilt from

where it had been thrown haphazardly across the coffee table. As he pulled back the folds of patchwork fabric, the upbeat tune of "Jingle Bells" halted on his lips.

Resting in the center of a large square of gold foil paper sat an antique cuckoo clock.

All the blood rushed from Luke's head as he fell to his knees in shock. It *had* to be his gift, didn't it? Which meant...

Glimpsing the corner of a gift tag protruding from the edge of the wrapping paper, he lifted it gently. Warmth radiated throughout his entire body as he read the four words written in Cassie's handwriting.

To: Sprinkles
Love: Ru

Luke blinked, not trusting his own eyes. He read the words again and again until tears blurred his vision.

Cassie loved him! Luke didn't know whether to whoop with joy or cry.

Pushing himself off the floor, Luke stood, filled with urgency.

He didn't care about the time or the distance.

He had to see Cassie.

❄

As Cassie collapsed onto the couch in her cramped apartment, a puff of dust escaped the faded gray upholstery. She didn't know a person even *needed* to dust a couch! Besides, she'd only been gone for... She tried to count off the days but gave up after she ran out of fingers. Her brain was fried after spending all morning, afternoon, and evening with Derek going over menu options, food vendors, and decor ideas. And although she hated to admit it, she'd relished every minute! Well, not *every* minute. She loathed spending time with

Derek. But the thrill of planning her dream coffee shop gave her goosebumps.

While she reveled in the day's excitement, Cassie's stomach growled. She'd forgotten to eat dinner. Padding barefoot into the kitchen, she rooted through her cupboards, stumbling upon a box of microwave popcorn. Not exactly a balanced meal, but it would pair perfectly with the Christmas Calendar's activity for the day. If she closed her eyes, she could still see it written in her grandmother's elegant script.

December 19: Watch It's a Wonderful Life.

Although confident she'd enjoy the movie, the evening elicited mixed emotions. Once the ending credits rolled, the Calendar would be over. It was the last activity Cassie could remember. Which meant, after tonight, she'd have to face the bitter reality. She'd failed, forfeiting her inheritance. While she didn't fully understand all the legalities, she knew Luke was bound by law to ensure she fulfilled the terms of the will. And without the Calendar...

Cassie shuddered, snuggling deeper into the plush throw blanket. After pressing play, she ripped open the bag of popcorn, barely noticing the mouthwatering scent of butter and salt wafting toward her with the steam.

She missed Luke. He'd texted her a few times to check in, and Cassie had promised to be back in Poppy Creek soon. At the very least, she wanted to return in time for Ben's school play on the twenty-second.

Then, she'd explain everything.

And hopefully, she'd have a few more answers to give Luke.

❄

As the ending credits rolled across the TV screen, Cassie ugly cried into the corner of the blanket. Both from how deeply the film had touched her heart and how homesick she felt.

Impulsively, she tossed back the blanket and sprang from the couch.

In a matter of minutes, Cassie had gathered her things and threw open the front door, ready to go home.

Derek stood on the other side.

"Going somewhere?" he asked, eyeing the coat in one hand and her purse and keys in the other.

"Uh, yes," Cassie stammered, completely caught off guard. "What are you doing here?"

"I thought I'd take you to a late dinner." Derek sniffed the air, stepping inside her apartment uninvited. "But it smells like I'm too late. Popcorn?"

Cassie left the door ajar, eager to get rid of Derek and be on her way. "I really don't have time to..."

Derek surveyed the empty bag of popcorn and the blanket puddled on the couch. "Movie night?"

Cassie sighed, slipping on her coat so Derek would get the hint. *"It's a Wonderful Life."*

"Classic." Derek nodded, smiling slightly as Cassie struggled into the sleeves. "Wait. Your hair is caught on your—" He reached for a strand of hair tangled in her necklace and froze. The blood drained from his face as his fingers coiled around the charm.

"I'll get it." Cassie hastily tried to brush his hand aside, but he wouldn't let go.

Color rushed to Derek's previously pale face. "Why do you..." His words faltered as if he couldn't bring himself to say them aloud.

Cassie opened her mouth to explain, but hesitated, realizing her feelings had completely changed. The necklace had lost all ties to her heart. It was merely a thing. A meaningless bauble. And one she no longer wanted. "Derek, let go."

"Tell me why you're wearing this." His tone was sharp, accusatory. And his flush deepened, a mixture of shame and confusion.

"If you would let go…" Cassie took a step back, eager to break Derek's hold and remove the necklace once and for all.

But as Derek followed, his toe caught on the edge of the rug.

He fell forward, ripping the necklace from around her throat.

Startled, Cassie released a clipped scream.

❄

Luke's heart pounded in his chest as the elevator rose to the seventh floor of Cassie's apartment building. The entire car ride he'd gone over what he planned to say, but when the metal doors slid open, his mind went blank.

All he wanted was to tell Cassie he loved her, kiss her deeply, and never let her go.

The hall light flickered as he approached Cassie's front door, and Luke was surprised to find it wide open.

Then he heard her scream.

Barreling into the apartment, Luke spotted a man lying on the floor. Cassie stood over him, shock etched across her face.

"Are you okay?" Luke asked.

Cassie nodded, her eyes widening even further at the sight of him.

That's all Luke needed before yanking the intruder to his feet.

"Easy!" the man grunted, cradling his nose. "Something might be broken."

"If it's not, it will be," Luke growled.

The man narrowed his eyes over his knuckles as if assessing his competition. "And *you* are?"

"You first," Luke demanded, one hand still around his collar.

"Derek Price. Cassie's business partner."

"That's a lie." It took all of Luke's self-control not to punch him right then and there.

"Ask her." Derek tilted his head in Cassie's direction.

Confused, Luke glanced at Cassie. "Cass?"

Cassie dragged her gaze from the floor. It appeared to take great effort for her to look him in the eye. "I can explain."

Stunned, Luke's grip slipped from the man's collar.

Derek straightened and headed for the door, clearly eager to escape further confrontation. "I'll see you tomorrow," he called out to Cassie over his shoulder before shooting a glare at Luke and storming out, still covering his nose.

The door slammed behind him.

For a moment, Luke didn't move. Every ounce of energy seemed to have drained from his body with the adrenaline. He didn't know what to say. Or think.

"Luke, what are you doing here?" Cassie asked, her tone soft, barely above a whisper. And the pleased, hopeful lilt to her question gutted Luke to his core.

He still wanted to wrap his arms around her and shower her with all the love and affection he possessed. But how could he? She'd left Poppy Creek to work with her ex. And didn't even tell him.

"I..." He paused, gathering his thoughts. "I came to check on you. To see how things were going with the Christmas Calendar." Never mind it was almost 10:00 p.m. And he could have waited until morning.

Cassie didn't seem to notice his illogical explanation. At the mention of the Christmas Calendar, her eyes pooled with tears.

The urge to comfort her overrode all other emotions, and Luke instinctively slid his arm around her shoulder. "Hey, what's wrong?"

They moved to the couch together, and once they sat down, the entire story spilled from Cassie's lips between sobs.

Luke listened in stunned silence as Cassie told him everything, from her mother's rehab to Derek's job offer to the destruction of the Christmas Calendar. His gut wrenched with each new confession, and he pulled her in closer, wishing she hadn't tried to carry the burden on her own.

"It's all such a mess. And it's all my fault." Cassie sniffled, wiping her eyes with the edge of her sleeve.

"It's not all your fault," Luke said firmly. "But why didn't you come to us for help?"

"I don't know," Cassie said weakly. "I suppose I'm used to figuring things out on my own."

Luke rested his chin on the top of her head. He could see how Cassie would feel that way. But he wanted her to know, from now on, that she could count on him. "I would have loaned you the money," he said softly.

Shifting her weight, Cassie tilted her head back, her gaze tender as she whispered, "Thank you."

Luke's breathing slowed as he held her gaze.

Before he could speak, Cassie blinked, her attention dropping to her hands. "I still can't believe the Calendar is gone."

"Not entirely."

"What do you mean?"

Luke smiled. "I've been doing my job for a long time. Do you really think I wouldn't have a backup copy?"

"Luke!" Throwing her arms around his neck, Cassie kissed his cheek. "You're amazing!"

Luke chuckled, savoring the lingering warmth from her lips against his skin.

The evening hadn't turned out the way he thought. But it had solidified one truth in his heart.

He couldn't be everyone's rock, no matter how hard he tried.

But he could be Cassie's.

CHAPTER 29

As Cassie's eyes fluttered open, it took her a moment to adjust to her surroundings. Sunlight streamed through the plastic blinds, dancing on the bare wall opposite the window. Cassie slowly sat upright, her gaze wandering from her plain dresser with the missing handle to her sparse closet. Nothing about the space felt like home anymore. And yet...

Warmth enveloped Cassie as her thoughts drifted to Luke asleep on the couch in the other room. Simply knowing he was nearby caused a contented sigh to escape her lips. Something about his presence set her heart at ease.

Slipping from beneath the sheets, Cassie snuck a peek in her tiny bathroom mirror. Her eyes looked a little puffy from crying, but after splashing some water on her face, and running her fingers through her hair, Cassie tiptoed into the living room.

Her heart skipped at the sight of the empty couch, but the familiar gurgle of her coffee maker calmed her concerns. Smoothing down the front of her rumpled T-shirt, she rounded the corner into the cramped galley kitchen.

Cassie's breath hitched in her throat at the sight of Luke, barefoot in jeans and a white undershirt. With his back to her, his biceps flexed as he reached into the cupboard overhead for two coffee mugs.

Cassie stole a moment to appreciate the sight of the man she loved—the man who'd come to her rescue, even after she'd left. Overcome with emotion, her throat tightened. She thought back to the words Luke shared the night of Pajama Christmas.

Love always hopes and always perseveres.

Words that had never held more meaning.

The coffee maker beeped, signaling the end of the brew cycle.

Startled from her reverie, Cassie gasped, and Luke spun around, smiling when he saw her.

"Good morning, sleepyhead."

"Good morning." Cassie blushed as Luke poured her a cup, and she accepted it gratefully. "Thanks." Inhaling the nutty aroma, she suddenly missed Frank.

Luke seemed to notice. "It's not the same, is it?"

"No," Cassie admitted, taking a sip. The locally roasted coffee she used to love now lacked flavor and body. She imagined every cup of coffee would dull in comparison to Frank's from now on.

"Well, don't worry. We'll be home soon."

Cassie's skin tingled at his words. "I can't wait."

Their eyes locked over the rims of their mugs and the tingles turned to shivers down her spine. With a single glance, he made her forget how to breathe.

Luke cleared his throat. "But there's something we have to do before we leave town."

"What's that?"

"I called Dolores this morning." His hazel eyes sparkled as he took a sip of coffee.

"And?"

"I asked her to look up today's activity on the Christmas Calendar."

Cassie's heartbeat skittered in anticipation. "What is it?"

"Perform an Act of Service. And I have the perfect idea."

Cassie smiled, barely stopping herself from kissing him on the spot. Of course, Luke had the perfect idea.

"There's a nonprofit down the street that serves meals to homeless veterans," Luke told her. "If we get ready quickly, we still have time to help with breakfast."

"Sounds perfect." Downing the rest of her coffee, Cassie set her empty mug in the sink.

"One more thing." Luke set his mug on the counter and reached into his back pocket. He withdrew Cassie's necklace, holding it out to her. "I found this on the living room floor."

Cassie stared at it a moment, then taking it from Luke's hand, she strode to the garbage can. Without a word, she stepped on the foot pedal that popped the lid and dropped the necklace inside.

As if she'd sent some silent signal, Luke's arms were around her waist, pulling her against him.

Their lips met with a breathless blend of urgency and tenderness.

Standing barefoot on the cracked linoleum in her cramped kitchen, with tangled hair and coffee breath, was not how she'd envisioned their next kiss.

But Cassie didn't care.

She slipped her arms around his neck, her fingers finding their home in the hair at the nape of his neck.

As far as Cassie was concerned, everything about the kiss was exactly as it should be.

Because it was with Luke.

❄

Luke tried to concentrate as they served pancakes and sausage links at The Forgotten Heroes Homeless Shelter. But in truth, he was still reeling from kissing Cassie. She turned him inside out, satisfying his soul, yet making him crave more. Even now, dressed in a hairnet and latex gloves, she set his pulse on edge.

"Luke." Cassie turned to him, a teasing smile tugging at her lips. "Bert claims the coffee here is the best in the city."

"That's a pretty lofty claim." Luke turned his attention to the scruffy veteran who'd returned for a second serving of flapjacks. "Are you sure about that, Bert?"

"I'd stake my life on it." The old man placed his hand over his heart.

"In that case, I'll have to give it a try." Cassie grabbed a small paper cup from the stack, and pumped a thimble-sized amount from the air pot.

"Come on. You gotta have more than that," Bert insisted. "I promise. Best coffee on the west coast."

"Whoa! The entire west coast, huh? We're really raising the bar." Luke laughed as Cassie filled her cup to the brim.

Luke watched with a fond smile as Cassie brought the rim to her lips, recalling the very first moment he saw her—the moment that changed everything. Amused, he wondered if she'd spit this coffee out, too.

Cassie's eyebrows lowered in hesitancy as she took a sip. But as the liquid touched the tip of her tongue, her head jerked up in surprise.

"See?" Bert nodded, a grin stretched across his weather-worn face. "I told you."

"It's that good, Cass?" Luke asked, still a bit skeptical.

"Not only that..." Cassie said slowly, taking another sip. Her eyes met Luke's with a look of confusion. "It's familiar."

"What do you mean 'familiar'?"

Cassie stared into the cup as though studying its contents for a clue. "I... I think I roasted this coffee."

Luke frowned. "How is that possible?"

Cassie handed him the paper cup. "I don't know, but taste it. It's my blend. The first one I made with Frank."

"Are you sure?" Luke tasted the sultry liquid, rolling it around in his mouth before swallowing. His palate wasn't nearly as refined as Cassie's, but it did taste vaguely familiar. And unbelievably delicious.

"Bert," Cassie smiled at the old man, "do you know where this coffee comes from?"

He shrugged. "No idea. It's here every morning, that's all I know."

"Will you excuse us for a minute?" she asked, grabbing Luke's hand.

Bert nodded, apparently content to return to his breakfast before it got cold.

Excitement illuminating her face, Cassie tugged Luke toward the kitchen.

❄

Breathless, Cassie pushed through the swinging double doors leading into the kitchen.

"You don't really think it could be..." Luke trailed off, following close behind her.

Cassie's eyes dazzled with the possibilities as she glanced over her shoulder. "I'm not sure. But it would make sense, wouldn't it? Frank never did tell me what he does with all the coffee he roasts."

Luke seemed to consider this as they paused in the chaos of the breakfast cleanup.

"Excuse me," Cassie addressed one of the volunteers. "Can I speak to whoever's in charge of the kitchen?"

The boy pointed to an older woman dressed in a white smock and hairnet. "That's Deb."

"Thanks." Cassie's pulse raced as they approached the woman checking off an inventory sheet on a clipboard.

She glanced up with a friendly smile. "Can I help you?"

"I hope so." Cassie snapped off the latex gloves, stuffing

them in her back pocket. "I'm wondering who your coffee supplier is."

"It's good, isn't it?" Deb said proudly. "But I'm afraid I don't know. It's an anonymous donation that gets shipped to us every two weeks."

Cassie's heart sank. She'd been so hopeful a moment ago. "Well, thanks anyway." Turning to go, a sudden idea struck her. Whirling back around, she asked, "Do you still have one of the shipping boxes?"

"I think so. But I don't know if it will do you any good. No name or company is listed on the return address. Only a PO box."

Cassie smiled, trying to calm the excited butterflies rollicking in her stomach. "Is it okay if we take a look?"

"Sure." Deb led them to the storage room, gesturing to a plain cardboard box resting on the shelf. "There you go. Let me know if you find anything. I'd love to thank whoever it is. The vets rave about the coffee here. And I'm pretty sure it's partially responsible for bringing a lot of them in off the street."

Hearing that warmed Cassie's heart, and she teared up. To hide her emotions, she concentrated on pulling the box off the shelf.

"Thanks," Luke told Deb. "We won't be long."

Cassie heard the squeak of Deb's white sneakers against the slick linoleum as she left them in the storage room. But she couldn't tear her gaze from the shipping label.

The town beneath the PO box blurred as tears filled Cassie's eyes.

Poppy Creek, CA.

Luke slid his arm around her shoulders. "It's Frank, isn't it?" he asked softly.

Cassie nodded, unable to speak past the lump in her throat. Taking a few deep breaths, she murmured, "It's so like him, you know." She sniffled, dabbing her damp cheek with her sleeve. "To do something like this and not tell anyone."

"Are you going to tell Deb?"

"No. It's not my secret to share." Cassie sighed. "Plus, while he's come a long way, I don't think we've fully cracked his shell yet."

Luke squeezed her upper arm. "Something tells me you're not going to give up until you do."

Cassie laughed as she wiped away a stray tear. "It's the Poppy Creek way, after all."

Love always hopes and always perseveres.

CHAPTER 30

Cassie knocked on Frank's front door, smiling to herself as she adjusted the box of baking supplies in her arm. So many things had come full circle since she first stepped foot in the quaint, quirky town of Poppy Creek.

She'd spent an unforgettable day with Luke in the city, then caravanned home, stopping a few times along the way. Luke claimed he wanted to check out the various fruit stands, but Cassie secretly suspected he wanted an excuse to hold her hand and steal a kiss. Which she didn't mind in the slightest! Truth be told, she hadn't stopped walking on air since their kiss in her kitchen.

Even her phone call to Derek, explaining she'd be gone for a few days, hadn't dampened her mood. She'd promised to carry out her duties—calling vendors and price checking equipment—and keep him apprised. Cassie hadn't mentioned she'd also be figuring out a way to pay him back to end their arrangement.

Luke had reiterated his offer to loan her the money, but Cassie still wasn't sure if she should accept it. Fifteen thousand dollars was a lot of money. A loan of that magnitude might be too much strain on a new relationship.

Cassie's heart fluttered at the thought. *A relationship!* They hadn't spelled it out in so many words, but with the way Luke looked at her, Cassie didn't have any doubts. He made her feel as though he'd been waiting all these years just for her.

The door swung open, and Frank cracked a smile before his gaze settled on the box. "What's that?"

"Baking supplies." Cassie slipped past him, taking the lead down the hallway toward the kitchen. "And hello to you, too," she teased.

Frank mumbled something incoherent, before he echoed, "Baking supplies?"

Cassie set the box on the kitchen table, whipping out an apron. "We're making a gingerbread house. It's today's activity on the Christmas Calendar."

"And why do I have to help?"

"Because," Cassie quipped simply, looping the apron over her head.

Frank grumbled but didn't object.

"If it makes you feel better," Cassie offered, "once we bake the gingerbread, we'll have some free time while we wait for it to cool. I thought we could try a new roast."

Frank's eyes gleamed, and Cassie could tell she'd struck the right chord of compromise.

❄

After the roast, they returned to the kitchen to check on the gingerbread.

"Perfect," Cassie said, testing the biggest square with the back of her hand.

"What about the extra dough?" Frank asked in a much more amiable mood.

"Oh, I'll just pop a few gingerbread men into the oven." Cassie attempted her most casual tone, so Frank didn't catch wind of the surprise. "It never hurts to have a few extra cookies, does it?"

Frank snorted, eyeing the enormous ball of dough. "That looks like enough to feed an entire naval squadron, but suit yourself."

Cassie grinned. "While I get these cookies into the oven, why don't you start frosting the walls together." She handed Frank the pastry bag of thick white icing.

He muttered a little under his breath, but couldn't hide the glint of delight in his eyes, and Cassie suppressed a giggle. He sure tried to be cantankerous, but he wasn't fooling her. Not anymore.

They worked together in peaceful silence for a few minutes until Frank cleared his throat. "I submitted my proposal for the second edition."

Cassie brightened. "Really? That's fantastic!"

Frank concentrated on his task, his head down. "I told my publisher I'd be working with a coauthor this time."

Cassie paused, the cookie sheet halfway in the oven. The heat blazed, tinging her cheeks bright red, but she didn't notice.

When the surprise finally subsided, she slowly slid the tray onto the rack. Closing the oven door, Cassie twirled around. "Frank... are you saying..." She didn't dare speak her thought out loud, in case she was wrong. After all, she *had* to be wrong. There was no way...

"I want you to write it with me."

Cassie's excitement bubbled to the surface, and she threw her hands into the air, a giddy squeal escaping her lips. The oven mitts went flying in opposite directions as she wrapped her arms around Frank.

He chuckled, patting her back while he gripped the pastry bag. "Don't get too excited. My name will still be bigger on the cover."

Cassie laughed, brushing a stray tear from the corner of her eye. "Sorry, I just can't believe it. This is so generous of you."

"You've earned it. Besides, I could use your help."

Cassie glowed from the inside out, barely able to contain her joy. She threw her arms wide, ready to envelop him in another hug, but he wielded the pastry bag.

"If you're this giddy already, I hate to see what happens when I tell you the rest of the news."

"There's more?" Cassie wasn't sure she could handle more good news.

Frank shuffled toward a kitchen drawer and pulled out a plain white envelope. Handing it to Cassie, he said, "As my coauthor, you're entitled to a portion of my advance."

Cassie balked, shaking her head adamantly. "Oh, no. I couldn't accept—"

He shoved the envelope into her hand. "Cash it or don't, it's up to you. But the money is yours."

Hesitantly, Cassie slid the check from inside the envelope. She gasped, gripping the back of the chair for support. *Twenty-thousand dollars!* Quickly, Cassie slipped the check back into the envelope, holding it out to Frank. "I can't take this. It's too much."

"If it makes you feel any better..." Frank's lips twitched. "That's not even half."

Cassie gaped at him, but Frank merely shrugged. "I'd give you more, but I had a feeling you were going to be difficult about it."

At first, Cassie didn't know what to say. Frank was calling *her* difficult? The irony caused a giggle to rise to the surface, transforming into a full-on burst of laughter.

Cassie laughed so hard she almost couldn't breathe. And before she knew it, Frank had joined her.

After a few minutes, they were both wiping tears of laughter from their eyes.

"Frank, I don't know what to say."

Before he could respond, a loud clamor outside drew their attention.

Frowning, Frank led the way down the hall toward the source of the commotion.

Throwing open the front door, he teetered in shock, and Cassie braced his elbow, grinning from ear to ear.

Five pickup trucks were parked in the driveway. Luke, Jack, Reed, and a few other men from town unloaded wood, tool-boxes, and other supplies while Penny and Eliza, along with her parents, unpacked paint cans and a plethora of rollers and brushes. Maggie, Dolores, and several women from their knitting circle carried enough cleaning supplies to spruce up a farmhouse twice its size. Glancing their way, Luke waved, followed by a few others.

"What—" Frank gasped, his gaze darting to Cassie.

Cassie smiled, her face glowing with affection. "Think we made too many cookies, now?"

Still stunned, Frank looked out across the driveway where a tiny construction crew converged on his front lawn, ready to mend his neglected house—and heart. "Why?" he croaked.

"Because, like it or not, you're a part of this town. And we care about you." Tugging on his arm, she added, "How about we brew a fresh pot of coffee for all these folks?"

Nodding slowly, Frank turned, his steel-gray eyes glistening.

As they headed back inside, Frank reached for her hand. Giving it a shaky squeeze, he placed it in the crook of his arm.

Side by side, they walked down the hall, accompanied by the sounds of life outside Frank's front door.

❄

A few hours later, as Frank served the group another batch of cookies, Cassie stole a minute with Luke.

Once they were hidden behind Luke's pickup, he scooped her into his arms, pressing a kiss to her lips.

When he finally released her, Cassie beamed up at him, breathless. She didn't think she'd ever get used to that.

"You're amazing," he murmured, pressing his forehead to hers.

Melting inside, she smiled. "So are you."

"I mean it, Ru." Pulling back, Luke gazed into her eyes intently. "You've changed everything. Since the moment you stepped foot in Poppy Creek, nothing has been the same. In the best possible way."

Cassie's heart stilled and time seemed to slow down as Luke took both of her hands in his. "Being with you these past few weeks, watching you fight for the important things in your life..." Pausing, Luke swallowed.

Offering encouragement, Cassie tightened her grip.

Luke took a deep breath, running his thumbs along the backs of her hands. "I've decided to do the same... Pursue something important in my life."

It took all of Cassie's strength to remain standing as anticipation weakened her knees. Was Luke about to...

"I've decided to quit my law practice and pursue my passion full-time."

It took a moment for Luke's words to sink in, but then a slow smile spread across Cassie's lips. "Really?"

"Really. And I have you to thank for it."

Cassie threw her arms around his neck, burying her face against his chest. Her heart swelled with happiness. She knew it must have been a difficult decision, and she couldn't be prouder. "I'm so happy for you, Sprinkles."

Luke laughed softly into her hair. "We make a good team, don't we?"

"The best."

"Speaking of teamwork..." Luke released her so he could let

down the tailgate of his pickup. "Ready to see the project we worked on?"

Cassie gasped as Luke lowered a stunning walnut rocking chair, the fresh polish gleaming in the sunlight.

"Luke! It's gorgeous." She ran a hand along the headrest, her fingers grazing the delicate carvings.

"Let's just hope Frank likes it," Luke said, grabbing one side. "Ready to show him?"

"Ready!"

She couldn't wait to set the two rocking chairs side by side, already hopeful a special person, one day soon, would come along to balance the pair.

CHAPTER 31

December 22 flew by like a flurry of snowflakes. And everything in Cassie's life finally seemed to be falling into place. She'd decided to cash Frank's check and had paid Derek back, much to his annoyance. He whined and complained, even though Cassie had emailed him a list of her top five food vendors, links to all the equipment he needed to purchase, plus the résumés of three ideal candidates for the management position.

With the uncomfortable conversation behind her, Cassie then spent the afternoon with Luke going over ideas to expand his office into a studio to display his work. Even though they hadn't been picking out grinders and espresso machines, Cassie felt content simply being in Luke's company.

To end the evening, everyone in town—including Frank—converged in the cafeteria of Poppy Creek Elementary to watch the kids perform *A Charlie Brown Christmas*. Which happened to not only be the annual Christmas performance for the entire elementary school *but also* the Calendar's activity for the day.

So far, Luke had been giving Cassie's tasks to her one day at a time. But on this particular morning, two days before Christmas, he'd called to say he wanted to keep it a surprise.

As Cassie waited for her morning cup of coffee to steep in the French press, she idly tapped her fingertips against the countertop. Checking the Christmas Calendar used to fill the four-minute brew time. But now, Cassie realized how much she missed it. And Luke's photocopied pages simply weren't the same.

Her fingertips grazed a nick in the butcher block, tilting the corners of her lips into a smile. She still wondered how the groove had come to be. Was it the slip of a knife? Or something else?

As her gaze traveled the rest of the kitchen, she observed other small details. How one gingham curtain was slightly longer than the other. And the tiny dent near the bottom of the white, retro-style refrigerator. So much life had taken place in the cottage. So many memories lingered in the nooks and crannies. Memories that didn't belong to her.

In a matter of days, the house would become Cassie's. And even though the cottage had already become her home, she realized very little in the space was actually *hers*. At least, not in the usual sense. For the first time, Cassie wondered what she would keep exactly as it was, and what she would make her own.

Perhaps she would spend the day figuring some of it out.

While she waited for Luke's surprise.

❄

Cassie stood in front of the vintage hall stand, peering past the aged patina of the antique mirror to assess her appearance.

She'd left her hair down, falling in loose waves around her shoulders, topped with her red knit cap, which made her lips and cheeks look even rosier.

Sticking with her basic black peacoat, she paired it with a red-and-green plaid scarf and a bejeweled poinsettia brooch she found in her grandmother's jewelry box. Somehow, she thought her grandmother would approve of the festive addition.

Cassie wasn't sure why she'd paid so much attention to the little details, except something told her the evening would be special. Ever since she'd received Luke's text that simply read, *Pick you up at 7. Dress warm*, she'd been buzzing with anticipation.

Cassie glanced at her phone, noting the clock denoted seven o'clock on the dot. Trying not to be impatient, she stuffed it back inside her coat pocket and fidgeted with a few wayward curls.

The faint jingle of bells outside drew her to the door. Swinging it open, Cassie's breath stalled in her throat.

Luke hopped down from a...

Cassie blinked. *A sleigh?* A real honest-to-goodness sleigh? Pulled by two magnificent Clydesdales, their reddish coats gleaming in the moonlight.

Luke grinned as he leaped up the porch steps to greet her. His gaze traveled from her beaming face to the brooch on her coat lapel, and he didn't bother to hide his admiration. "You look beautiful." Slipping his hand around her waist, he bent to kiss her softly, stealing her breath for the second time.

When their lips finally parted, Cassie gripped his shoulders, still a little wobbly on her feet. "We're going on a sleigh ride?"

"Technically, it's a carriage. Sleighs don't do so well without snow."

As soon as the words left his mouth, large feathery snowflakes drifted from the sky, as if on cue.

"You were saying," Cassie teased.

"Wow. I don't think snow was in the forecast for tonight."

"Grandma Edith probably ordered it just for us."

Luke laughed. "You're probably right."

"It won't ruin your plans, will it?"

"Not at all! I always plan ahead, just in case."

As Luke helped Cassie climb into the carriage, she saw what he meant. Several thick, heavy blankets lined the seat and she spotted a thermos filled with what she suspected to be Sadie's famous hot chocolate.

"Ready?" Luke asked, climbing in beside her.

Cassie beamed her approval. "I can't believe a carriage ride was on the Christmas Calendar!"

"It's not." Luke grinned, tapping the reins to signal the horses.

They whinnied, whipping their black manes as they trotted forward.

"It's not?" Cassie echoed in confusion.

"We're on our way to the Christmas Calendar's activity. The carriage was my idea."

Touched beyond words by his gesture, Cassie planted a kiss on his cheek.

"I guess it was a good idea," Luke chuckled and Cassie snuggled in closer, pulling the blanket around them.

As they traveled down a quiet one-lane road, the soft jingle of bells complemented the peaceful silence of their surroundings. Moonlight reflected off the bright white snowflakes, transforming them into glitter cascading from the sky. Enraptured by the sight, Cassie didn't even notice the sting of the cold air against her cheeks.

"We're almost there." Luke transferred the reins to one hand so he could slide the other around her shoulders, pulling her into the warmth of his body.

A contented sigh escaped Cassie's lips, her wispy breath disappearing into the stillness of the night as she cuddled closer.

As they rounded a bend in the lane, the pines grew denser until one final curve in the road led them to a small clearing in the trees.

Cassie clutched Luke's hand, unable to believe the spell-binding scene before her.

In the distance, hedged by a thick forest, a single pine stood draped in golden twinkling lights.

"What is it?" Cassie whispered.

"It's called the Wishing Tree." Luke hopped down and looped the reins over the hitching post. Reaching inside his pocket, he withdrew two slips of paper and a pen before climbing back into the carriage. Handing one slip to Cassie, he said, "You write down your wish, roll it into a scroll, and tie it on the tree."

Cassie stared at the blank white space. What could she wish for? All her wishes were already coming true.

Luke passed her the pen and pulled two strings of twine from his coat pocket, using one to wrap his scroll.

"You already finished yours?" Cassie asked.

"Yep. I knew exactly what I wanted."

As he gazed into her eyes, Cassie shivered.

Attributing it to the cold, Luke said, "Write yours down and we can head back home. The snowfall is getting heavier."

Cassie pressed the pen to her lips in thought, smiling as a silly idea sprang to mind. Hastily, she scribbled down her wish, then rolled the slip of paper as directed.

"You stay here, where it's warm." Luke held out his hand for her scroll. "I'll go tie these to the tree."

Cassie snuggled beneath the pile of blankets while Luke trotted through the snow and hung their wishes on the sparkling branches.

Glancing around her fairy-tale surroundings, Cassie savored the crisp scent of pine and freshly fallen snow, attempting to capture every exquisite detail of the moment.

So far, the evening had been beyond perfect.

And she had a feeling the magic had only begun.

❄

After a serene ride back, stealing kisses along the way, Luke pulled up in front of the cottage. Extending his hand to help Cassie down from the carriage, Luke's heart hammered against his chest.

As he led her toward the cottage, he paused a few feet from the front steps, gazing at the enchanting Victorian adorned in ethereal, shimmering lights.

"Remember the first evening we ever spent together?" Luke asked.

Cassie smiled, her eyes soft and dreamy. "The day you helped me decorate."

"That's the day I started falling in love with you."

Luke heard Cassie's sharp intake of breath, and he turned to face her.

Her stunning green eyes peered up at him, searching, as snowflakes gathered on her long lashes.

"Ru…" Luke said, his voice husky.

But before he could say another word, a sharp trill startled them both.

"I'm so sorry!" Cassie fumbled inside her coat pocket. As she withdrew her phone, the color drained from her face.

"What's wrong?" Luke asked.

"It's… the rehab center."

"At this time of night?" Luke glanced at his wrist, realizing he wasn't even wearing a watch.

"I'm so sorry," Cassie repeated. "I'm worried it's—"

"It's okay. Answer it." Luke reached for her free hand, in case she received bad news on the other end.

Squeezing back, she answered the call on speakerphone, a gesture of trust and intimacy that warmed Luke's heart, even in the falling snow.

"Hello?"

"Cassie Hayward?"

"Yes."

"I'm sorry to call you so late. I'm the night receptionist at Snyder Sobriety Center, and it's just come to my attention that no one has contacted you regarding your mother's belongings. Seeing that it's almost Christmas, I thought you'd want to be notified as soon as possible."

"My mother's belongings?" Cassie wavered slightly, and Luke gripped her hand a little tighter.

"Yes, your mother left all of her belongings behind. We haven't been able to reach her, but you're listed on all her forms."

"I don't understand." Cassie pressed a hand to her forehead in confusion.

Luke's stomach flipped as the pieces clicked into place.

"Is my mother no longer at your facility?" Cassie didn't seem to notice the snowflakes collecting on her phone screen, so Luke gently brushed them aside, careful not to disrupt the call.

A rustling of papers filled the speaker before the receptionist spoke again. "Let's see...your mother checked out on December 20, during her seventy-two-hour trial period."

Cassie's lower lip trembled and she squeezed her eyes shut.

Luke wanted to do something—anything—but he didn't know how he could help. Wrapping his arm around her, he slowly led her up the front steps, out of the cascading snowflakes. He sat on the top step, easing her down beside him.

"Ma'am? What would you like us to do with your mother's belongings? Would you like to pick them up?"

"Um," Cassie started, her voice shaky. "No. That's okay. You can keep them. Or give them away. It doesn't matter."

A brief pause preceded the woman's response. "Very well. Thank you for your time. And have a merry Christmas."

"Merry Christmas," Cassie said hoarsely before the call ended.

Leaning her head against Luke's shoulder, Cassie cried in his arms.

Luke didn't tell her it would be okay. Or that it would all work out in the end. He simply held her, letting the tears fall.

If life had taught him anything, it was that some things were out of your control. And when the difficult times arose, having someone by your side made all the difference in the world.

CHAPTER 32

Waking up the morning of Christmas Eve evoked bittersweet emotions for Cassie. Although she had countless reasons to celebrate, the news of Donna's departure from rehab left an ache in the pit of her stomach. She'd tried calling her mother, but each attempt went straight to voicemail.

However, there was a silver lining in the darkness.

Since Donna left rehab within the seventy-two-hour window, except for the deposit, the fee would be credited back to Cassie's account. Leaving Cassie with more money than she'd ever had in her entire life. Such news would have elicited excitement, were it not for the painful situation surrounding the sudden windfall.

Throwing back the covers, Cassie slipped out of bed, determined to break through the cloud of sadness shadowing an otherwise perfect day. She had plans to meet Eliza, Penny, Maggie, and Dolores at Sander's Farm to prep the enormous barn for the Christmas Eve dance later that evening. Which was also the Calendar's activity.

The dance!

It suddenly occurred to Cassie that she didn't have a single thing to wear! Her thoughts drifted to the elegant, emerald green gown displayed in Penny's shop. What were the chances it was still for sale now that Cassie could actually afford it? She made a mental note to stop by Thistle & Thorn on her way to Sander's.

Her mood slightly lifted, Cassie padded into the living room to restock the fire, when her gaze fell on a beautifully wrapped package resting on the coffee table. Intrigued, Cassie removed the note tucked inside the red satin bow.

Merry Christmas Eve!
Don't wait to open it.
~ Sprinkles

Grinning like a child on Christmas morning, Cassie tore away the red-and-green striped wrapping paper. Luke left her a present! And it wasn't even Christmas yet.

Lifting the lid of the white gift box, Cassie's breath faltered as a corner of emerald-green lace hid beneath the tissue paper. The thin paper rustled as Cassie flung it into the air like confetti, revealing the breathtaking gown underneath. How had Luke known?

Cassie's lips twitched as she imagined Eliza gleefully pointing Luke in the right direction. A truer friend than Eliza didn't exist. And Cassie couldn't wait to thank her in person.

Nestling the gown back in the box of tissue, Cassie hummed softly.

The hurt and disappointed slipped away as easily as the silky lace slid from her fingertips. She'd spent a lifetime wallowing in the pain and rejection of her past.

This Christmas, she would choose a different path.

One she wouldn't walk alone.

❄

That evening, Cassie doubled-checked her appearance in the mirror above her grandmother's dresser. Although it wasn't full-length, it was the largest mirror in the house.

To her delight, the gown fit like a dream, hugging every curve as though it were made for her. Paired with simple black heels, on loan from Eliza, the delicate lace gently grazed the floor.

The elegant cap sleeves draped off her shoulders, drawing attention to Cassie's bare neck. Her fingertips brushed her collar bone where the heart charm had once rested. Its absence represented a lifted burden. And Cassie almost regretted covering up with her grandmother's vintage mohair stole, but the soft ivory fabric paired perfectly with the gown and provided a modicum of warmth against the chilly winter night.

Twisting a strand of hair between her fingertips, Cassie tucked her grandmother's pearl-studded comb behind her ear, sweeping her long dark curls off to one side. Taking one last glance in the mirror, Cassie couldn't help a satisfied smile. Her thick black lashes and berry-red lips gave her an Old Hollywood style appearance reminiscent of Vivien Leigh. A resemblance her date would certainly appreciate.

The deep rumbling of a vehicle outside drew Cassie to the front door, her heartbeat skipping in anticipation.

Tugging the stole around her shoulders, Cassie beamed as she threw open the door.

Frank's Chevy convertible gleamed in the moonlight as he climbed from the driver's seat.

"Merry Christmas Eve." Cassie smiled, suddenly feeling shy as Frank blinked in awe.

"You look just like your grandmother," he murmured, holding out his hand. He stood tall and gallant, clothed in full-dress uniform, complete with shimmering medals pinned above his left breast pocket.

Cassie accepted his outstretched hand and placed a kiss on his cheek. "You look very dashing."

"It's the only formal wear I own," he mumbled.

But Cassie noted the pleased glint in his eye as he escorted her through the crunching snow.

When they approached the car, Cassie reached for the door, pausing in confusion. "Frank, there isn't a handle." Cassie hoped he wasn't about to remove the canvas top and make her climb over the side of the car in her gown.

Frank chuckled, bending to access a hidden button in the chrome trim.

The door popped open.

Her eyes sparkling, Cassie smirked. "Well, aren't *you* full of surprises?"

"This car was my first purchase after my book hit the best-seller list." Frank helped her slide onto the buttery upholstery. "Have you thought about how you're going to spend your advance?"

"Not yet," Cassie admitted. Deep down, she longed to open Poppy Creek's first coffee shop. But there wasn't a single space for sale or rent.

"You'll think of something." Frank shut the door, shuffling around to the driver's side.

Cassie pushed all thoughts of her dream coffee shop aside.

Tonight, she only wanted one thing.

To see the look on Luke's face when she entered the dance wearing his gift.

※

Luke nearly choked on his chilled apple cider the moment Cassie waltzed into the room arm in arm with Frank. She looked... stunning? Radiant? Breathtaking? He couldn't think of a single word that would do her beauty justice.

Wiping his mouth with the back of his hand, he set his glass on a nearby table, rushing to greet them at the door. Reaching for her, Luke froze, taking a second to soak up every single detail of her appearance. "Wow, you look..." He still couldn't conjure up an adequate adjective.

"For Pete's sake," Frank grunted. "Tell her she looks beautiful and kiss her already."

"Yes, sir." Luke slid his arms around Cassie's waist, kissing her deeply.

Frank cleared his throat. "That'll do, sailor."

Pulling apart, Luke and Cassie laughed.

"You really spruced up the place," Frank told Cassie, scanning the expansive barn with an appreciative glance.

"She did a great job, didn't she?" Luke admired the dozens of pine-scented garlands and wreaths bedecking the barn's interior, particularly impressed with the hundreds of paper snowflakes dangling from the ceiling.

"It was a group effort." Cassie blushed as she focused her gaze on the ten-foot-tall Christmas tree. "And it was women like Maggie and Eliza who really went above and beyond. After spending the morning decorating, they filled the dessert bar with their delicious baked goods."

"Speaking of Mom..." Luke spotted Maggie across the room where she chatted with a pretty older woman dressed in a burgundy organza gown. "There's someone she'd like you to meet." Locking his fingers with Cassie's, Luke led them toward the dessert table.

Maggie's entire face lit up when she saw them approach. "Sweetheart, you look dazzling!" After kissing Cassie on both cheeks, she turned her attention on Frank. "And don't you look handsome in that uniform!"

Frank mumbled something incoherent before adding, "Merry Christmas Eve, Margaret."

"Frank, have you met Beverly Lawrence?" Maggie's hazel eyes twinkled as she gestured toward her friend. "She's the town librarian and knows more interesting facts than a contestant on *Jeopardy*."

"I prefer *Wheel of Fortune*, myself," Frank muttered.

Luke suppressed a groan. Wow, Frank really wasn't getting the hint.

Beverly smiled, her porcelain cheeks turning pink. "Me, too."

Frank cocked a peppery eyebrow. "Did you watch last night's rerun?"

Beverly giggled. "You mean when the contestant didn't recognize the famous line from Shakespeare?"

"I almost threw my dinner plate at the TV," Frank admitted with a wry grin.

"So did I!"

Grasping Cassie's elbow, Luke shot a meaningful glance at his mother and slowly backed away, leaving Frank and Beverly to chat alone.

"Well, don't they make an adorable couple?" Cassie whispered.

"As long as Frank doesn't find out one minor detail."

"What's that?"

"Beverly doesn't like coffee."

Cassie's hand flew to her mouth, stifling a laugh. "Oh, no. That might be a deal-breaker."

"You think so?" Catching Eliza wave at them across the dance floor, Luke steered Cassie through the crowd of swaying couples. "And what if I didn't like coffee? Would you still love me?"

As the words floated from Luke's lips, time slowed down. His heart thumped above the four-piece band so loud he was certain Cassie could hear it hammering.

The night of their first kiss, Luke held back. He'd told Cassie he was *falling* in love with her, but she deserved more than that. She deserved the truth.

In the middle of the crowded dance floor, Luke took hold of Cassie's hands.

She gazed up at him, her eyes searching his.

"Cassie Hayward," Luke began, his voice thick with emotion, "I am hopelessly in love with you."

A soft smile tugged at the corner of her mouth. "Hopelessly? Why, Luke Davis, you know better than that."

Baffled, Luke's mouth fell open. "I..."

Cupping his chin with her fingertips, she murmured, "Love always hopes, remember?" and pressed her lips against his.

Luke melted into her kiss, savoring the knee-weakening taste of her.

Gently pulling back, she whispered, "I love you, too."

As Luke took her in his arms, the silky notes of "The Christmas Waltz" filled the air, cocooning them in the melody.

Holding Cassie against him, Luke swayed, humming along with the lyrics.

This year, Luke had a pretty good feeling his New Year dream would come true.

CHAPTER 33

C assie's eyelashes fluttered as her surroundings drifted into focus, the edges hazy as though she was still dreaming.

Outside the window, delicate snowflakes swirled in playful patterns in celebration of Christmas morning. Cassie burrowed deeper beneath the soft sheets, grateful she'd donned the flannel pajamas Eliza had given her the night of Pajama Christmas.

Christmas... the word danced in Cassie's mind, teasing a smile from her lips.

In the past, the day had conjured nothing but heartache. But now...

Hope and happiness swelled in Cassie's chest, and she pressed a hand over her heart, certain she would burst with joy any second. In a few hours, she would join Luke at Maggie's house, along with Frank and Dolores. Eliza and Ben said they'd stop by, too.

This year, Cassie would spend Christmas with family— people who loved her.

Stretching her arms overhead, Cassie beamed, basking in the glory of the morning and the promise of things to come.

Curiously, the tantalizing aroma of warm-from-the-oven cinnamon rolls and freshly brewed coffee tickled her nose. Ready to explain the sensation as the sheer force of her imagination, Cassie snuggled deeper beneath the covers.

Then the silky notes of Nat King Cole's "The Christmas Song" floated up the staircase, luring Cassie out of bed.

Heart skittering in anticipation, Cassie's fingers curled around the smooth banister. Had Luke come for her? A smile curved her lips, crinkling the corners of her eyes. As she slowly descended the stairs, her Christmas tree came into view, the star on top glittering brightly.

Cassie's pulse quickened as she neared the last step, each chord of "The Christmas Song" accompanying her movement. Pausing at the bottom, Cassie's breath caught as her gaze settled on Luke, surrounded by Maggie, Dolores, Frank, Ben and Eliza, each wearing a set of pajamas identical to her own.

"Merry Christmas!" they shouted in unison.

Happy tears pooling in her eyes, Cassie admired her newfound family gathered around the twinkling Christmas tree. The snowfall beyond the bay window provided the perfect backdrop to the most beautiful sight she'd ever seen.

"You're here." Cassie's voice broke with emotion.

Luke stepped forward, cupping a mug of steaming coffee. "We thought you should spend your first Christmas in Poppy Creek at home."

Moved beyond words, Cassie leaped into Luke's arms, wrapping her arms around his neck.

Grinning, Luke tried to save the coffee from sloshing onto the floor. But as Cassie's lips found Luke's, his concern slipped away.

Ben's less than subtle exclamation of, "Ew," eventually pulled them apart.

Giggling, Cassie slid her arms from around Luke's neck, hugging everyone else in turn.

When she finally reached Frank, he tugged the collar of the gaudy pajamas mumbling, "They made me wear this getup."

"It suits you," Cassie said, smiling fondly.

Frank grunted, but his gray eyes twinkled. "Merry Christmas, Cassie."

"Merry Christmas, Frank."

She embraced him warmly, content with his awkward back-pat.

As they broke apart, Eliza looped her arm through Cassie's, leading her to the sofa. "It's time for presents."

"Oh! Let me get—"

Before Cassie could retrieve the gifts she'd set under the tree, Eliza gently shoved her into the plump cushions. "Sit. You're opening first."

Cassie laughed. "You're a little pushy for Santa's helper, aren't you?"

Eliza smirked, her face glowing with excitement. "Sorry, but none of us can wait another second."

Touched, Cassie's throat tightened as they all gathered around the crackling fire, festively-wrapped packages in hand.

"Me first! Me first!" Ben skipped toward her, thrusting a thin, flat rectangle into her hands. "I wrapped it all by myself."

Cassie hid a smile, noticing Ben had secured several mangled scraps of wrapping paper together with way more tape than necessary. But as the pieces fell away, Cassie's hand flew to her heart.

A stunning silver frame displayed a colorful drawing.

Ben curled up next to her on the couch, proudly pointing to his masterpiece. "That's me. And that's you. We're building a snowman. See?"

Cassie nodded, tears stinging her eyes.

"That's the pen we used for his nose." Ben's finger tapped the glass above a bright orange streak depicting the highlighter pen. Tilting his pink-cheeked face to look at her, he asked, "Do you like it, Aunt Cassie?"

Swallowing past the lump in her throat, Cassie draped her arm around Ben, pulling him into a hug. "I love it. It's perfect."

Ben beamed, throwing his arms around her.

Resting her chin on top of his head, Cassie closed her eyes, hoping to capture the moment in her memory. She couldn't imagine any present topping the one she'd just received.

"It's my turn next." Dolores eagerly placed a large gift bag on Cassie's lap.

Setting Ben's picture frame on the coffee table, Cassie removed the red and green tissue paper. Laughter spilled from her lips as she withdrew a knitting starter kit. "I was just thinking the other day since I'm staying in Poppy Creek, I'd better learn how to knit."

"Now, I can teach you." Dolores's eyes gleamed behind her glasses.

"I can't wait." Cassie smiled her appreciation, surprised to find she actually meant it.

"Our turn!" Eliza cheered from her perch on the arm of the couch. She nudged Maggie, who sat beside her.

Reaching across Ben, Maggie handed Cassie a small red stocking. Her fingers curved around Cassie's for a moment, squeezing gently before pulling away.

Turning the stocking over, a long brass key fell into the palm of Cassie's hand. Confused, Cassie searched Maggie's face.

Maggie smiled with motherly affection. "It's the key to the bakery."

Cassie stared at the aged metal, its sheen dull and scratched from wear, still uncertain what it meant. Was Maggie making her a manager? The thought that she trusted her to open and close the shop touched Cassie's heart. "Thank you, Maggie."

"It's really a gift from both of us." Maggie reached for Eliza's hand. "When I hired Eliza, the intention was she'd take over for me one day. I wasn't sure when that day would be, but..." Misty-eyed, she patted the top of Eliza's hand. "When you girls took over for me the other day, I realized I enjoyed having some time for myself. So, after a lot of consideration, I've decided to retire. And I can't think of two better women to take over the business for me."

Dumbstruck, Cassie's gaze darted between Maggie and Eliza.

"What do you say, Cass?" Eliza asked. "Do you want to be business partners?"

"I—" Cassie grasped for the right words, but her brain wouldn't cooperate. "I… don't know what to say."

"Then say yes," Maggie supplied. "Of course, Luke will help us make it official. And if it makes you more comfortable, we can work out a small price constructed as a payment plan from the profits."

Cassie thought of the money sitting in her bank account. Assuming Eliza had a little saved, they could make a fair down payment to Maggie and still have money to remodel. She drew in a shaky breath. This couldn't be happening…

"Well, Cass?" Eliza leaned forward eagerly.

Clutching the key, Cassie's eyes sparkled with a wellspring of emotion. "Yes! I'd love to be business partners."

"Yay!" Eliza bounced on the arm of the sofa, nearly toppling off in her enthusiasm.

"Thank you," Cassie whispered, reaching across Ben to embrace Maggie.

Ben giggled, and squirming out from under them, escaped to join Luke on the loveseat.

Eliza took his place, completing the group hug. "I'm so glad you said yes! And Mags, you'll still be around all the time, right?"

"Of course, I will. I suspect you'll have to come up with a new name, though." Maggie wiped a happy tear from the corner of her eye.

"That's true! Any ideas, Cass?"

"The Calendar Cafe," Cassie blurted without thinking. Her

hand flew to her mouth, heat spreading across her cheeks. Where had that come from?

Eliza clapped her approval. "It's perfect! Three hundred and sixty-five days of deliciousness."

Cassie laughed. "And without the Christmas Calendar, none of this would be possible."

Her eyes glistening, Maggie squeezed her hand. "I can't think of a more perfect name."

The three women huddled together, celebrating their new venture.

Frank cleared his throat. "I believe that brings us to my gift." Slowly rising from the armchair, Frank shuffled toward Cassie, unceremoniously plopping a simple craft bag in her hands.

The enticing aroma of freshly roasted coffee rose from the loose seal, but it wasn't the contents of the bag that caught Cassie's attention.

Cassie's Blend was printed neatly across the front of the bag in large, bold letters. Grazing her fingertip over them, Cassie met Frank's gaze. "Thank you."

"I figure you'll go through several pounds a week. We can develop a few different blends if you want. And something special for the espresso, of course."

As the implication of his words settled, Cassie's eyes widened. "You mean..."

Digging his fists into the pockets of the pajama bottoms, Frank shrugged. "If you want to serve some other brand of coffee at your cafe—"

Leaping from the couch, Cassie flung her arms around Frank and pressed a kiss to his scruffy cheek. "Thank you! Thank you! Thank you!"

Cassie expected Frank to pull away, embarrassed by her outburst, but his shoulders relaxed and he leaned into the embrace. "That clause of Edie's," he whispered in her ear. "It changed my life, too. And somehow, I think she knew it would."

A sob nearly escaped Cassie's lips as she buried her face in Frank's neck, inhaling the faint aroma of coffee that seemed to permeate his entire being. "I think you're right," she whispered back.

Pulling apart, they each wiped stray tears with the edges of their matching pajama sleeves.

"You have one more gift." Frank nodded in Luke's direction.

As Cassie turned, she noticed Ben had vacated the spot beside Luke.

With a tender smile, Luke patted the cushion next to him.

Seated side by side, Cassie's thoughts swirled wildly as he handed her a small, square-shaped box.

"Merry Christmas, Ru."

Heart fluttering, Cassie tried to control the tremble in her fingers as she untied the velvet bow. What could it be?

She thought of the cuckoo clock wrapped beneath the tree. Even though Luke confessed to already seeing it, he still wanted to open it Christmas morning so he could fully appreciate the meaningful gift. She'd happily obliged, adding a special collector's edition of *Home Alone*, including a voucher for a Christmas movie marathon next year.

She'd never known gift-giving could garner so much joy.

Finally reaching the box beneath the wrapping, Cassie tentatively lifted the lid.

A gasp escaped her lips.

Luke scooted closer, placing his hand on her knee as her fingertips gripped the red satin cord.

Slowly, Cassie withdrew an exact replica of the cottage, each intricate detail of the ornament carved by hand. "Oh, Luke," Cassie breathed.

"I thought we'd continue your grandmother's tradition," Luke said softly. "And there's something else inside."

Cassie's gaze flickered to Luke's face. Could it be?

He gestured toward the miniature red door.

Drawing in a deep breath, Cassie eased the door open and peered inside.

Her breath caught, and as she tilted the ornament, a glittering gold necklace slid into the palm of her hand.

"I thought you could use a new one." Lifting it gently, Luke held it up for her to see. Light reflected off the charm shaped like a tipped coffee cup. The delicate chain appeared to loop through the handle and tiny diamonds sparkled along the rim.

But the engraving in the center garnered all her attention.

Two simple letters that made her heart sing like a Christmas choir.

Ru.

"Do you want to put it on?" Luke asked.

In response, Cassie pressed her lips to his, lacing her fingers through his hair.

Tenderly cupping the side of her face, Luke returned her kiss, speaking the depths of his love without a single word.

❄

Contentment filled Cassie's heart as she topped off her coffee mug, once again admiring the colorful poppies splashed across the smooth, white porcelain. Laughter and chatter carried into the kitchen from the living room, along with the triumphant notes of Andy Williams's "It's the Most Wonderful Time of the Year."

Cassie would have to agree. Oh, how things had changed.

"There you are." Luke strode across the kitchen, scooping her into another kiss.

As their lips parted, Cassie chuckled. "Miss me already?"

"More than you know. And I have another gift for you." Luke handed her a plain manila envelope. "The last day on the Calendar was Celebrate with Friends and Family. I think you've accomplished that, don't you?"

Cassie met Luke's gaze, her pulse pounding in her ears. Her

fingers trembled slightly as she peeled open the seal. Even though she'd been working toward this moment all December, she couldn't believe it had actually arrived. She hesitated as her fingertips met the sharp edge of the paper.

Luke bent and kissed her forehead. "Do you want a minute alone?"

Reaching for him, Cassie shook her head.

Luke slid an arm around her waist and lovingly brushed aside a loose curl.

After taking a couple of deep breaths, Cassie slid the top sheet from the envelope. As she gazed at the deed to the cottage, her vision blurred. She'd finally received her inheritance. Yet, holding the deed in her hand felt so surreal. As if, in some strange way, Cassie had already received her inheritance. And it had nothing to do with the four walls surrounding her.

"There's more," Luke said, as though reading her thoughts.

Cassie withdrew a second sheet of paper, her breath faltering as the handwritten letter came into focus. Wiping her damp cheeks with the edge of her sleeve, Cassie blinked back the impending tears, not wanting to miss a single word.

My dearest granddaughter,

You've made it. Of course, I knew you would. You're a Hayward. Which means you're too stubborn to quit a challenge. I just pray you're not too stubborn to have a change of heart. Christmas is a gift. But like any gift, you have to accept it. Call it a clause, if you will. You can have the tallest tree or the brightest lights, but if you don't have Hope in your heart, it's all for naught. But then, I suspect you know that by now.

Merry Christmas, my dear. Until we celebrate together one day. In the meantime, I'll leave you with words paraphrased from our good friend, Charles Dickens.

May you keep Christmas well.

All my love,

Grandma Edie

Cassie heard Luke sniffle, and glancing up, caught him wipe a stray tear from his eye.

Her own eyes glistening, Cassie gently set the letter on the butcher block. "She sure was special, wasn't she?"

"She was." Luke turned Cassie to face him, brushing a tear from her cheek. "You okay?"

"I only wish I could have met her. Or, at least, thanked her somehow." Every word from her grandmother's letter had permeated Cassie's heart. As she'd carried out the different tasks over the last few weeks, something had changed inside her. And Cassie knew it had nothing to do with the activities themselves.

"Come here." Taking her hand, Luke led Cassie to the doorway.

"What are you doing?" A smile teased Cassie's lips as she gazed up at him.

Holding both of her hands in his own, Luke tipped his head toward the ceiling.

"Mistletoe?" Cassie laughed. Then, suddenly, her eyes widened. "Wait. How did you…"

Luke flashed an impish grin. "I may have snuck a peek at your wish. 'Finally kiss Luke beneath the mistletoe.'"

Blushing, Cassie made a move to swat his arm, but Luke wouldn't release her hands.

"Excuse me, but I believe I have a wish to fulfill."

As he lowered his lips to hers, Cassie closed her eyes. The sensation of his deep, tenderhearted kiss flooded her with warmth, and vivid images flashed through her mind.

Luke rescuing her from the attic.

Their bodies sprawled in the snow.

The comfort of his strong, steady embrace.

A stolen kiss in swirling snowflakes.

So many memories shared.

And Cassie hoped, so many more to come.

"Wow," Luke breathed, finally pausing to catch his breath. "Can we keep the mistletoe all year?"

Laughing softly, Cassie nudged his shoulder playfully. "Since you cheated, you have to tell me your wish now."

"Sorry, no can do."

"But that's not fair!" Cassie tried to pout, but she couldn't stop smiling.

Eyes twinkling, Luke held her gaze. "I promise, you'll find out soon."

Something in Luke's expression caused Cassie's heart to flutter. Or maybe it was the tender way he ran his thumb along her finger. Whatever the reason, Cassie tilted her chin toward Luke and closed her eyes as he kissed her once more.

But this time, different images flashed before her.

Visions of hope for the future.

EPILOGUE

E liza loved New Year's Eve. Especially this year.
  She could practically smell the tantalizing aroma of
fresh starts and endless possibilities carried on the crisp winter
night air.

Pulling the collar of her plum-colored peacoat tighter
around her neck, she shivered, more from excitement than the
cold. A combination of space heaters, two bonfires, and nearly
every resident in Poppy Creek huddled together in the town
square, created a cocoon of warmth. All eyes were on the clock
tower of the courthouse, counting down the seconds until
midnight.

The dulcet notes of "Auld Lang Syne" complemented the
collective expressions of hope and nostalgia, and Eliza swayed
along with the melody.

The coming year would be different. *She* would be different.

Although Poppy Creek embraced her and Ben, showering
her with love and support even during her unexpected preg-
nancy, she saw the way people looked at her. Their smiles
could never quite hide the pity in their eyes.

In high school, she'd spouted all her grand plans with the
confidence of youth—go to culinary school and study abroad

in Paris under the tutelage of a renowned pastry chef before opening an artisan bakery in San Francisco.

Then, one wrong choice had changed everything.

Not that Eliza regretted Ben for a second.

Catching sight of a little boy tugging his father's arm, begging to be lifted onto his shoulders, Eliza's stomach churned with doubt. She'd debated bringing Ben tonight. But he could rarely stay up this late. And since Sylvia preferred watching the New York City ball drop on television, Eliza let Ben stay home with his grandparents.

Home... Eliza's feelings regarding that particular word were complicated. She'd lived in the two-story, periwinkle-blue farmhouse all her life. But she never expected to raise her family there. Or to still be living with her parents going on twenty-seven-years.

Her chin instinctively raised a little higher as the thought of owning her own bakery sprang to mind. Finally, she'd make something of herself! No more "poor Eliza." She'd be a businesswoman, able to stand on her own two feet. Maybe then everyone would stop trying to fix her up with older, more stable men. If she wanted a relationship—which was a huge *if*—she could find one on her own.

Yep! Look out, Poppy Creek! The next year would be full of changes!

And not only for her...

Eliza stole a glance in Luke and Cassie's direction.

Cassie stood in front of Luke, leaning against his chest while his arms were wrapped around her, holding her close. Eliza couldn't help a small sigh, noting the way Luke rested his chin on top of Cassie's head. The two lovebirds seemed to melt into each other, as though they existed as one person.

Jealousy niggled at Eliza's heart, but she forced it aside. She was happy for her friends. Truly, she was. But whoever said it was better to have loved and lost was a cold-blooded liar.

Eliza took a deep breath. She couldn't entertain that line of thinking.

Tonight was about Luke and Cassie.

Eliza noticed a few more heads turning in their direction. Okay, more than a few. The entire town seemed to shift focus from the clock tower to the blissfully unaware couple.

Heat crept up Eliza's neck, coloring her cheeks. She shouldn't have said anything. Luke told her in confidence. But then, he should have known better than to share a secret with her. She'd only been able to keep one secret her entire life. Solely because she didn't have a choice.

With only a few minutes left until midnight, the townspeople collectively held their breath in anticipation.

Luke slid his arms from around Cassie and cleared his throat.

"What's wrong?" Cassie turned to take in Luke's nervous expression.

Maggie and Dolores sniffled, linking arms as they gazed on with the rest of the crowd.

"Is everything okay?" Cassie glanced from Maggie and Dolores to Frank, then Eliza.

Flashing a reassuring smile, Eliza surreptitiously slid her cell phone from her coat pocket, swiped open the camera app, and pressed record.

Luke took both of Cassie's hands in his. "Everything is more than okay. In fact, I can only think of one thing that could make this evening better."

The crowd gasped as Luke dropped to one knee.

Cassie's hand flew to her throat, her fingertips curling around the necklace Luke had given her for Christmas.

Reaching into his coat pocket, Luke withdrew a tiny velvet box. "I realize we haven't been together long, but I couldn't envision another year without you as my wife. Cassie Hayward, would you make my Christmas wish come true by saying yes?"

Luke slowly lifted the lid, revealing a stunning antique diamond ring.

Eliza stole a glance at Frank, whose steel-gray eyes glistened with unshed tears.

Dabbing at her own eyes with her scarf, Eliza had trouble keeping the phone steady.

The first time Luke shared the touching story, Eliza cried for five straight minutes. Luke offered to purchase Edith's ring at any price, but Frank refused payment, insisting the ring was meant for Cassie.

Cassie's green eyes sparkled as brilliantly as the tiny emeralds encircling the oval cut diamond as she held out her hand. "Yes, of course! Yes!"

The final yes came out as a sob as Luke scooped her into his arms.

Their lips met as the clock struck midnight.

Cheers and applause erupted as large confetti cannons burst, shooting rice paper poppy petals into the air.

Other couples joined Luke and Cassie in ringing in the New Year with a kiss as the string quartet once again performed "Auld Lang Syne" in concert with the chime of the church bells.

Eliza slipped her phone back inside her pocket as others around her recited lines from a classic Alfred Loyd Tennison poem:

"Ring out the old, ring in the new, Ring, happy bells, across the snow; The year is going, let him go; Ring out the false, ring in the true."

For the first time since hearing the age-old adage, the words struck Eliza at her core.

Ring out the false, ring in the true.

And that's when she saw him.

A dark figure blurred by bright red petals fluttering to the ground.

It couldn't be...

Her heartbeat stilled as she peered closer, desperate for a definitive view.

But as suddenly as the figure appeared, he vanished from sight.

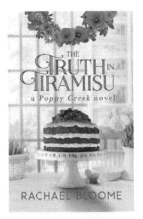

Read the rest of Eliza's story, and learn more about your favorite Poppy Creek characters (including what happened to Donna Hayward), **in *The Truth in Tiramisu*.**

SPECIAL BONUS OFFERS

DEAR FRIEND,

Thank you for reading *The Clause in Christmas*. If you enjoyed Luke and Cassie's story, I would be so grateful for an honest review.

If you'd like to spend more time with Frank and Beverly, you can sign up to read their bonus love story, *Poppy Petals*, by joining my newsletter at www.rachaelbloome.com/secret-garden-club. You may even recognize a few key characters from my sweet and heartwarming novella, *Puzzle Pieces,* which is also free to download along with hours of additional exclusive content.

Thank you again; you truly make writing these stories worthwhile. As always, I would love to hear from you. You can reach me anytime at hello@rachaelbloome.com. And don't forget to visit my website where you can download your own printable version of the Christmas Calendar.

Until next time...
Blessings & Blooms,

ACKNOWLEDGMENTS

✳

My deepest, heartfelt thanks to everyone who helped make *The Clause in Christmas* come to life, particularly my husband, parents, and constant cheerleaders: Lynn, Melissa, Rachel, Savannah, and Starla.

A huge thank you to my critique partners, Dave and Gigi. You not only helped shape this story with your wonderful insights, but were a consistent source of support and encouragement. Your friendship means the world to me.

I would also like to thank the kind and generous online writing community, especially my close-knit writing family on Instagram. You brought me into your circle of knowledge and friendship, and I couldn't be more grateful.

This novel wouldn't be what it is today without the incredible skills of my editor, Beth Attwood; proofreader, Krista Dapkey with KD Proofreading; and cover designer, Ana Grigoriu-Voicu with Books-design. You ladies made this story shine.

A final thank you to everyone who invited me into their home by reading this story. You've made this dream possible.

ABOUT THE AUTHOR

Rachael Bloome is a *hopeful* romantic. She loves every moment leading up to the first kiss, as well as each second after saying, "I do." Torn between her small-town roots and her passion for traveling the world, she weaves both into her stories—and her life!

Joyfully living in her very own love story, she enjoys spending time with her husband, adorable daughter, and two rescue dogs, Finley and Monkey. When she's not writing, helping to run the family coffee roasting business, or getting together with friends, she's busy planning their next big adventure!

EDIBLE KINDNESS RECIPE

❄

This recipe is near and dear to my heart.

Every year, my kind and generous mother-in-law makes several batches of this delicious fudge and hand-delivers festive tins to each of her neighbors. It's become a treat they look forward to eagerly and inspired one of the tasks on the Christmas Calendar.

This year, I'm sharing the recipe with you. And I hope it will inspire a similar tradition of spreading kindness and Christmas cheer... along with a scrumptious, mouth-watering treat!

INGREDIENTS

3 cups sugar

¾ cup butter, room temp

5 oz evaporated milk

12 oz chocolate chips (can substitute peanut butter chips or other flavors)

10 oz marshmallow crème OR 7 oz marshmallow crème and 3 oz small marshmallows

1 tsp vanilla

1 cup chopped walnuts, if desired

INSTRUCTIONS

Line 9 x 13 pan with foil. Extend foil over edges an inch or so. Place in freezer.

Combine sugar, butter, and milk in a large glass bowl. Microwave 8 minutes, stopping every 2 – 2 ½ minutes to stir. Remove from microwave.

Drop a little of this mixture into cup of ice-cold water. Mixture should be at the soft ball stage. If not, return to microwave for 30 seconds and test again.

Remove from microwave.

Stir in chocolate chips until melted.

Add marshmallow crème/marshmallows. Stir until blended.

Add vanilla.

Because fudge is creamiest when it cools quickly, stirring is of utmost importance. If you have a KitchenAid or other industrial strength mixer, pour the fudge mixture into the mixing bowl and blend for several minutes on a medium speed. Otherwise, stir by hand until mixture cools a bit.

Add nuts.

Remove pan from freezer and spray with cooking spray. Spread fudge mixture into cooled pan, and return to freezer for several hours. Remove from freezer. Lift foil from pan and place on cutting board. You may need to let it soften for 5–10 minutes.

Using a straight edge (not serrated), cut fudge into squares.

Fudge can be frozen for months, to savor whenever you get a craving for a special treat.

Enjoy!

CHRISTMAS CALENDAR

❄

DECEMBER 1

Decorate the House

DECEMBER 2

Cut Down a Christmas Tree

DECEMBER 3

Decorate the Christmas Tree

DECEMBER 4

Bake a Mince Pie

DECEMBER 5

Build a Snowman

DECEMBER 6

Attend Pajama Christmas

DECEMBER 7

Go Sledding

DECEMBER 8

Make Mulled Wine

DECEMBER 9

Random Act of Kindness

DECEMBER 10

Go Ice Skating

DECEMBER 11

Make Eggnog

DECEMBER 12

Read A Christmas Carol

DECEMBER 13

Have a Snowball Fight

DECEMBER 14

Send a Christmas Card

DECEMBER 15

Go Caroling

DECEMBER 16

Buy a Christmas Present

DECEMBER 17

Wrap Presents

DECEMBER 18

Look at Christmas Lights

DECEMBER 19

Watch *It's a Wonderful Life*

DECEMBER 20

Act of Service

DECEMBER 21

Make a Gingerbread House

DECEMBER 22

Attend a Christmas Pageant

DECEMBER 23

Wishing Tree

DECEMBER 24

Christmas Eve Party

DECEMBER 25

Celebrate with Friends and Family

BOOK CLUB QUESTIONS

❄

1. What do you think the title of the novel means?

2. What theme(s) do you think the author was trying to convey?

3. What was your favorite scene? And why?

4. Which relationships did you enjoy the most? What did you like about them?

5. Who was your favorite character? And why?

6. Did any of the characters surprise you? Did your opinion of them change throughout the novel?

7. Does Poppy Creek remind you of any place you've lived or visited? In what ways?

8. Would you want to live in a town like Poppy Creek? Why or why not?

9. Luke and Cassie fell in love relatively quickly. Did you find their romance believable? Why or why not?

10. Can you paraphrase Edith's letter to Cassie? What do you think she was trying to express to her granddaughter?

11. The Christmas Calendar was all about festive traditions. What Christmas traditions do you enjoy with your family?

12. What does Christmas mean to you?

13. What do you think is the overall message of the novel?

14. Which characters would you like to see get their own stories in the future?

You can email your questions for the author to hello@ rachaelbloome.com.

A SEASON OF HOPE

❋

Luke 2: 8-14.

"And there were in the same country shepherds abiding in the
field, keeping watch over their flock by night. And, lo, the angel
of the Lord came upon them, and the glory of the Lord shone
round about them: and they were sore afraid. And the angel
said unto them, Fear not: for, behold, I bring you good tidings
of great joy, which shall be to all people. For unto you is born
this day in the city of David a Savior, which is Christ the Lord.
And this [shall be] a sign unto you; Ye shall find the babe
wrapped in swaddling clothes, lying in a manger. And suddenly
there was with the angel a multitude of the heavenly host
praising God, and saying, Glory to God in the highest, and on
earth peace, good will toward men."

Made in the USA
Columbia, SC
24 October 2023

24888109R00174